BLOOD ROUGE

BLOOD ROUGE

By
JEZA BELLE

RESOURCE *Publications* • Eugene, Oregon

BLOOD ROUGE

Resource Publications
An Imprint of Wipf and Stock Publishers
199 W. 8th Ave., Suite 3
Eugene, OR 97401

www.wipfandstock.com

PAPERBACK ISBN: 979-8-3852-1948-3
HARDCOVER ISBN: 979-8-3852-1949-0
EBOOK ISBN: 979-8-3852-1950-6

05/15/24

To my first siblings:

The oldest who slayed all of the dragons before the rest of us,
with a heart of gold.
The middle who beat up bullies and became the patriarch.
The sweet girl who made me laugh a lot.

"There comes a time when suddenly you realize that laughter is something you remember and that you were the one laughing."

—Marlene Dietrich

Contents

Acknowledgements

Mitch Olson—for making me a believer that I could actually write and for being a special and inclusive mentor.

My partner in life—for always supporting me.

Dylan Garity—for being a fabulous editor.

Thomas Evans Photography—for the press photo.

Wipf and Stock / Resource Publications—for being brave, bold, and flat out ballsy.

PART I

Der Concealer

Friedrichshain-Kreuzberg

"Lick my *arsch*, shit fucker!"

Those were the last words I heard before the butt of a Karabiner rifle slammed into the back of my head, which until that moment was covered only by a blond bob.

As I felt blood mingle with the bleached horse hair, the Nazi soldier pushed me and our small group toward a row of cattle cars that sat on a lonely train track in Friedrichshain-Kreuzberg, Berlin. The railway line was barely visible through the dense fog that clung to the railyard.

I could feel the soldier's hot breath on my cheek as he leaned past me and reached out with his free arm to slide open the door to one of the cars.

Metal screeched on metal, piercing the night air, as if crying out from the pain that I felt in my skull.

"Now you can go get fucked by your *Juden* friends, you pink pussies!" he screamed, as he and another *Sturmtruppen* herded us inside.

The red-faced Nazi glared at me, then spit at my legs, growling, "*Stück scheiße.*"

He slammed the door shut, and my eyes took a moment to adjust to the dim light in the damp box. Suddenly, my left satin-lined kitten heel buckled, and I collapsed in a heap on this mobile barn's floor. It was sprinkled with weeks-old straw that smelled of piss and death.

My Lucas, with his stained brown suit jacket, bent wire glasses, and a bloody nose, pushed past the dozen others to come to my side. As he reached me, the wig fell off, and my own recently grown-out ashen locks spilled out. These were mated now with a mixture of both caked and runny blood.

Seeing the state of my head, he reached down and tore off a piece of the frills from my brown chiffon dress with green leaves and little orange flowers that I had proudly stolen earlier in the day from the Hertie Department store on Leipziger Straße. The shop was formerly owned by that nice Jewish man Herr Tietz, until they aryanized it a few years back and gave it to that fat *miststück*, Herr Karg, with the beady eyes and pasty skin.

Lucas tied one long piece around my wound. He licked a smaller piece to moisten it, then dabbed my cheek, sweeping off the dried eyeliner that had mixed with soft peach concealer and spilled down my bruised face where I had been struck earlier during the raid on the Rote Schwein, or Red Pig. The bar had become my second home. It was at the Red Pig that I had not only finally become my true self, but also become *die blaue blume,* the blue flower of Schöneberg. A blossom who now sat in cold waste that came from heaven only knew what creatures had been locked inside this forsaken crate before us.

"I told you, Josef. Anke warned us about the *Staatspolizei* . . ." His baritone voice trailed off.

Such a strong timber for a thinly framed man, I thought to myself as I began to push off from the floor with my legs until my back was against the hard wall of the cattle car.

I reached up and pulled the frames of his glasses off his face and twisted them back into form before returning them to hook perfectly behind his ears. The train car shook as the engines roared to life.

One of the group of bar patrons began to sob. "They're taking us away. Oh my god, they're really taking us away!"

Several men ran to the sides of the car and began banging on the wood-planked walls. They yelled out, begging for anyone in earshot to release them. Their cries were drowned out by the responding silence.

The train bucked forward, and those who weren't already on the floor like Lucas and me started to fall over each other as we lurched toward the unknown.

"Only God knows what they will do to us when we arrive," Lucas said as he looked me over head to toe. "To you, Josef. To you!"

This was one of the things I loved most about Lucas. He was ever attentive, reliable, loyal even, no matter if his own life was in danger. He had proven his love for me and had stepped up to protect me more than once.

I helped Lucas to pull off his jacket, which I folded up in my lap like a pillow. Then I guided his frightened head down onto my legs to rest. I turned my own head to look out between the rough wooden boards onto the quiet city of Berlin, shrouded in white gauze. It was the middle of the night, and nothing stirred but our fears. A lonely whistle sang a sad good-bye to the city I had suffered hard and grown up fast in, as the last few lights that twinkled through the fog slowly faded from view.

After a few minutes, I looked down to where the shoe that had broken its heel when I was shoved onto the train sat among the dark and rancid straw. Reaching out, I picked it up and examined it closely.

And here I am again. I chuckled to myself as I looked at the shoe. *Without a home and uncertain about my future.*

I sighed from the weight of all I had experienced, exhaling into the open the memories of the last few years of my life. Then I leaned my rattling head back against the planks and closed my eyes.

Treptow

I stood in front of my bedroom mirror and admired my shapely legs. For a boy who was days away from his eighteenth birthday, I was what one might consider pretty, with wide, baby-blue eyes and sandy-colored hair that was shorter on the sides but thick and tousled with waves on the top. With one knee perked up in front of the other, my ankles showed off a pair of black leather heels with ribbon laces and little cutout holes. The heels looked especially good against the newly refinished black and white tiles my stepfather, Herr Füchs, had just installed on the second floor of our Berlin home, in the pricey Treptow district.

"Josef?"

I was startled back to reality at the disappointed voice of my mother calling me from down the stairs.

"Josef!" she yelled.

I kicked off her heels and ran down the hallway into the bathroom, where I slammed the door shut and locked it.

A few heavy clip-clops later, I could see the shadow of my mother's feet under the door. She rapped on the wood with a few short bursts from her knuckles.

"Josef, it's time for school," she announced.

Satisfied that I had my audience, I glided over to the white porcelain toilet, where I lifted the seat, leaned over, and stuck my fingers into my mouth.

My throat gurgled a cry as I retched loudly, pushing up last night's dinner of liver dumplings and *spaetzle*. The revived egg noodles were broken as they spilled out of my stomach and into the toilet water, though my mother had made them ever so delicately the night before.

I could hear her sigh with exasperation. "Josef, you've already used that trick twice this week, and I will not fall for it again." Her foot stomped on the floor just on the other side.

I looked back, then turned around and heaved some more.

"You are in perfect health!" she declared.

We both remained still in our spots. Me, hoping she would give up, go away, and let me stay home from school for the day. Her, waiting for me to open the bathroom door and get on with it.

"When you finish with your dramatics, your lunch is with your books in the kitchen." She let out another loud sigh.

I wiped the spittle off of my mouth with the back of my hand and rolled my eyes, resigning myself to one lost battle out of the likely many that today would present me with. Most of my days in this house and in my life in Treptow felt like war.

Standing up straight, I walked to the door, turned the knob and stood looking my mother in her eyes. Helena Dietrick-Füchs was a boxy woman, a true German *mutter*, with the birthing hips to prove it. Her face, though, was stately and chiseled. She had high cheekbones and deep blue eyes like sapphire that were set off by her pin-curl waves of ash, as if she were the direct descendant of *Frijjō*, the old Norse Goddess of love and beauty. Her beauty was the only thing I had been thankful to inherit from my mother. The fact that her arms were crossed over her chest meant that this morning's incident would not go without reproach.

"Really, Josef. What would Herr Füchs say?" she questioned. "He will not have a sissy hiding under his roof, too afraid to go to school every morning!"

Her words stung and caused my face to crumple up in an effort to fend off the attack.

Recognizing the hurt in my eyes, my mother uncharacteristically stepped forward and wrapped her arms around me. It was a rare moment of warmth and it left me unsure of how to respond, so I awkwardly hugged her back, taking in the scent of Fleurs de Rocaille, a pleasant mixture of gardenia meets lilac.

Helena kissed me on the forehead and whispered, "Remember, Josef, everything you do reflects on us."

So this was not a gesture of love she was embracing me with after all, but rather a quiet warning, meant for my ears only.

I pushed her off. "You mean it reflects on *you*."

My mother's face tightened up to weathered stone. "Your body is changing into that of a man now, Josef. Act like one!"

"You're even beginning to sound like Herr Füchs." I responded bitterly.

Helena stepped back and looked at me with regret. "When your father, Josef Der Alter Dietrick, died soon after the great war, I was lucky to find a bachelor willing to marry a woman like me who already had a child." She lowered her voice to a harsh whisper. "Especially the way he died."

My father's suicide two years after the war ended was a subject we almost never broached, and I had no desire to now. "But Herr Füchs also had a child, so it's not like you were any worse off than him, a widower."

"True, though his wife died of natural causes," she replied, bitterness seeping through her words. "Plus, in a city of untold thousands of war-widowed women who were scratching for every bachelor, Herr Füchs had his pick of fräuleins. He could have easily gone with someone without attachments, one less mouth to feed or body to clothe." She looked off down the hall, casting a palpable sadness.

"Still, just because you had a child already, I can't see you being treated like his slave—cooking, cleaning, and sewing like you're the housemaid, as if you should be lucky to scrub his undergarments . . ."

I had barely finished speaking when the full weight of her palm swept across my face.

"You see this dress I wear?" She was whispering still, but it came out like a howl. "This cameo on my breast? The fine furniture in this house? We would have none of it without Herr Füchs!"

Recomposing herself, my mother pleaded, "Please, Josef, behave! I cannot ever go back to living penniless as we did in those dark days after your father's death. You are too young to remember such times."

I clutched my cheek in a mixture of shame and defiance.

She clasped her hands together as if praying. "I'm begging you, Josef. Do all that you can to avoid drawing attention to yourself here, else you risk your mother being destitute again."

I considered her words. It must not have been easy being a woman. Dependent on looks, the type of home you provided, and the good graces of a man, no matter his disposition or conduct. The alternative though, in my mind, was freedom, even if it meant living poorly, living on crumbs.

To Helena, status and stability mattered more than silly things like dignity and love.

Knowing I had lost the second battle of the morning, I loudly blew the air from my lungs out between my teeth and threw my hands up in surrender.

"Fine," I said, then stomped past her and down the stairs.

When I reached the large kitchen on the first floor, I noticed my books tied together with string, sitting on the thick wooden table. The acidic smell in the air of cabbage slow-braising in apple cider vinegar for Herr Füchs's supper that evening only served to increase my annoyance. Next to my books was a metal lunch pail with a cloth napkin covering the food my mother had prepared.

I grabbed the stack of books with one hand and swept up the lunch pail with the other.

As I turned around, there stood my stepbrother. Marteen was a dark-haired boy whose smiling face made his eyes squint tightly, giving him the look more of a weasel than a person. Nothing made Marteen squint harder than me in any kind of troubling situation.

My mother alighted the stairs in the hallway and looked down at the two of us. Marteen unnarrowed his eyes when he saw my mother, sharing an innocent look with her. The exchange belied their delicate dance, whereby Marteen pretended to tolerate and even adore my mother, while Helena played at being doting and deferential, denoting the importance of staying on the good side of Herr Füchs's natural-born son.

Marteen walked over and kissed her on the cheek, wishing her a good day. I shook my head in disgust at the two of them and this charade. Not being able to stand the farce a second longer, I darted down the hall, directly past the duo, heading for the door. As I stepped through the frame, I allowed the heavy oak to slam shut behind me.

It wasn't but a second later that the door swung back open, and the pair followed. My mother stood on the portico and watched Marteen run to catch up with me in the front yard.

Ever mindful of appearances, Helena proudly swelled her cameo-pinned breast, as if she were just another ornament on the porch of our well-appointed, three-story home with its brick facade. My mother presented herself well any time she stepped outside, as one never knew if there might be early-morning neighbors looking in our direction.

Marteen caught up with me and put his arm around my shoulders. We reached the black, wrought iron gate that had been hammered into a wilderness scene including a deer leaping over forest trees. My stepbrother looked back at my mother, the two of them in smiles, while I fumbled to open the gate latch. I could feel Marteen slowly tighten his supposedly friendly grip around my neck.

Helena looked on and waved at us warmly when she spotted Frau Corper, who lived two doors down, walking by with her Dandie Dimont, Pepper, its short legs and long body zig-zagging past us as we exited the gate.

I smiled at Frau Corper with effort, then pushed the gate shut and turned to walk toward school. Marteen continued his embrace, increasingly tighter.

Our house was on a street that ran along the River Spree. On the surface, it was a peaceful walk from the Füchs's home on Ekhofstraße, our quiet lane, to the school. The emerald-green water was lined by willow and alder trees that had been perfectly curated as if they were select museum pieces delicately propped along the water's edge. A hen mallard and her chicks floated by as Marteen took one last peek over his shoulder to make sure the coast was clear.

Satisfied that we were out of sight, with the one arm he had around my neck and shoulders, Marteen flung my body around, throwing me back several feet. As I recovered my balance, he shouted out, "You didn't think that whole arm on your shoulder thing meant something, did you, big sister?

I sighed and shook my head at this ongoing morning routine.

At that moment, a small group of boys rounded a corner and ran down the street, jostling and joking their way toward Marteen and me.

Seeing them, he continued, "Good. Now count to twenty before you walk to school. It's bad enough that we have to live together. I don't need any of my friends thinking we hold hands and tiptoe through *die tulpin* as well."

Marteen held up his hand, palm down, and tipped it back and forth in a gay manner. He laughed to himself at his comedic brilliance, then ran down the block to meet his friends halfway.

In the group I could see Bruno and Bren, two thick twins who each resembled big blocks of Emmentaler cheese, the kind with all of the pock-marked holes. Mother and I had used to live cheaply on Emmentaler before she imprisoned us to a life of *Bratapfel*, bier, and bitterness, I thought to my-self as the bobble-headed twins tackled a laughing Marteen to the ground.

Another boy approached and stood over all three of them, watching them fight and play. This was Tielo Tielgel, their leader. Tielo was what many would call the picture of German male perfection. His short brown hair framed his square jaw and movie-star good looks, save the small scar he had above his lip on the left side of his face. They said he got it while reel-ing in a predatory asp fish off the River Spree when he was much younger. The spiny creature was said to have broken violently across the water just as Tielo landed it, only to find the lure no longer in the fish's mouth but hooked into his own upper lip. Though he was not even ten years old, Tielo pulled the hook out of his mouth without a cry, then stomped on the asp repeatedly until there was nothing left but grizzled bone, scale, and fin.

Tielo gave the other boys a moment to play around, then beckoned them onward with a deep grunt toward the large brick school that stood off in the near distance.

I followed slowly behind and watched the four friends dip into the building with the weathered white sign that read *Berlin Jungen der Schule*. I approached the door without hurrying, until my steps reached the point that I could lag no further. I had no choice but to enter, so with reluctance, I did.

While my eyes adjusted to the light, my ears could hear the distinctly disappointed tapping of Headmaster Baeur's walking stick on the floor in front of me.

The stick came into focus, attached to the white-haired man, whose back bent over so far that his body more closely resembled a Ü than that of the leader of a boys' school.

"Young Herr Dietrick," Headmaster Bauer wheezed.

"Ja, Herr Bauer?" I tried to sound innocent, but we both already knew the outcome of our short encounter.

"When I was a sergeant in the Franco-Prussian war, I would have my charges flogged for tardiness . . ." he began.

He took a loud breath, which was my opportunity to move this along.

"Am I late then, Headmaster Bauer?" I inquired.

"Not presently, but if you do not step to, you will be so, and then I will have no choice but to apply the Prussian procedures!" Headmaster Bauer stood up straight at attention, then tapped the bottom of his cane down hard onto the floor, where the metal on marble sang out.

The Prussian procedures, to most of us boys at the Berlin Jungen der Schule, were a glad welcome compared to hearing Headmaster Bauer drone on about military maneuvers from years gone by. To be frank, bare-assed swats from fresh pine twigs were far preferable to endless war stories about Chancellor Bismark and the Battle for Wissembourg.

"Yes, Headmaster Bauer," I said quickly, then moved toward my class-room door, which I hesitantly opened.

The bare-walled room contained one solitary stand-up chalkboard and a middle-aged teacher who sat furiously studying a book in the corner. I looked out at the nine young men who were already sitting, taking all of the chairs except for one empty stool in the corner. The group of students included Marteen, Tielo, Bruno, and Bren, all continuing their jovial banter from their walk, and five other pimply boys in various states of pre- and post-pubescence.

I skulked over to the open seat to the sounds of barely whispered snickers and outright laughter with pointed fingers from the others, as Herr Roth, our teacher, stood up from his desk in the corner.

"Now *jungvolk*, turn to page eleven of our books."

We all took our books and pencils out and began to copy what Herr Roth had written on the board.

As we spent the morning working through the dactylic hexameter of Virgil's *Aeneid*, little bits of chalk would periodically bounce off of the back of my neck whenever Herr Ross turned to map out the rhythmic scheme on the large slate that faced the room.

Each time a fleck of fine-grained limestone landed on me, plucked from a stick that Tielo had pilfered when he entered the classroom, re-pressed giggles would erupt behind hands held up to cover the mouths of the boys, who delighted in seeing me used for enjoyment.

I sank lower into my seat, hoping that would minimize the target and that they would all soon lose interest.

When Herr Ross turned back to us, he scolded me for slouching and informed me I was to wash the classroom windows after school.

I glanced back at a beaming Marteen, who was all teeth, while Tielo leaned back in his chair, winked at me, and blew me a kiss.

The rest of the day went as such. Wherever I went, there were my tormentors, ever ready to stick out a foot to trip me, to push past me briskly, knock me into walls, or whisper under their breath words like *tunte* or *shwul.* I tried to ignore them, but there was something that cut deep about being called homosexual in this way.

I would try my best to walk between the shadows, making it a point to leave classrooms well after the others, giving me mere seconds to get to my next location before I would be considered late.

When I arrived home an hour late from school, my uniform was spotted from the lye and water I had used to wash Herr Ross's windows. My mother was tsking at my entry, and it was clear Marteen had already announced my sins to the household.

"Go upstairs and change for supper, you *böser bub*," she scolded in a hiss. "I asked you to go one day without making problems." She looked back over her shoulders to make sure no one else had heard her. Then she straightened her black dress and headed back into the kitchen.

After I had changed I came back down the stairs to join Herr Füchs and Marteen at the dinner table. The dining room had a fine dark cherry table that was tonight covered in white, a Battenburg lace in a swirling cut-out pattern. Herr Füchs sat at the head of the table, reading a newspaper. All I could see above it was thinning silver hair that barely covered the liver spots showing on his aging head.

When I sat down in one of the side chairs, I took the cloth napkin that was perched atop my place setting and unrolled it delicately. Herr Füchs lowered his paper only slightly and watched me covertly as I refolded the linen, first diagonally, then in half before neatly laying it across my lap with what some might call an elegant flare. His eyes shut heavily, as if he could erase the sight of this eternal bother from his life.

With a sigh, he crumpled the paper up as Helena swooped in with a platter of crispy breaded veal cutlets. She stabbed two with a large silver fork and dropped them onto the bone china plate with pink roses and greenery that sat in front of her husband. Without a word of acknowledgement, Herr Füchs put his left arm out and nudged my mother back out of the way while he grabbed the large bowl of long-simmered red cabbage that she'd started on the stove that morning.

Throughout dinner, Helena scurried to and fro to ensure both the senior and junior Füchs were well attended to. When she got up to get some rolls for the table, Marteen looked my way and gave me a small, twinkling smile before he purposefully dropped one of the schnitzels onto the floor, then let out a surprised yelp.

"Oh goodness," he exclaimed, "I dropped part of my dinner."

Helena rushed to his side and bent over to begin cleaning from the floor the crumbs that had separated from the cutlet. "It's alright, Marteen," she soothed him, "accidents happen."

Marteen laughed silently in my direction, pointing to my mother at his feet.

Once she had cleaned the mess, she returned with a fresh piece of meat for my stepbrother, setting it on his plate in replacement.

When Herr Füchs had cleared his own plate, Helena brought out a fresh pie made with apples carted in from Hesse. These were crisp and sweet, the perfect addition to cinnamon and pie crust. As she placed it on the table and began to slice it up, Herr Füchs turned to address me directly in a stern tone. "None for you, Josef," he reprimanded while he took a slice on a small pie plate from my mother's hands. "When you can go without problems in school, you can enjoy the fruits of my labor."

He emitted a moan of delight as he heaped a large forkful into his mouth.

"I wouldn't be much of a father figure trying to raise men," he mumbled through a mouth filled with goodness, "if I allowed you to cause problems while living in my household and then be rewarded for any misbehavior." A crumb flew out of his mouth and landed violently in front of me as if to directly condemn my existence.

"You can go up now and get ready for bed," he finished with a final chew.

Not wanting to cause any more problems than the day had already presented me with, I nodded, then removed myself from the table. On the second floor of the house, I entered the bathroom and shut the door behind me. The rare moment of reprieve was met with a bracing splash of cold water to my face as I washed myself thoroughly before bed.

After I was clean, I sat on the edge of the bathing tub, holding the small bottle of almond oil my mother used as part of her nightly regimen, and rubbed some into my cheeks. The faintly sweet, nutty aroma filled my nose, and I wondered why the instruments and rituals of beauty were only assigned to womanhood.

When at last I opened the door of the bathroom, I was greeted by Marteen, who stood down the hall, bent over with his pants around his ankles.

"This is what I think of you, Josefina, and your mother." He laughed hysterically as his bare buttocks, which were lightly covered with a spattering of dark fuzz, shook at me from his guffaws.

I rolled my eyes and slid past him, shutting the door to my small but private bedroom firmly behind me.

As I threw my body onto the bed, I sighed aloud and looked up at the ceiling. I was alone at last, yet the presence of those in my life still consumed me.

Heavy thoughts pressed in on my head, asking me why I was so reviled. Had I done something to deserve their treatment, or was there just something wrong with me? If living meant always waiting for the next harmful blow to be inflicted, it was no wonder my *vater* had chosen to depart this world early and on his own terms.

Where was I to go in this life, though? At the end of this year, I was to sit for my final set of exams. I had already begun *Berufsschule*, the internship Helena had set up for me at Herr Füchs's furrier shop two times a week, which would become a full-time position come the spring. I would then trade one set of chains for another, only this set meant I would never get even a moment's respite from the Füchses, not that I found much presently between Marteen at school and him and his father in our home.

I fell asleep fitfully to the haunting sounds of boys laughing, their cruel barbs reverberating through my mind.

SEVERAL MORNINGS LATER, I rose from my bed and remembered it was my birthday. I found I did not have the energy to face anyone in the household, so I got myself dressed and tried to leave the house quietly without being noticed.

As I eased the door closed behind me, I began to head toward the gate, certain I had managed to avoid everyone, when Helena opened a large window and yelled out, "Josef!"

Surprised that Helena even remembered my day, I turned back to face the house, certain she wanted to put on some kind of show for the neighborhood so she could play the doting mother celebrating her child's big day.

"Don't forget you are working with Herr Füchs today after school!"

"Oh shit!" I muttered to myself. Not only had she completely forgotten what day it was, but she'd assigned me to spend it working for that *verdammter* too.

"Once you finish up, be sure to run by Frau Marlow's to pick up the lace I ordered," she finished yelling over the lawn.

Her dismissal from her mind of anything that might put me at the center of her day now completed, I rolled my eyes and stormed off to school.

I arrived in Latin before everyone else, so I took a seat at the back of the room, hoping it would lead to an uneventful morning, as I would no longer be the subject of chalk-throwing target practice.

When the rest of the boys shuffled in, I found myself studying Tielo closely. He possessed such power of persuasion over the others. The way the moon commanded the tides, Tielo's presence seemed to draw the others toward him. They ebbed and flowed with the direction of his attention.

Marteen said that Tielo did not actually live in Treptow like the rest of us. Instead, he walked over each morning from the rough-and-tumble Neukölln neighborhood, where he was rumored to live with an alcoholic father in a room loaned out to them by a Lutheran bishop. The bishop, hoping to save their souls, insisted Tielo attend Eucharist and our school in exchange for the living space. His mother was long dead, and it was said to be a home of disarray and delinquency.

Perhaps this air of danger and compacted masculinity was what intoxicated the others, as if Tielo wore a musty cologne that activated the other boys' glands with some form of virile attraction to brotherhood and manliness.

A few months back, Tielo came over to visit Marteen at our house after school. They were in Marteen's bedroom next to mine, so I pressed my ear up against the wall to listen with great interest to Tielo's tall tales of sexual experiences. Marteen tittered with excitement while I overheard Tielo brag about his supposed rompings, as he meted out his knowledge of *titten* and vaginas gleaned from personal experience. His musings entertained me through the drywall and ecru paint, and I found myself oddly aroused by the thought of Tielo's scarred lips touching my own.

I was lost in my thoughts and observations of Tielo, and my attention to him in Latin that morning did not go unnoticed. When he realized I was staring in his direction, Tielo halted his conversation with his friends and licked his lips seductively and winked at me. Of course the others found his actions hilarious, giggling and following suit. Whenever Herr Ross turned his back during instruction, I was met with sexual gestures, batted eye-lashes, and kisses blown in my direction.

The rest of the morning dragged by, a swirl of maths, *philosophie* and *politische*, and near-constant bullying.

At last the *mittagessen* had arrived, and we were all permitted a thirty-minute break to eat and socialize.

The sun shone like a spotlight on a stage as all the boys barreled out of the front door of the building for lunchtime. I followed behind, my eyes cast downward to my feet. The others ran right past me, laughing at inside jokes and making plans for what they would do with their free time as soon as they finished their meals.

I was only a few feet outside the door when I slammed directly into Tielo's taut body, causing his lunch pail to fall to the ground with a clatter.

I began sheepishly, "I'm sorry, Tielo, I was not looking whe—"

A strong, closed-fist punch landed squarely across my jaw before I could finish. My own lunch pail fell, its contents scattered across the ground. I could taste blood from my lip as I reached up to cover it with one of my hands.

"I think you meant to bump into me, didn't you?" Tielo said loudly, turning toward the already-gathering crowd. Bruno and Bren had shown up just in time to be perfect audience members, and they howled with laughter for their much-admired main performer.

"I believe that you wanted to touch my penis!" Tielo said, grabbing his crotch and shaking it for good effect.

He continued in a high-pitched voice, "Everyone knows you want to make love to boys like me, Josefina! We all saw you admiring me this morn-ing in Herr Ross's class. Do you like me, Josefina?" Tielo sang out. He started to prance around on the tips of his feet, then followed this up by kicking his heels in the air as if frolicking at a traditional Bavarian *Zwiefacher* dance.

Tielo stopped when he eyed a cloth napkin on the ground that had fallen out of my pail. It was wrapped around a slice of meat pie, which he picked up and studied. The pie was filled with ground beef and the remain-ing cabbage from last night's dinner. Tielo gave me one of his cool-eyed winks, then opened his mouth and took a giant bite out, moaning with ecstasy at the taste.

"That's my lunch . . ." I started to say, just as my legs were swept out from under me. Bren stood behind me and laughed at his brave act in the center ring. Tielo came closer, until he was standing over me. He spit the chewed-up pie directly into my face, and the crowd roared in hysterics.

He leaned over me in the dirt and threatened in a deep whisper that only he and I could hear, "Stay away from me, or one day I'll show you what I do to little girls." The threat echoed softly. I could smell the sauteed onions and the yeast from the bread's dough on his breath.

The other boys picked up Tielo's fallen pail and walked off together. They pulled him along and clapped him on the back as they headed away to enjoy the rest of their lunch break.

I crawled to what was left of my food and began to pick each item up, dropping them into my pail. I looked back toward the school entrance to see Marteen, who stood there with his mouth turned up. His look was one of disdain, and his small eyes shimmered with enjoyment.

Marteen shook his head in disgust and went back into the building, leaving me to my dirt-ridden meal.

I got up and slunk behind the side of the school building, where I leaned against the hard brick and sat down against its cool walls in the shade.

▼

HOURS LATER, I WALKED down Isenstraße, Treptow's main road. I stopped to drool over the Dresden Stollen cakes that were being sold at Hoffman's bakery. The sight of the sweet cakes dusted with soft sugar and filled with plump raisins, folded in rum, vanilla, and cardamom, made my mouth water. These were a warm and welcoming distraction from my day at school, and I wondered what the other boys of Treptow ate with their families in celebration of their eighteenth birthdays.

Alas, I could put off the afternoon no longer, so I walked on, kicking at the small rocks in the street as I made my way down the road until I reached the window of Füchs's Furrier Shoppe, where my eyes widened. In between the multipaned glass panels stood a mannequin in a long fur coat that could only be described as the color of snow for both its lush softness and blinding whiteness.

A young lady exited the shop, and the sound of the door shutting jarred me back to the moment, so I approached the entrance and went inside.

Herr Füchs looked over the shoulder of a plump woman in black fur who was smiling at herself in a long mirror. She made such a sight next to the thin, gangly body of the shop's owner. From behind the glasses perched on his long, thin nose, Herr Füchs's eyes squinted like Marteen's in my direction.

"At last, Josef," he said with a sense of exasperation. "You took too long getting here. There's a pelt of silver fox sent today from Moscow in the storeroom." He pointed toward the back of the store. "Go prep it for use," he commanded.

"Yes, Herr Füchs," I responded with great boredom.

He volleyed back, "I'll be there when I finish with the *fräulein* here to check on your work."

It was a stark reminder that whenever I was in his presence, Herr Füchs constantly looked over my shoulder and waited to judge me for any movement he considered inappropriate, any mistakes that I might make.

The storeroom was a windowless space at the back of the shop. One hanging bulb dangled over a small wooden table in the center of the room. All along the sides stood racks and racks of beautiful furs in various shades and hues, made from the pelts of animals such as wolf, rabbit, bear, mink, and fox.

I dropped my pail and bundle of books onto the table and turned to face a hook with a fleece of glimmering silver. I reached for the coat and brought it to the table, where I began to brush it out in preparation for Füchs to pin it into a frame before it would get sewn onto an appropriate jacket.

While I brushed out the fur, I spotted another white ermine identical to the one in the store window hanging on the opposite wall of the store room. I shook my head to resist the temptation and went back to brushing. But before long, my strokes slowed and I found myself staring out at the pure tone of the coat, as if called by the sirens toward their crashing rocks.

With no more hesitation left in me, I set the brush on the table and approached the fur, taking it off the wall. Next to the now-empty hook stood a floor-length mirror, and I held the white softness up to my cheek as I looked at myself, rapturous in this delicacy of the senses.

I swung the coat around my shoulders and placed my arms through its sleeves. Beauty stared back at me from the mirror. My smile faded as I noticed the scab on my lip from where Tielo had punched me earlier. Not to be denied this exquisiteness, I pulled my right arm up to my face until the cut was covered with soft fur and only the image of my face framed by allure and the mystery of the coat remained.

A gigantic guffaw unleashed from the entrance to the storeroom. Startled, I looked up in the mirror to see Marteen doubled over in a fit of giggles. After a moment of cackling, a look came across my stepbrother's face as if he had suddenly solved Einstein's Theory of Relativity. He gave me a good smug glare that let me know he had a plan that was bound to hurt me, then gasped as if he'd seen a ghost and yelled furiously, "Hurry, father! You must see Josef. Hurry!"

He gave me one last glance of revile, then finished his performance, shrieking, "Josef thinks he's *ein mädchen!*"

Herr Füchs was at the door in less than two seconds, leaving me no time to remove the fleece from my body and place it back on the hook. There was nothing left to do but stand there, caught. The man turned to Marteen calmly and directed him, "Finish up with the woman in the front, Marteen. I want to speak to Josef . . ."

Marteen stood there transfixed, in a state of elation.

"Alone," Herr Füchs declared loudly.

The door closed behind a sullen-faced Marteen, who left his father, me, and the fur to our demise.

Herr Füchs began to slink across the floor toward me.

"I've been a good husband to Helena," he declared, to himself as much as to me, it seemed. "I've tolerated your antics, Josef. But I can only do so up until a point."

My stepfather crept closer. I stood grounded in embarrassment at being caught, though I was growing concerned about his nearness to me.

"Although you are getting older, your girlish mannerisms are not only refusing to fade, but now you are blatantly flaunting these deviances in my own shop." He spat. "The very house of trade that provides your mother with the money to clothe and feed you."

He was almost at me. "I'll not stand for it any longer!"

Herr Füchs was upon me. He reached out and clutched my arm through the white fur and squeezed. I tried to pull away, but I could not break free from his viselike grip.

With his other hand, my stepfather removed his belt from his waist.

Leather sang out into the storeroom's stale air before it landed with a crack on the parts of my legs that the ermine did not cover.

"It is no wonder your own father left you. One would rather be dead than have a fucking pansy in their home!"

I screamed in pain as six quick, furious lashes broke my skin.

"That will do for now," Herr Füchs declared, throwing me onto a heap of hairy scraps on the floor. He put his belt back on and stood over me. "I will see to the rest of your punishment at home after supper!"

He exited the storeroom, leaving me to sob into the white coat.

After a minute, I stood up, threw the fur onto the floor, and pouted my way out of the backroom into the main shop.

Marteen waited for my emergence with wide, thrilled eyes. He choked on a chuckle as I stormed past him and his father to the entryway. I pulled the door open, stepped outside, and slammed it behind me.

Shoppers and townsfolk of all stripes and with all purposes walked to and fro in front of me, unaware of the pain and humiliation I had just endured. I could feel the redness cover my flushed face as the urge to scream at the top of my lungs rose up through my throat—not just at my situation but at the whole world.

Before it broke the air, I choked my feelings back down to my stomach and let my feet begin to move. I felt the wind in my hair as I furiously ran along Isenstraße. When I no longer felt cobbled pavement beneath my feet, I slowed to a breathless walk. Grass and mud were beneath me now as my body moved closer to the bank of the River Spree.

The slosh of water filled my shoes as I stepped into the river, farther and farther into its murky arms, which comforted me and whispered to me that the farther I found myself from the shore, the quicker all my pain would end. When at last I was up to my shoulders, I looked down at my reflection, staring back at me from the stillness of the Spree's shimmering mirror just a few inches away. Scrunching up my face, I lifted my hand up out of the deep and slapped the water hard. My shameful image, now covered by dozens of tiny radiating ripples. I was left with but a few choices. I could continue forward into the water until I could no longer feel the bottom beneath me, letting it take me from this life and into the world my father had chosen to enter not long after my birth. Or, I go back to the uncertainty of certain misery.

After several silent moments, I turned and waded out of the river.

Once I had fully emerged, I found my way over to a tall tree and fell down at its trunk. The hard bark pinched into my skin. I leaned my back against it with all my might, letting it pierce my flesh. Then I closed my eyes and began to cry.

▼

MY NECK GAVE WAY, causing my head to snap downward. This sudden motion jerked me awake as I sat there, my back still pinned against the tree I had sat down at sometime earlier. I shook the sleep off of my eyes. The bright daylight that had been shining down when I fell asleep was gone, and now only a small beam of sun was left as it sank beneath the western bend of the river in the distance. The darkening blue triggered something in my memory, and I let out a gasp and darted to my feet.

"The lace from Frau Marlow!" I suddenly remembered.

I dusted the dirt and leaves off my body, then began to walk along the edge of the river in the direction of her house.

I heard a twig snap to the left of me, and turned my head around to find Marteen, Tielo, Bren, and Bruno standing there in a semicircle that blocked me off from everything but the river, which was beside me.

Bruno called out to me with a sing-song voice, "What are *you* doing here, Josef?"

He seemed to have no interest in any answer. The pack of wolves began to inch toward me, scowls on their faces and growls on their breath.

Marteen piped up next. "Why did you leave the shop so quickly?" His voice was playful, innocent.

"He probably had to meet up with his boyfriend," Tielo explained, flicking a cigarette from his fingers onto the ground.

All of his parroting puppets laughed.

Marteen turned to the others. "You should have seen the little princess earlier today—all dressed up like a proper matron in her furs." He looked back to me in disgust. "Not only did this creature"—he pointed my direction—"and his whore mother move into my own mother's house . . . but this *thing* repays my father's kindness for taking in these homeless bitches by prancing around like a dancing queer right in his face—at his own shop!"

"Herr Füchs's kindness?" I laughed nervously.

This seemed to trigger Marteen. He stumbled toward me, yelling, "You ungrateful cunt!"

Tielo reached up and put his hand on Marteen's shoulder to steady him.

"Marteen, I already promised your sister here earlier that I would be the one to show her how men handle women if she was to come near me again." Tielo gave me a quick wink.

Marteen smiled at him. "Well then, get him!"

I turned to the river, hoping to run into it as my only means of escape, but in the blink of an eye, all four of these *biests* were upon me.

"Pin him down," Tielo commanded sharply.

The others readily obeyed.

Marteen sat on my head, smashing my left ear and cheek into the dirt and pine needles of the forest floor. Bruno and Bren each grabbed one of my arms until I was fully prostate, held down with nowhere to go.

I tried to look behind me with my one available eye to see what was happening. Then I felt Tielo reach under my waist and begin to unfasten my pants.

"What the fuck are you doing?" I screamed out between gasps of air.

Cold air hit my lower body as with one tug, Tielo yanked off my pants, exposing my nakedness to the group.

I struggled to little avail. I was trapped, bare assed and red faced.

I thought their humiliation would stop there, but then I heard the sound of Tielo's own trousers hit the dirt.

My jaw clenched tightly, and I cried out in pain as Tielo entered me from behind.

My fingers clawed at the dirt, and behind me I heard Tielo panting with excitement as he penetrated deeper and harder with each thrust.

"No," I begged through tears.

With one loud grunt, the boy collapsed in a heap against my buttocks and fell onto my back. After a moment, he stood up and hoisted his pants back around his waist.

Time stood suspended as a trickle of blood seeped out between my legs, mixing with the dirt beneath me.

"Shit, you got blood on me, you nasty pig," Tielo said, wiping me off the front of his pants. He looked around to the other boys, whose faces were frozen somewhere between fear and exhilaration.

The blood did not matter. Nothing mattered. Nothing ever would matter again.

I lay there perfectly still, no longer resisting.

"Who's next?" Tielo inquired.

No one moved.

"Suit yourself." He shrugged. Tielo took a cigarette out of his jacket and lit it up. After a few puffs, he walked off into the darkened air, whistling proudly to himself.

Bruno let go of me first. He picked my pants up off of the ground. Seeing this, Bren freed my other arm, and the two of them ran off, playing tug-of-war with my trousers as they departed.

At last, Marteen stood up from my head. He stared down at me for a long minute before slowly setting off to find his group.

I lay there for what seemed like hours. Salty tracks spilled down my face until they reached my crusted lips, matted down with silt.

With what little I had left in me, I pulled myself to my feet and started to limp toward the river. After a few seconds, my limp became a run, and I dashed into the water, where I began to scrub furiously at the blood between my legs.

Then I hobbled back onto the land and walked through the trees in silence. Up against a willow, I finally came upon my trousers, stained with bloody hatred and mud. I pulled them on one leg at a time, moaning from the soreness of my body and my soul. From there, I wandered along the river's edge toward our house on Ekhofstraße.

IT WAS FULL DARK as I squatted in the spindle bushes outside the Füchses' home. Lost in a vacant stare as I contemplated my next step, I hardly noticed Helena come out onto the portico and place her palm above her eyes to scan the night sky.

"Josef?" she called out into the darkness. "Oh, where is that boy?" she muttered to herself, stomping her foot on the red-painted timber.

I rustled my head up above the hedges and whispered a single word. "*Mutter*."

Helena looked down among the shrubbery, confused. "Josef?" She stepped forward and widened her eyes in disapproval. "What are you doing down there?" she exclaimed. "You are late for supper." When I didn't respond quick enough, she continued, "Did you get the lace from Frau Marlow?"

"Shhh," I insisted, motioning for her to come closer to the bushes. In a hushed tone I urged, "Mother, you have to come with me. We have to leave now!"

Helena chuckled. "Josef, what are you talking about?" A knowing look swept across her face. "Ah, Herr Füchs said there was a problem at the shop." She stomped again. "And you have promised me repeatedly that you would behave, Josef."

My lips began to quiver. "They attacked me, *mutter*."

"Who did? Who would attack you, Josef?" She laughed in disbelief.

"First Herr Füchs, then Marteen and his friends . . ."

My mother cut me off sternly. "That's enough! Stop this story. Stop telling me this silliness at once."

Peering down, she noticed the cut on my lips, my torn and filthy pant legs.

"What happened to your trousers?" Her brow furrowed.

I replied, "I am trying to tell you . . ."

She walked off, back into the house. A second later, she reemerged with a fresh pair of pants, which she tossed down at me. "Put these on—quickly," she hissed.

Helena scanned the street for any nosey neighbors while I swapped out my torn pants for the clean ones. "The dramatics never stop," she sputtered. "I cannot have you come inside and have Herr Füchs find you in such a state." Content that no one had seen me, she made her disappointment clear. "What if someone was out walking and had seen this foolishness out here, Josef? You, in the hedges, changing clothes?"

"But Marteen—"

"What about Marteen? You must have done something horrible to him, and this must be why Herr Füchs is so upset with you."

A snort shot out of my nose. "Wait, you think I did something to him?"

My mother crossed her arms over her chest and stared down at me. "It's always something, Josef."

I stared in disbelief at her unwillingness to even consider me or my point of view.

"Never mind Marteen for a second, Mother." My whisper was transitioning into a yell, so I shook my head to reset my approach. "Let's leave. Maybe we can go to your sister in Dusseldorf? We would be safer there," I implored.

Her eyes widened into frightened saucers. "Leave Herr Füchs? Go to Dusseldorf?" She shook her head definitively. "No! Whatever you have done to upset Herr Füchs and his son, you must go inside now and fix it.

Tell them you are sorry for everything that you have done to cause them to be upset with you. I am certain they are justified in their reasoning."

My mother stepped back and pointed toward the door of the house. "I will not jeopardize my own comfort—or yours, Josef—any longer. Go inside and apologize at once."

I stood there among the leaves, unmoving.

"At once, I said!"

When I did not move even still, Helena proclaimed, "I am warning you. If you do not go inside now, I will consider myself childless."

Tears of resignation stung my eyes. When at the crossroads, she always chose to be my mother second.

Seeing my unwillingness to move, her own eyes glossed over as if I were already dead and gone.

"You would abandon me? After everything I have just been through?" I cried.

She stared coldly off into the distance.

"Where will I sleep? It's cold outside!" I blurted.

Helena let out a sigh. "Wait here."

She went back in the door again briefly and came out with her own black fur coat in her hands. She tossed it down to me in the bushes.

"I'll tell Herr Füchs that you pinched it. There's my grocery money in the pocket." With little feeling, she said, "That should at least feed you for a day or two, until you come to your senses." As I picked the coat off the ground, Helena muttered, "Now, you have made your choice and I have made mine."

The woman who had given birth to me turned to leave. "I must go in and clean up after Herr Füchs's supper," she said to herself, and disappeared into the Treptow home.

A loud bang rang out as she slammed the door shut behind her. Pepper, the neighbor's dog, began to bark out into the night.

I sat and cried in the bushes, mumbling "*Mutter*" over and over again. After all of the years of emotional neglect at her hands, I now knew I no longer had a mother. In many ways, I never really had.

PART II
Der Lidschatten

Erfurt

We had been on the train for two days already when it came to a jerking halt. Assuming we had reached our destination, Lucas and I stood up with the others, facing the door. Fear spilled out in cold morning breaths.

The same door that had shut us away tore open, throwing blinding sunshine into our dark, dilated eyes. In the bright light, the outline of a man clutching a toddler in his arms became visible. The young girl on his hip had her hair tied up in a bright pink ribbon, which was swallowed in the scene of dirt brown and the musty odors of unwashed men.

Outside, some muffled commands could be heard, followed by a woman's blood-piercing scream.

A single gunshot echoed, followed by the sound of the train door shutting to close once again.

Remembering my own feelings upon entering this mobile prison, I stepped forward to our newcomers.

"Where are you from?" I called out from the darkness.

"Erfurt," came the quiet response.

Erfurt was located in the central part of Deutschland, so we scanned our minds furiously to think where we could be headed, having come so far from Berlin yet still so far from anyplace else. Surely this medieval town somewhere between the Harz mountains and the Thurngian forest was not to be our final destination.

"Here." I reached out to the man. "Let me help you." I beckoned them to the side, quietly humming. "There's a seat along the wall by us."

When I reached my hands out to take the young toddler from his father, the man's eyes seemed to adjust to the darkness. Disgust registered on his face as he saw me more clearly. He clutched his daughter tighter and backed away suspiciously from Lucas and me toward the other side of the car. When his back hit the opposite wall, he sat down, never once taking his eyes off of me.

"Fuck him," Lucas said angrily when he saw the look of hurt cross my face. He pulled me back to our side of the convoy, leading me by the arm and reassuring me. "You are better off not helping those who think this way about you."

The train whistled and heaved, and Erfurt, like the many other *dörfer* and *stadt* we had passed in the slow-moving days since we left Berlin, was left behind.

Off we rolled into the distance, as I again found my spot against my own wall. I sat there and looked at the man and his child. She leaned her ribboned head against her father's body. A shiver ran across my frame. I thought to myself how sad it was that even in these worst of circumstances, men still found ways to separate from each other, to lead with fear and hatred.

I cupped my hands together and pulled them up toward my mouth, blowing into them for warmth.

Baumschulenweg

I blew warm air onto my cold, numb fingers as I walked over the iron-truss Baumschulenbrücke Bridge, which led from Treptow to Baumschulenweg. When that didn't work, I pulled the sleeves of Helena's fur down as far as I could to cover my digits from the icy night wind, which blasted across the Britzer Canal with a particular menace.

I had already walked aimlessly through southeast Berlin for more than two hours after my mother had turned me to the streets, and my tired legs and my sore body needed rest. At the end of the unknown road I was on stood a dingy, sloped building with a small sign that read *Gasthaus Kreuzberg*. I could carry on no longer. I needed a safe space to lay my head, so I headed toward the inn and walked inside.

A dank smell matched the dim interior, which consisted of a small lobby with a worn wooden counter that looked as if it hadn't been cleaned since the Spartacus Uprising in the earliest days of the Weimar Republic.

A small, fat woman with whiskers on her chin and a gray, wiry mustache hobbled out of a nearby door. She examined me from head to toe. I can only imagine what she thought as she looked upon a teenage boy in an expensive fur coat with a busted lip and a bruised face.

"What do we have here?"

I could barely get the words out from exhaustion. "I need a room for the night."

"Aren't you a little young?" She sounded suspicious. Reaching over the counter, she brushed the fur that covered my chest with her gnarled fingers. "A bit oddly dressed to be in such a place alone and so late," she wheezed.

Exhaustion had taken my manners away. "Just tell me how much it is for a room," I snapped.

The woman waddled over to a sign on the counter and turned it around to show me. *Zimmers – Zwei RM.*

Two Reichsmarks? Now that I saw the amount in print, I realized I hadn't even contemplated how I would pay before I walked in. I stood there dumbfounded and silent.

"Well, how much do you have?" she prodded.

Hesitantly, I reached into Helena's right coat pocket and desperately I pulled out a mess of coins and lint that I then dumped onto the counter.

Fingering the coins one by one, I counted, "Ten, twenty, thirty, forty, fifty . . . seventy two Reichspfennings." I declared it as if I were rich.

The old woman grunted through a scowl. She started to shake her head, but then I felt something in the coat's other pocket.

The corners of my mouth turned upward as I slammed a bank note onto the countertop. "Oh, and ten Reichsmarks too!"

A sinister smile crept between the woman's gray whiskers.

"Perfect. I happen to have one small room left. It is late, but on account of you seeming so nice, I'll give it to you for the rate of ten."

Before I could respond, she whisked the banknote off of the counter and into her sagging bosom.

"Wait," I said, "ten Reichsmarks for one night? I thought the sign said two!"

Ignoring my alarm, the woman pulled a key from one of the many hooks along the wall.

"I accidentally showed you the summer rates. The winter rate is ten," she explained. "Now then, are you from Berlin?" She hobbled her way out from behind the counter and toward a stairway.

"Um . . . yes," I replied reluctantly, following her to a narrow set of steps that let out a loud creak when I put my first foot down.

The old lady continued to question me on our way up, her words emerging between heaving breaths. "If you don't mind my asking . . . What's a fair thing . . . like you doing . . . away from hearth and home?" As we reached the top, she stopped to hack out a deep, dry, crackling cough.

"I do not have a home," I informed her sadly.

"Oh, I see. So you are all alone then?" she asked with a face of interested innocence.

We reached a doorframe, where she presented the key she'd taken from downstairs to a tarnished brass lock, wiggling it in with zest.

A small click, and then the door flew open.

"No relatives to stay with, even?" she pressed.

When I shook my head, she smiled and led me into the space.

The room was small, but it was a palace compared to walking aimlessly on the streets. A small bed abutted a wooden table with a lamp. Yellow curtains swirled with the breeze in the window on the far wall.

"I serve bread and cheese in the morning, half past seven," the old woman said.

She looked me over and reached out to touch my fur again, then pulled her hand back to tightly clutch her chest that held the money. She shut the door behind her as she left, and I was surprised to next hear the jiggle of the lock once again.

Why would she lock me in here?

I shrugged, as being locked into a room to rest seemed like a treat to me after everything else I had been through that day. I walked over to the window, peeled back the curtains, and stuck my head out into the night air.

"Safe at last," I whispered, letting a sigh of relief out into the cold air before pulling my head inside and yanking the window shut.

I plopped myself down onto the brown woolen cover that was spread across the bed and reached down to untie the laces from each of my shoes. After kicking them off, I pulled my body up to a pillow and clutched it tightly. I could smell the faint odor of the person who had stayed on this bed last—a combination of sweat, hard work, and aching muscles.

I switched the lamp off, then lay back in the security of this small, protected place.

Earlier, I'd had no time to contemplate the pain I felt in my rectum, but as I lay there, the bitterness of the day welled up in my eyes. I closed them tight and let it all out, as I sank into a deep, exhausted sleep.

THE LOUD THUMPING OF a fist on the door startled me from my slumber. The room was dark, and I was still in my clothes, lying on the bed.

A key jangled. The door swung open, and a beam of light entered the room. I recognized the illuminated frame of the old woman who held a lamp in her gnarled right hand, but the other two bodies outlined there were a mystery to me.

I jolted up as two police officers came into view. They approached me with menacing scowls on their faces.

"That's him!" shrieked the old woman from behind the officers. "That's the little thief!"

At the word "thief," the officers pounced on me.

Each grabbed one of my arms, and they dragged me off the mattress and toward the door.

"He must have climbed in through the window after he stole my mink from the lobby!" she wailed through thick tears.

"What is going on here?" I begged, as I was flung around like a ragdoll.

The officers at last placed me upright on my own feet. I felt the steady ground beneath me and stepped back.

The first officer looked me over, then looked back at the hag. "I see he *is* wearing your fur coat, Frau Stracken, just as you described it."

The second officer snarled, "Take that coat off, now!"

"But this is my coat," I explained.

"Yeah and I'm the fucking Kaiser reincarnated," Officer Two chortled.

The old woman and the other officer laughed.

Officer One took a baton off his hip and began to slam it repeatedly into the palm of his left hand as a warning.

I looked back and forth between the old woman, whose discolored teeth were showing in between a fake cry and a full laugh, the second officer with his wide shoulders and muscular arms, and the first officer, beating this weapon in his hand like a war drum.

Grimacing, I sprang backward across the bed toward the window. I threw it open and had one leg over the ledge when the second officer's hand gripped me around the ankle and yanked me back onto the bed. I could feel the skin where Tielo had violated me earlier rupture once more, spilling more blood onto my pants.

Officer One slammed me across the body with his baton while officer two held me down.

"This is my coat! My mother gave it to me!" I screamed in between blows.

I sent out a kick that landed in Officer One's gut, sending him and his stick hurling off of me and the bed. Officer Two yanked me back onto my feet like I was a wilted weed.

"Either you hand over that coat, *junge*, or you are going to jail" Officer One declared as he caught his breath.

My eyes welled up. What more could be taken from me this day?

I slowly pulled the sleeve off of my right arm, stripping it of the sole act of warmth Helena's reaction to my recent rape had allowed her. Doing the same to the left, I looked into the eyes of the wicked Frau Stracken, then dropped the fleece onto the floor at her feet.

The wrinkled crone bent over with a gymnast's flexibility and vaulted the fur up into her arms, clutching its warmth against her cheeks.

She gave me a knowing smile. "Now that I have got my fur back, get this thieving trash out of my inn," she instructed the officers.

They grabbed my now-bare arms and dragged me out, across the rickety hall and down the narrow stairs. At the front, one officer opened the door, and then they both hurled me outside like piss from a bucket.

With a thud, I hit the cold stones.

My bottom was sore from Tielo's sexual assault, my legs ached from the switches of Herr Füchs belt, my face burned with shame from the wretched thievery of Frau Stracken, and my soul wept from the abandonment of my own mother.

Being manhandled and tossed out on the ground by two officers seems almost anticlimactic after a shit day like today. I found myself laughing, in a near state of delirium.

In the distance, I could hear the faint clopping of strangers' feet, moving farther away into the night. Likely headed toward their warm homes, I pondered with jealousy. I was alone, except for the wiry rat I watched scurry across the street and up under the ledge of a dilapidated wooden residence.

A soft moan escaped my mouth as I lifted myself up onto shaky legs. I skulked along the edges of the inn until I reached the corner, then turned and scanned the perimeter of the streets in front of and then behind me from side to side. Content that I was alone, I reached down and pulled my right sock off, lifting my bare foot into the air. As I returned it to the icy pavement, I pulled a wad of bills out of my sock and smiled.

"Just enough leftover grocery money to get to Dusseldorf." I sighed aloud with great contentment.

Happy that I still had the means to get away from this city that had forsaken me multiple times this day alone, I put my sock back on and limped off without shoes down the street and into the night.

Schöneberg

The morning broke with a slight red tone that shone between the cramped buildings. A single ray fell on my crumbled body where I lay behind a pile of trash in an alley that ran alongside a butcher shop. I let out a small, groggy groan, feeling the dryness of my throat.

Just then, a bucket of chicken bones flew across my sore legs.

I sat up. "Hey! There's somebody here, you know."

A straw-haired young man with thin gold wire glasses approached and peered down at my trash-lined body.

"Are you alright?" he inquired.

His eyes were a warm green, filled with honesty and concern.

"Do you happen to know where I am by any chance?" I yawned.

"Are you asking me what street you're on?" He leaned closer to question me.

A slight nod of my head, and he responded, "Lohmulenstraß."

I shook my head, "Lohmulenstraß in Schöneberg?" I lifted my back up off the grimy floor. "I must have walked all night."

My bare feet stared back at me. No shoes, and now I had no socks, and as such, I definitely had no more Reichsmarks to get to Dusseldorf. I rolled my eyes back in my head and let out an exasperated sigh.

The young man wrinkled his nose. He must've caught a more pungent whiff of me. "Are you lost?"

His smile was warm, so I found myself speaking without thinking. "No. I just became disoriented, so I sat here to gather my whereabouts and must have fallen asleep."

He put down the bucket that he had used to carry the slop he'd accidentally thrown across my legs. Then he reached out a hand, attached to a slight but strong arm lined lightly with blond fuzz.

"Let me help you up."

As I clasped his hand with my own, he continued, "My name is Lucas."

When I stood up straight onto chicken bones and muck, I replied, "I am Josef." I started to dust the alley and its trash off of my torso.

"Forgive me, but are you sure you are really lost, and not simply homeless?" Lucas pushed, as he looked me over head to toe.

My eyes narrowed. "Absolutely not," I gasped, indignant.

Here I was, a bedraggled teenager, hair unkempt, barefooted, sleeping in trash, yet this good-natured man, who had to be around twenty years of age, just winked, nodded, and played along with my guardedness.

"Well, 'just disoriented' Josef, I can offer you a meal and a basin to wash your face in this morning, if you would like. It's not much, but it will be warm, and it will get you out from the alley, at least for a few hours." He chuckled.

For the first time in more than a day, maybe in eighteen years, I could feel my shoulders drop just a bit from the constant high-intensity tension and worry they were used to.

Unfamiliar with kindness, I responded softly. "Um, I would greatly appreciate that. Are you sure?"

"It's decided then," Lucas said, turning to walk out of the alley. He called back, "Follow me."

I hurried behind him dutifully and soon fell into a trance at the sound of Lucas whistling to himself. We walked along the busy street past the large butcher shop. The whistle felt safe and comforting, he the pied piper leading me, his street rat, out of Hamelin.

After a few short bars of his tune, Lucas stopped in front of a long brick building. He flung open a door to one of the flats and waved me for me to follow.

We entered a sparsely decorated living room, where a long brown sofa that looked to be made of itchy burlap sat in the center of the room. There was a round table with short legs in front of the couch, which was covered in piles of fabric and folded clothing. Toward the back of the room, a small brown piano with peeling varnish stood against a wall. The hooks beside it were populated with both male and female coats and hats. The room ended with a square table and four chairs in a small kitchen area.

Lucas led me to the kitchen and instructed me toward a white basin, which he filled with clear water from the chipped blue pitcher that sat beside it.

"Wash your hands and face here," he directed, then moved toward the small doorway on the other side. I could just make out a narrow set of stairs leading upward. Lucas leaned in and yelled, "Anke! Come down here and eat before I leave."

I pulled the cool water up over my face, letting the drops splash off the tears and dirt of Treptow and that old bitch who stole my coat. When they were clear of the water, I turned to see a hot loaf of brown bread on the small table. Lucas was cutting it into three chunks.

He plopped a steaming piece onto each of three plates, then pointed me to a seat. He pulled a tray of butter out from behind a covered shelf that ran under the basin, which he placed on the table in front of me.

Just as I sat down, a thin young woman emerged from the stairs. Her eyes widened at the sight of me.

"Anke, this is Josef," Lucas shared. He looked over to me. "And Josef, meet my sister, Anke Strechburg. We live here together."

I stood up and dried my hands on my pant legs, then extended one out. "It is a pleasure to meet you."

Anke gave me a hesitant look before taking my hand and shaking it lightly. She resembled Lucas, though I thought she must be a bit older. Anke had pale skin with wary gray eyes that seemed to be searching mine for any hint of criminality. Her thin face was framed by long, wispy hair, the same shade as her brother's. Though the siblings looked similar, Anke did not have Lucas's aura of trust and benevolence. Rather, she seemed like someone who had been tasked with the care of her younger brother and would see to his safety and comfort whatever the cost to herself.

"Lucas was so kind as to offer me a little food and a place to wash up?" It came out more as a question for her to answer, and the stiffness of her body revealed her disapproval.

She sat down at one of the other seats and picked up her bread with both hands. As she pulled a smaller piece off with two of her fingers, she let out a quiet sigh. "That sounds like Lucas."

He slapped some butter on his own bread. "Say nothing further on it. The world is dark enough. We must spread what little sunshine we can to those we meet."

Anke and I both looked at him, unsure of what to do next. "Now eat!" he commanded.

She gave me a suspicious look, then began to nibble on her food.

Having not eaten a bite since the morning before, I devoured my bread within seconds, as both siblings looked on in surprise. Not to be impolite, they made no verbal mention of my animalistic attack on the food, but they did share a curious glance.

"Are you new to this area then, Josef?" Anke inquired.

I stopped chewing, but I only responded with silence.

Lucas interjected. "Um . . . no. Josef is just . . ." He raised one eyebrow toward me as if to ask permission. "Passing through?"

"Oh!" Anke exclaimed. "I see. Then you are just here temporarily on your way somewhere else." She sounded relieved.

Lucas and Anke looked back and forth between each other and me, but I remained silent, the tension of the pause only growing.

My lower lip quivered. "I didn't want to say before, when you asked me in the alley, but I actually am homeless." I hung my head until my chin touched my neck. "Newly and unexpectedly homeless, that is."

Lucas stabbed the bread knife into the butter, where it stood up straight. "In that case"—he turned to Anke—"I may as well tell you the truth. I found Josef sleeping behind the slop bin."

Anke looked at her brother with fury. After a few seconds, though, she settled her face back to a more relaxed state and probed me further. "What happened to your home that sleeping behind our slop bin was the better option?"

Unable to share more, I sat again in silence.

"Do you have any relatives with which to stay?" she pushed.

"My aunt lives in Dusseldorf, but that's six hundred kilometers away . . . and someone stole the train fare I had in my sock to get me there." I sighed.

"So what exactly are you planning to do then?" asked Lucas. "You cannot take a train with no money, and you cannot walk there with no shoes."

I shrugged. "After I'm finished here, I suppose I will head to the train station and see if someone could buy me a ticket."

Lucas looked incredulous. "You mean beg? That would take a lot of pennies from strangers to get that kind of fare."

I shrugged again.

"Well, do you have any skills, or anything you know how to do, Josef? Like something you could work at to earn the money for your ticket?"

"I only worked in my stepfather's shop. He was a furrier, and I was in my last year of studies at the *schule* when . . ." My words faded as pain crept across my tightening brow. "I was preparing to sit for my examination." I stared off vacantly into their small apartment.

Lucas eyed his sister with a look of determination that urged her to speak. After a moment, she loudly and resignedly released the excess air from her lungs.

"Seeing that you worked for a furrier," she began, while her smiling brother looked on, "I could use some temporary help darning socks and mending coats if you're amenable. The girl I worked with recently married and moved away. She left me with much work on my own." Anke nodded toward the pile of fabric on the table in the small sitting room.

"Anke is a seamstress," Lucas announced.

She stood up from the table and approached a trunk in the corner. Opening its lid, she pulled out a dress of blue and yellow flowers. "I also make dresses to sell in the *gendarmenmarkt*, but that's only when I can afford some extra fabric." She held the delicate creation up to her neck.

My eyes widened. "That is beautiful work. I can tell you have real talent."

Anke folded the dress back up and put it into the trunk. As it clicked shut, she turned to me and said, "The pay would be minimal. Ten Reichspfennings a week, plus room and board."

I was unable to stop the smile that burst onto my face. However, when I saw the brother and sister smile to each other as well, my own grin receded back into darkness and mistrust. *People do not just do nice things for others without some ulterior motive,* I told myself. I thought back on all I had experienced just recently.

"That is kind of you, but regrettably, I must decline," I stated with force, putting down the last of the bread I had planned to eat. "I forgot that I had already written to my aunt in Dusseldorf. She left a standby ticket for me to use at the station, so she will be expecting me."

I pushed my chair back from the table and stood up. "Besides, apart from yourselves, I have found little kindness in Berlin."

I tried not to let on that I was aware that they were up to no good. The memory of Frau Stracken was a painfully fresh reminder to me that people just could not be trusted. I would not allow myself to believe any longer that their offer here was for anything but selfish gain. No, they must have meant to use or hurt me in some way.

Lucas frowned at my rejection, but I just kept talking. "I should be going, especially if I hope to catch the next train." I began to back away toward the door, the boards creaking as I dragged my feet across them.

Anke tilted her head in sympathy, as if she understood my fear. "Well if you change your mind, Josef, you know where we live."

"Thank you again for your hospitality and your offer. Maybe we will meet again someday," I said as my body reached the door. Lucas raised his hand and called my name as I turned to exit, but I did not stop to listen. Instead, I fled for the safety of the streets. Here, I could not be trapped by anyone. I had nothing left to take, not even anything on my feet. I was alone, but I was free.

I hurried away from their home, in what direction, I cared not.

After I had walked for some time, I sat by a fountain to catch my breath. Nearby, a woman in a dark gray woolen suit, with a bowl-cut hat that came just past her ears in the same fabric as the suit, paused in her own stroll. She pulled black gloves off and milled her hands about in her black leather handbag until she came out with a long cigarette and a lighter.

I admired her as she drew the cigarette hard into her red-lipsticked mouth. The tip began to sparkle with fire as a man in a suit of an even darker gray approached her and the two began to talk. He was as handsome as she was, and she threw her head back to let out a delighted purr at the man's inaudible words.

Without realizing it, I had stood up from the fountain, and my body had begun to mimic this woman's movements. First, I imagined a cigarette held theatrically between my index and middle fingers. I turned my hand over to flick ashes to the ground and noted how the coat of the arm of her suit pulled back just at the wrist to reveal a splash of pink skin. Then I threw my own head back like hers, mirroring that seductive laugh. I spread my legs slightly and pushed one hip out to my side.

The man and I were both mesmerized by this woman's movements, though for different reasons. She said little with her voice, as far as I could tell, but her body spoke in tones at once sharp, seductive, and tender. There was an intoxicating power in her presentation, a power that made him want to have her and me want to be her.

An older man pushed past me loudly with a wooden cart filled with apples, and when he was gone I found myself once again alone by an unknown fountain in the middle of a neighborhood that I did not know the name of, somewhere in Berlin.

A small bag jostled out of the man's back pocket as he scurried by. I did not have time to both pick it up and call out to him, as he was gone around a street corner before I even had the bag in my hands. I peered inside to find a massive jumble of coins.

"Dusseldorf!" I exclaimed. That old man's loss was now my gained trip out of this city and to a new life with my aunt.

I turned my head over my shoulder one last time to find the woman in gray locking an arm around the man's and they walked off together down a road in the opposite direction.

Clenching the bag tightly, I strode in the direction of a sign overheard that pointed toward the train station.

After a few minutes, I stopped in front of a fabric shop window. In the display sat a bolt of the same blue and yellow flowers that Anke had used on the dress she had created back on Lohmulenstraß. I looked on at the fabric until a boxy female clerk approached the display window from inside the store and smiled at me. I nodded with embarrassment and continued my walk.

The Anhalter Bahnhof stood towering over my approach, clothed in white stone and built right into the city's old customs wall. As I approached, men and women darted in every direction, and the sound of metallic announcements projected over the speakers.

I paused to watch a brown and red chain of train cars chugging out of the station. A little girl waved from one of the windows. She was held tightly around her waist by a relative of some sort. As the train picked up speed, a pink ribbon flew off of one of her pigtails and landed at my feet, and then she disappeared with the train down a line of tracks carved out between the bustling streets.

AS MY HANDS WERE completely full, I landed a series of loud kicks on the bottom of the door with my foot. The door swung open, and Lucas's mouth dropped when he saw me standing there in new hard toe black shoes.

The sun was almost setting, and I had returned to Anke and Lucas's flat.

"Josef?" Anke cried out as she rushed forward to help me with all of the packages in my hands.

Lucas threw an arm around my shoulder and ushered me toward the couch while Anke placed the boxes and bags on the table.

"What is all of this?" she asked with merry suspicion.

I lifted up a box and pulled the lid off to reveal the entire bolt of blue and yellow flowered fabric I had eyed in the window earlier.

"I figured for the cost of a train ticket, one could make five dresses to sell at the gendarmenmarkt."

Lucas and Anke shared a look of surprise that quickly turned to smiles.

"Perhaps with the sale of those, I wouldn't be such a burden if I lived here and shared this flat," I added.

"Does that mean you are staying?" Lucas asked.

"If you will have me?" I arched one brow upward.

Lucas looked to his sister for her decision. After a moment's reflection, which included another glance at the flowered fabric, Anke declared, "Of course!" She stood up. "You can start working with me tonight in fact. But first"—she moved toward the kitchen—"it is time we celebrate the growth of our family with some dinner."

Anke pointed toward the small stairway near the kitchen and ordered her brother, "Take Josef upstairs in the meantime and show him the bedroom while I set the table." As we made our way across the room, she added, "You and Lucas will share the larger room; I will switch to the smaller room now that there are two of you, as I don't have as much need for the extra space."

Lucas darted up the stairs, with me right behind him. The sound of dinner dishes hitting the table echoed from below as we stepped into the larger of the two small rooms. It had a double bed with a tarnished brass frame. A small round window sat at the top of the far wall, just enough to catch a drop of sun or moonlight. This bedroom seemed like heaven.

I turned to him. "I want to thank you, Lucas."

"For what?" He sounded surprised.

"For taking me in of course—for sharing your food and now your room."

Lucas sheepishly kicked at his feet. "It's nothing. You were in need, and so were we to be honest. Anke cannot do all that mending and sewing on her own."

"Truly, I was desperate, and you came to my rescue." Inside, though, I felt as if I were Ann Darrow and he Jack Driscoll, helping me down a vine and away from the great ape Kong's terrible grasp.

"It's nothing." Lucas blushed.

No, it was everything. His acts made me feel like I mattered to someone, and that could never be nothing.

"I do not know how I will repay you, but one day, Lucas, I will do for you what you did for me here today."

Anke's voice punctuated the heavy air. "Food is ready and on the table!"

The smell of stewed meat hit my nose as we headed back down the stairs and into the kitchen area. My brain tried to catch up with my eyes, as there were only two places set. My face fell at the sight. My earlier prediction that everything was not as it seemed crept back into my mind, as I was clearly not fully wanted for supper despite their lulling words of welcome.

Anke sat at one place setting and motioned for me to sit at the other.

I looked across at Lucas, unsure why I was being offered the empty seat and not him, but he was already grabbing his coat off of a hook on the wall by the piano.

"Well, I'm off," he announced as he flung the coat around his shoulders and headed for the door.

With a confused shake in my voice, I asked, "But are you not eating supper?"

Lucas walked over behind his sister.

"My brother teaches piano," she explained, "and several nights a week he works at a booze bar." She emphasized the last two words, as if to convey some kind of lurid meaning that flew right past my half-cocked head.

He bent over to kiss Anke on one cheek, and then he shared, "They feature doll singers and such."

"Doll singers?" I asked. This was a term I was as unfamiliar with as I was with the words "booze bar."

When he finished kissing his sister, Lucas started back toward the door. "I'll take you with me one night if you are interested."

His voice was hurried, and his footsteps picked up urgency. "For now, though, I've got to run—no dolls or drinks tonight, just Frau Anderson's fat pig child, Tomás. If I'm not there to teach *der dickwanst* piano by half six, the Frau will squawk like a bird roasting alive on a fire pit." He waved his arms in the air like a bird trying to put out flames.

With that, the door opened and slammed shut, leaving Anke and me to giggle alone over our steaming bowls.

Chunks of meat sat in thick brown gravy punctuated by small bits of cubed potato and rough-cut carrots. Anke picked up a spoon and pulled some of the hearty fare toward her mouth. She blew on the spoonful to cool it, then stated, "Go ahead and eat up, Josef. After dinner, I will teach you how to do a basic stitch."

Her mouth formed a near-perfect O as she scooped up her dinner and began to chew.

I hadn't eaten since I left the flat earlier that morning, and Anke's chewing caused my own mouth to water and smack with anticipation for the fare. It didn't take me long to shovel hot spoonfuls of the stew into my maw.

Once our bowls were cleared of their contents, I helped Anke carry them to the counter, where we placed them in a large tin basin filled with water. She rinsed each dish and spoon thoroughly, then placed them upside down on a thin towel to dry.

"Come on over to the sofa, Josef—I will show you only something simple for tonight." Anke motioned for me to join her as she headed toward the sitting room.

I followed behind respectfully. She was more than a short-term acquaintance, or even my flatmate; she was also now my employer.

Once Anke was seated, she pulled out from under the table a simple silver sewing kit. She handed me a needle and some white thread, then picked up a similar set herself. Motioning with her fingers, she demonstrated and instructed, "First pick up the *nadel und faden*, just like this." She held each in a separate vise between her index finger and thumb. I followed along.

"Good," she continued. "Now just like that, you slip the thread right through the needle." Her thread broke through the small hole at the end with a quick and steady motion. When I attempted to do the same, my thread got jammed up and went sideways, escaping the narrow hole by what seemed like a meter.

Anke chuckled. "It's okay, Josef. Once you get the hang of any of what I will teach you tonight, it will become second nature." She put her needle and thread down and grabbed hold of my hands, which still held my own materials.

"Now, take the thread and dip it quickly on your tongue," she ordered me, guiding the thread up toward my mouth.

I could not help but to laugh, and Anke used that moment to attack my opened mouth with the thread. She swiped it on my exposed tongue, and we both tittered as she guided my thread into the eye of the needle waiting patiently in my other hand.

"There you go." She released my hands and clapped lightly. "Now take the thread out of the needle and try again on your own."

In quick order, I had rethreaded the needle and was ready for my next set of instructions.

Anke next took out a piece of black fabric scrap and demonstrated how to do a backstitch. Within minutes, I was an expert, pushing the needle down into the fabric, then pulling the thread through, then forcing the needle back up mere millimeters away. We practiced this and the simple forward running stitch over and over again until my instructor graduated me to a brief class on sock mending, where one stitched a box of thread over a hole in a sock.

Once class was over, we sat in a sweet silence, needling time away, me at a small pile of hosiery and Anke repairing the arm of a man's jacket she'd been hired to stitch back to life.

It seemed like only minutes had passed when Lucas burst back in the door. He greeted us breathlessly, and Anke rose from her mending to fix him a bowl of the stew we had enjoyed earlier.

After Lucas had regaled us with tales of Frau Anderson and her Tomás in between bites, Anke announced it was time for everyone to go to sleep for the night.

"We are not Deutsche Bank with its unlimited holdings, and so it is time for our expensive electricity to be drawn down." She pointed toward the stairs and hit a switch in the living room. "Lights out!"

The three of us headed up the small, dark set of stairs. Anke turned to the right and closed the door to her room behind her. Lucas and I continued to the left and did the same.

"How many times this evening did you prick your fingers?" Lucas chortled, as he made his way across the room, dimly moonlit from the high window.

A small click, and then the room was flooded by the soft glow of a small bronze lamp that stood atop the knotty pine bureau by the bed. He began to undress.

"Only a few times." I spoke softly, standing paralyzed as his bare back faced me. Unexpectedly, he continued past his shirt, removing each item of clothing, dropping them onto a thin chair with a round seat and an arched wooden back. Within seconds, Lucas was completely naked, his firm, slender body just feet away from me.

He turned over his shoulder and laughed. "Why are you just standing there, silly?" He dashed to the bureau and pulled out two pairs of men's pajamas, both of them white with light blue pinstripes.

He tossed a pair at my face, then pulled his own pair of pants up over his smooth, white bottom. Soon after, he jumped into the bed and yanked a book off the top of that same bureau and began to read.

I nervously made my way over to the chair Lucas had placed his clothes on and began to strip. After peeling off my shirt, I threw a pajama top on and buttoned it down swiftly. Then I stood there, unsure of what to do next.

Lucas looked up from his book and sighed. "Josef, if this light is not off in the next ten minutes, we will have Anke demanding our blood." He went back to his book, adjusting his glasses by pushing them slightly further up his nose in order to read better.

I shuffled from foot to foot before unfastening my pants. As they fell to the floor, Lucas, peered over his book and let out a small gasp. The sight of the welts on my legs from Herr Füchs's belt were a bright, puffy pink.

He put his book down onto the bedsheet and leaned over to look at me more closely. As he did, his throat emitted a loud gulping sound, and his eyes landed on the dark red stain that sat on the inside of the seat of my trousers. Treptow's humiliation of me was now complete.

"You are injured," Lucas said, lifting himself out of bed and making his way over to me.

I recoiled when his hand touched my shoulder. My face turned darker than the stained shade inside my pants. I snatched the pajama bottoms and threw my legs into them, facing the wall all the while, unable to look into Lucas's eyes.

"No," I said, "It is nothing. I fell a few days ago . . . and I . . ."

His warm hand was on my shoulder again, and this time I did not flinch away but was grounded by it. The connection unlocked the flood I had been holding back now for days.

I could not speak through the tears, so we both stood there, his face to my back and his hand on my shaking shoulder.

"It's alright. You do not have to tell me if you do not want to or do not feel ready."

He bent down and gathered up my soiled clothes. There he folded them into a small pile and deposited them on the floor by the chair.

"Just know this, Josef," he said, "whatever happened before, you are safe here. Anke and I will not hurt you . . . I will not hurt you."

Lucas returned to the bed. He put his book up on the bureau and pulled back the covers next to him.

"Come rest now. I am certain Anke will work you like a Russian peasant all day tomorrow, so you will need your sleep."

I wiped the tears away with my sleeve, then slinked toward the mattress and slid in, my back to Lucas. He turned off the lamp, and we were left in silence and darkness.

▼

IN A BLINK, a light yellow stream came through the little bedroom window and landed on my cheek. I yawned and stretched from what felt like a hundred years of slumber.

Sitting up in the bed, I scanned the room to remind myself of where I was. When my eyes landed on the chair, I widened them at the thought that Lucas had seen my shame laid out in blood on my trousers. When I dropped my eyes to the chair legs, my pile of soiled clothes were no longer there. A pile of freshly laundered items stood in their place.

I curiously made my way over, bent down, and pulled the fresh delicacies up to my nose and inhaled. Content that the smell of blood and beatings were finally out of my life, I slipped the new clothing on with a smile, then headed toward the door.

The siblings were already seated at the table, sipping on cups of strongly brewed coffee. The scent assaulted the room with morning energy. Lucas looked up from a newspaper and used his free hand to push an empty cup my way. He returned his nose to the print, while somehow managing to find the handle of the hot pot of black liquid that sat in the center of the table. He scooped it up then dropped it down next to my cup without so much as a glance.

Anke stood and walked to the counter, where she cut off a giant hunk of bread. She plopped it onto a plate, which she set in front of me.

"Guten Morgen!" she sang as she returned to her seat.

I looked across the table at them and delighted in my newfound family.

Once breakfast was finished, Anke and I sat for hours mending shirts and socks. As the day faded, Anke finished her stitching on a silk blouse that shined with a bright green luster. She put the garment down and rose to fetch a drink of water from the kitchen.

The sheen of the fabric called to me. I peeked back to see her turned away as she sipped from a cup, and I seized the opportunity to snatch the emerald piece that lay before my eyes. I rubbed the soft silk between my fingers and gazed with admiration at the rich, jeweled tone the silk fibers managed to capture.

Lost in the moment, I was startled by Anke's return. She now stood directly behind me. "Frau Lempf's husband brought her that silk all the way from Peking this summer."

My cheeks reddened, knowing that I had been caught romantically touching the blouse. I quickly put it back where I found it.

"I'm sorry. I just wanted to touch it . . ." My voice faded.

Anke smiled brightly. "It is quite alright, Josef. That silk is very beautiful, and you clearly have good taste!" She came back to her seat on the couch.

My shoulders relaxed. "Ever since I was little, I have always liked the feel of fine fabrics. Silks, satins, furs. I suppose it is silly," I pondered aloud.

"It is not silly at all!" Anke insisted. She studied my face for a bit, then continued. "You know, some boys, Josef, possess an . . . artistic spirit. A gentle soul that is too special to be defined by the rigidity of man."

Unsure of where this conversation was headed, I nervously picked up a beige sock and began to thread a box around the hole that was open in the toe.

Anke continued undeterred. "Lucas possesses some of that spirit too." My face was stonelike. I worked hard to keep it as unresponsive as if it were the lifeless, holey sock in my hands.

"That is why I knew when he brought you home that you and he would become good friends."

Anke reached over and put her hand on top of my own. I stopped my sewing and looked up into her eyes.

"After all, everyone needs friends, Josef. Even gentle souls."

Her words were as soft as Mrs. Lempf's blouse, but they were as strong and as reassuring as the great wall that surrounded the country that beautiful green silk had journeyed from.

The moment was broken as Lucas clattered down the stairs from the bedroom and across the kitchen to the hook with his coat.

"I have to be at the bar for rehearsal before tonight's show," he panted. He darted back to the kitchen table and grabbed an apple out of the bowl.

"You can't just have an apple for dinner!" Anke said as she got up and dashed over to the stove, stirring a large spoon into the big pot that sat over the burner. "Sit and eat for a few minutes," she demanded, pointing at a chair.

Lucas chomped a bite out of the apple in his hand and jumbled out the words, "No time." In between chews, he looked back at me and mumbled, "Want to tag along?"

I looked to Anke, unsure if we had more work for the night.

Her brow furrowed in consideration, and then she relented. "I can finish up the last items for tonight by myself." She pointed the spoon at me. "You go and have some fun!"

As I stood up, she placed the spoon back in the pot and grabbed another apple out of the bowl.

"Josef," she called.

As I turned around, she tossed the apple toward me, and I reached out and caught it with a laugh.

"You may as well eat one for supper too. The beer they serve at the Rote Schwein is too strong for an empty stomach."

Lucas and I ran out the door and into the early evening air, hustling swiftly down a side street.

"Have you ever been to a bar, Josef?" he asked between steps.

"No, never."

He nodded. "Ah well in that case, I was going to warn you that this is not like just any bierhaus in Berlin." He stopped and brought a hand up to his chin to consider. "Then again, I suppose you do not know what any bierhaus is like if you have never been inside of any of them before."

"What do you mean? What are you talking about that it's not like others?"

"In most bars, you have a bunch of drunk men who tell tales of war and make plans to hunt and fish for the big one," Lucas explained.

"I'm not sure I understand. What is it like at the Rote Schwein then?"

Lucas started to walk again, so I hurried to catch up.

"Well the men *are* hunting and fishing for the big one here too . . ." He laughed aloud.

I shook my head. "I am confused."

Lucas threw his arm around my shoulder. "It's what they call a cabaret."

"Where beautiful women sing and perform?" I asked with the wide eyes of innocence.

"Something like that." Lucas smiled big, then tousled my hair.

He led me down many streets, laughing in anticipation at my baptism into Berlin's underground bars.

"We must take all precautions to not be followed or lead anyone to the doll bars," Lucas explained as we walked. "Most of these have already closed shop, but the Rote Schwein still exists, for those who know how to find it."

At last we reached the road Lucas was leading me toward, just off Nollendorfplatz. He stopped to scan in both directions before pulling me down an alleyway. We passed a dark and frightening figure in the shadows; I could not make out if it was a person or one of those American carnival creatures I'd read about once in a pamphlet. A half-man, half-demon kind of thing.

I shook off the sight in time to follow Lucas down a small set of stairs that led to another, even darker alley, then through a courtyard and over to a small brick hallway. At the end of the hallway stood a heavy wooden door that looked as if it had been made from the shields of Vikings, battered with the blows from the axes of Francish enemies.

At the door, Lucas rapped three times with his middle knuckle.

A small peephole toward the top opened, revealing only a solitary faded blue eye. The hole closed just as quickly, and several loud latches turned on the other side of the door. A creak broke the still night air, followed by the smoke of cigarettes and the laughter of men spilling out from the establishment's confines.

Lucas pushed me inside, and I found myself staring up at the eyes of a towering man who sported a ginger-red pirate's beard.

I looked out over the dimly lit room as my nose took in the smell of stale beer that had seeped its way into the floorboards over many years of use. Men in dapper suits of various shades of brown and black stood around or sat on stools, engaged in conversations ranging from serious to hysterical.

Captain BlueBeard, as I had titled him in my mind, slammed the door shut thunderously, and its sound caused all speaking to cease. Everyone turned to get a good look at the fresh meat Lucas had brought in from the street. After a moment where I felt awkwardly on show, everyone went back to their conversations.

Along the wall nearest the entrance, I spotted a large wooden carving of a fat pig, its tusks covered in peeling red paint.

Lucas came up behind me and slapped me on my back. "Now this, my dear Josef, is the Rote Schwein, our proud cabaret and home of the finest dolls!"

He twirled me around in delight and led me by the arm toward a long wooden bar. A gray-bearded man with gentle eyes nodded from behind it as we made our way over.

"I see you brought a friend!" he exlaimed to Lucas, slapping two glasses down onto the slab of scuffed wood. He filled the glasses to the brim with an amber liquid topped with a frothy cloud that looked like soapy bubbles.

"Wolfe," Lucas said, "I would like to introduce you to my good friend, Josef." He pushed me toward the bar. "Josef is staying with Anke and me for a while. So, I imagine that you will be seeing a lot of him for the time being."

Wolfe wiped his hands onto a soiled apron, then reached one out to firmly shake mine.

"A pleasure to meet you."

"You as well."

A younger man with dark hair and eyes ran to and fro behind Wolfe, clearing away the empty glasses of patrons. He would whisk the steins off the bartop, then turn to wash them in a soapy basin before neatly stacking them again in a row. "And this is Johan, our barback," Wolfe said, pointing to the young man, who lifted an elbow and his chin as if to say "hallo" between the soapings.

He turned back to Lucas and scowled. "If I were you, I would hurry up and head backstage. Miss Sauerkraut is turning to pure pickle brine by the minute. She thinks you forgot that she has a show to perform this evening."

Lucas rolled his eyes, then picked up one of the glasses of foamy beer and handed it to me. The other he grabbed and chugged out a giant sip before gripping it tightly and heading across the room, past a worn black piano and toward a small door along the wall.

I followed behind him, staring with wonder along the way at both the beer in my hands and all of the men carousing around the room. Not a woman in sight. Curious.

As we entered the side room behind the piano, a pair of women's hose lay across a chair, a bra splayed itself on the floor, and various nighties and scantily assembled dresses were strewn on hooks and tables.

An older man with skin of leather sat in a green dress in front of a shattered mirror. The man cast a glaring glaze into the looking glass that reflected back at Lucas with fury.

He lifted a cigarette that rested between two stubby fingers whose nails were dabbed with red nail paint up to his ruby lined lips. He pulled hard on the butt, then exhaled a long line of smoke into the mirror, which fell apart when it hit his rebounded image.

The man emitted a sound from his throat that sounded like gravel being scraped across the ground by bicycle tires. "I thought I would have to send the Gestapo out for you," he grumbled.

Lucas set the beer glass down on a mirror stand near the man and placed a hand on his hip. "There, there, Miss Sauerkraut, is that any way to behave in front of a stranger?" he reprimanded.

The gruff man looked over to me and grunted.

"My bestest of friends Josef, meet the one and only, Miss Salley Sauer, also known as Miss Sauerkraut. Berlin's best and worst doll."

Sally giggled at Lucas's introduction and purred, "You bad boy." The guy turned to me and pointed with his hairy, cigarette-holding hand. "You there, little boy!"

I stood there, mesmerized at the sight of this battleworn man who was dressed as a woman—except for his bald, glowing head.

"Hallo? Boy?" Sally snapped his fingers.

I looked into his eyes.

"Yes, that's it—you." Sally motioned me over.

"Do you mean me, sir?" I asked nervously.

"Sir?" Sally laughed thunderously. Then he abruptly stopped and stared at me. "In this bar you will always refer to me as a lady. I'm a she in these walls...absolutely never a he! Is that clear child?"

I felt a lump in my throat so I nodded.

"Now, let us start again." Sally said. "You, little boy!"

"Yes...Miss," I stammered.

"Now go grab that sheet music from under that yellow robe over there." She pointed, and I meekly walked to the paper and picked it up.

As I came closer to Sally to hand it over, I slowed my already measured pace.

Sally reached out her hand and sucked her teeth before stretching out and snatching the papers from my grip.

"I'm not a creature from a Grimm's fable, darling."

She rolled the sheet music up, then walked over and slapped Lucas on the behind with it.

"Next time, do not be late," she rebuked him. "I'm too old of an artisté to have to worry about whether or not the help will arrive in time for my show!"

Lucas began to laugh, which started a chain that moved on to Sally with her heaving roar and then on to me. I could not help but to join in on the delight of this ludicrously new experience.

After a moment, Sally abruptly stopped and commanded me once again. "Now, be a good little *kleiner junge* and bring Mama a glass of water from over there by my hair." She pointed toward the black bob that sat on top of a statue of a Greek goddess.

Sally took the hair from my hands a moment later, pulling it onto her head and standing up. "Enough pitter patter." She stamped her stubby-stockinged feet on the floor. "Let's get out on the stage. I'd like to be home early. My dear Maximillian has been away to Magedeburg and returns in the morning. I would like to get in at least a few hours of rest tonight, so I look fresh for him."

She started to shuffle toward the door, stopping only to plop on some black low heels. "It's not so easy to look beautiful anymore on just a handful of winks and a few liters of bitter coffee," she said before snatching a green boa off a lamp and throwing it over one shoulder. With a wink toward Lucas, Sally marched out the door as if she were entering the Colosseum to thunderous applause.

"Come on," Lucas called out to me as he ran toward the door as well, "you'll love this!"

Unsure of what was happening, I followed behind in wonder, like a child seeing a butterfly take flight for the first time.

The bar full of men once again fell silent as Lucas sat down at the piano. Sally had already thrown one arm and her torso over it in a dramatic pose. The dim light was cut further by the haze of cigarette smoke, which gave Sally a softer look. You could almost see an alluring beauty on her face from years gone by if you squinted hard enough.

I inched my way backward, unwilling to turn my eyes away from Sally and Lucas, until I was at the edge of the crowd. What were they going to do?

Sally had already managed to put the crowd under a trance before a note was played or a song was sung.

Lucas began to stroke the keys, bringing forth a haunting tune. With his hands, he carried us all on an emotional journey. I had no idea that the piano could sound so stirring, nor did I realize that the man I was sharing a bed with was so talented, dare I say even mysterious. His usually slight frame seemed full-bodied and virile as he worked and tamed the instrument with great passion.

I remembered then that I had only known Lucas for mere days. What did I really know about him, if anything at all?

The music trilled sadly, and Sally swept her head and arms upward until she stood erect, staring off toward an unknown sight in silence. At a break in the notes, in a low and still gravelly voice, she began to sing:

Love may come.
Love may go.
New love is like the falling of fresh white snow.
One minute it is there
and then it melts and goes.
But the memories fill your heart
till it overflows.
Love may come.
Love may go.

As Sally sang, an image of my mother flashed before my eyes. It was my seventh birthday, and she held her hands over my eyes and led me forward. When she dropped her hands, we were standing together in front of the Zoologischer Garten Berlin, where I had been begging her to take me. We had little money in those days, so Helena had scrimped and saved until we found ourselves joyfully flitting from cage to cage, taking in the wondrous sights of the animals in each of the zoo's enclosures. It was the one time I felt as if Helena was really happy to have me in her life. We ended the day eating flavored ice, mine a strange bitter lemon that I could still taste in my mouth after all these years. *Fitting, as all of my memories with her have that same taste now.*

The piano ended softly, and I found myself, like many of the other men around me, with damp cheeks. People shot up from their seats and burst into loud applause, yelling out, "Bravo!" and "Gut!"

Sally took a bow, then stood and blew kisses out to her supporters before walking to the door of her dressing room, where she disappeared.

Lucas ran down to me. "What did you think?" He sounded near breathless in anticipation of my answer.

I dried my tears with the back of my hands. "I have never experienced anything like this before." It was all I could say.

He gave me a look of understanding, then led me back to the bar where we had met Wolfe earlier. Lucas motioned to the man for some drinks, and I felt a puzzled look cross my face

"How can a place like this even exist?"

"The Rote Schwein is nearly impossible to find," Lucas said with a chuckle, as Wolfe deposited two more beers in front of us. "You have to know exactly where to look for it, or else it's just another door on any other building in any other part of Berlin."

"But the Nazis?"

As I spoke the words, Lucas's smile faded.

"Up until a few years ago, homosexuals were left alone in Berlin—they were even well regarded" he said without emotion. "Once the Nazis came into power, there was a great purge of the doll bars and homosexual establishments. Now, this is the last of them . . ."

Fear crept up my leg and escaped through my lips. "Maybe we should go home then."

"Relax. Even if we were raided, all they would do is smash a few tables and make a big fuss. Old Wolfe here would probably have to pay a big fine, but again, they would have to find us first."

After a pause, Lucas shook the heaviness off and brought a smile back to his face. "Never mind all of that. For tonight, let's not think of Nazis or anyone else."

He handed me his glass of bier and picked up the other from the bartop. "Instead let us focus on all the bier we have left to drink and all of the songs Sally has left to sing!" He lifted his glass in a toast. "Prost!"

It clinked against mine, and then he drew it back toward his mouth and began to guzzle.

I considered his words and his actions for a second, then shrugged. Lifting my own glass, I returned a yell of "*Prost!*" and tackled the amber liquid with the same ferocity as my pianist friend.

We slammed our empty glasses onto the bar together, and Lucas yelled out to Wolfe, "Two more!"

SEVERAL HOURS AND MANY biers later, Lucas somehow helped drag me back to our flat and physically pushed me up the stairs toward our bedroom.

He shushed me sternly when we passed Anke's door as I sang out between giggles, "Love may come. Love may go!"

Lucas led me to the chair and instructed me to sit down. I obeyed, and as he helped me take my shirt off, I hiccupped, *"Memories fill your heart . . . it overflows."*

I let out a peal of laughter as he hoisted me up and guided me to the bed. With one arm, he held my frame up to stop it from falling over, and with the other he pulled back the covers, then steered me onto the bed. He swung my legs up and pulled the sheets over me.

Lucas headed to the other side of the bed, where he quickly stripped down and threw on his pajama bottoms, then slid in beside me.

"I had so much fun!" I lifted my head up off the pillows and sat up.

Lucas took his glasses off and put them on the bureau. "I am glad you did."

"The Rote Schwein is so much fun!" I declared emphatically.

He patted me over the covers on my leg.

"Yes, it is, Josef. Yes, it is." He spoke softly, as if trying to help me lower my own volume.

"Sally Sauer is so much . . ."

"Fun?" Lucas asked.

This made me giggle harder.

"Lie back and rest now. It will be morning soon, and you have darning and sewing to do, as Anke will not care anything about bier or Miss Sauerkraut."

I slid back down on the mattress and settled my spinning head onto the pillow, closing my eyes. I was just about to drift to sleep when an urge burst up from inside of me. I swooped my body back upright.

"What happened?" Lucas asked, groggy with sleep already. "Is everything alright?"

I leaned over. "Everything is perfect." I gave him a quick peck on his lips, which tasted of bier and sweet security.

Lucas lay there with his eyes now wide open as I turned over, scooted down, and snuggled myself into the pillows with a smile.

▼

A FEW WEEKS LATER, Anke, Lucas, and I strolled through the eastern meadow of the Stadtpark Schöneberg. The sun shone brightly as we began our walk at Martin-Luther-Straße and headed at a gentle pace toward the Volkspark Wilmersdorf on Kufsteiner Straße. Mothers pushed their baby carriages, and lovers kissed on a park bench along the way.

A vendor was selling popcorn on a path, and Lucas and I followed behind Anke as she ran to buy a large bag of the warm, salty kernels.

"You work well with Anke," Lucas remarked. "Do you think you would like to be a seamstress or a tailor yourself someday?"

I stopped walking to consider. "Hmm," I thought aloud. "I have never given much thought to anything really, as I never had plans of my own. Helena always seemed to decide everything, and I just did as told, usually without question."

"What exactly happened with your mother? You say she abandoned you, but what does that mean?"

"Let's just say she's always had one person on her mind—herself." I let out a short, subdued laugh as we continued our walk. "She would be the first to tell you, and quite loudly at that, that she did everything for the two of us once my father died. But she had a habit of never thinking beyond herself and where, or rather who, would provide her with her next meal. For as far back as I can recall, she was hustling to get herself a man. And not just any man, but someone well-off. Whatever she had to do to get a leg up on the other women, she did willingly."

We paused to sit on a bench, and I continued. "In some ways, I cannot say I blame her. It is hard to be a woman in this world, especially a widow with a child. But for my mother, I was more of an afterthought, just something in the way of getting what she truly desired."

I bent down and plucked a wild dandelion from near my feet. As I pulled its petals off one by one, I felt Lucas's soft gaze upon me.

"One time she had a romantic liaison with a jeweler whose family used to be the personal crafters for the house of Hagen prior to the republic. Nothing sent Helena's emotions into a flutter quicker than the *Bildungsbürgertum* and the *bourgeoisie*. She loved the thought of nobility even though it had long been abolished—the shine of former alignment still sparkled for her like the jewels this one man crafted."

"The jeweler did not know about me, so Helena would often leave me with our neighbor, a woman named Frau Teubert and her two children. The Frau hated me with a passion and would beat my legs with a broom if I made too much noise or interrupted her own children in any way. In turn, her little girls, knowing what would happen if I was not silent, would pinch my arms whenever Frau Teubert left the room, twisting my skin hard until I yelped. The Frau would then rush back to the room to beat me like she did her rugs. I did not dare speak up to my mother, though she sometimes left me for days, for fear she would gladly choose to send me to a *waisenhaus* or an orphanage if she was forced to decide between confessing to the jeweler that she had a child or continuing her dalliance with her secret held tightly until she could convince the Herr to wed her."

With the petals all plucked from the flower, I stood up. "Such was life with Helena." I reached out a hand and helped Lucas to his feet. "Some people get mutters who dote. I got one who convinced only herself she cared about me. I was forever and always in the way." I tossed the naked stem onto the ground and stepped on it, pushing it into the grass and dirt.

We started to walk again. "How about you?" I asked.

"How about me, what?" Lucas raised his eyebrows.

"You asked me what I wanted to be. What about yourself?"

"I have always wanted to be a concert pianist," Lucas declared, his eyes seeming to disappear on an unknown stage in his own mind. "But . . ."

"But what?"

We stopped walking again.

"I attended music school for a short while. Until our parents died."

I gasped. "Forgive me, Lucas. I have been so consumed with my own survival that I never even asked why you and Anke were living together on your own"

He gave me a sweet smile.

"It is okay, Josef, it is okay. I don't like to talk much about it, but I will tell you. Our parents joined a Lutheran mission to Togoland when we were young. They decided to leave us behind for the first year with relatives. Unfortunately, they died of malaria within a few months of their arrival."

"I am so sorry."

He continued, "Once the money they had set aside to care for us ran out, the relatives dropped us off at an orphanage, and what I had learned on the piano as a child was all that I would ever learn from any teacher, at least in a school setting."

This surprised me. "How do you play so beautifully then?"

"Whatever I learned formally was enough for me to figure the rest out by ear and by error." He looked wistfully into the distance. "Someday, I hope to play beautiful music in a great big concert hall, instead of silly songs at a dingy bar for dolls."

Just then, a kernel of popcorn bounced off his cheek.

We both turned to see Anke returning with her treat. She lifted some up to her mouth to chew. "Why such gloomy faces?" she joked.

"I was telling Josef about Mother and Father."

His sister stopped chewing, and a look of sadness came across her face.

"I have not thought of them in quite a while," she admitted.

"Maybe we should walk home now," he said.

Shaking her head, Anke declared, "I will not have such nonsense." Her smile returned, and she looped one of her arms into one of each of ours and began to march us forward with her in the middle. "I have got my two favorite escorts with me, and I am not quite ready to go back to stitching yet," She smirked, and her eyes twinkled. "At least not without a little fun."

Anke unhooked our arms, then threw some more popcorn into each of our faces. She started to run away, her laughter fading as she sprinted toward the center of the meadow.

Lucas raised an eyebrow as a question, and I replied with a nod. With that, we both ran off after Anke, catching up to her within seconds. She stopped and threw the rest of the bag's contents into our faces as we tackled her together in a fit of laughter onto the gentle grass.

We lay on the ground and looked up at the sky together, Anke holding my hand in her right and her brother's in her left. We were all deep in our analysis of the clouds when she blurted out, "I met a boy."

"Wait, what?" I sputtered.

Lucas and I jolted upright and looked down at her with wide eyes. I settled my legs under my body, placed my elbows on my knees and my palms on my face, and then prodded her forward. "Let's begin with when?"

"It was several weeks back," she said, sitting up as well. "The meeting was both tragic and magical"—her face furrowed—"so how does one tell of something so happy when one must also tell of something so horrible? I could find such few words, so I have not said any up until now." Her voice grew faint, and her eyes full of terror. A strange shiver went up my back.

Lucas reached over and clasped her hands, which they held together in her lap. "There's no other way than to just say it," he pressed her.

"It was last Thursday. I was on my way back from the *gemüsemarkt*. I had just bought some beets to pickle . . ."

"Go ahead, Anke," I encouraged, moving quickly from elation over hearing about her new lover to fear of whatever unknown she was withholding.

She looked right through me. "I was almost past the book shop when the Nazis pulled up right in front of me, in two jeeps. Their tires had barely screeched to a halt when four or five of them jumped out and headed in my direction." She quivered. "I dropped my bags, and the beets rolled everywhere."

Lucas squeezed her hands tighter, "It's alright though, Anke. Go on . . . the Nazis?"

She turned to her brother, her eyes now dotted with tears. "Oh Lucas," she gasped, "it was not me they had come for."

Her head turned back toward the past, and her voice lowered. "Edsel, the butcher's son, ran out of his family's own shop next door. He rushed to my side to help me collect the fallen beets, but I just stood there paralyzed."

"Edsel?" I broke in. "What a curious and masculine name, Anke."

I had hoped to lighten the mood, but she continued on as if she hadn't heard me.

"Only seconds had passed when"—she shivered—"two loud bangs pierced the air." Her chin lowered to her chest, shaking. "The soldiers ran out of the shop as quickly as they had run in. An old woman came out after them, screaming that they had killed her husband, but—one of the Nazi soldiers just shot her dead." Her eyes became vacant as she lifted them again. "Right there. In front of me."

Anke took a shallow breath. "A small crowd had gathered, and the one who shot the woman glared at us as if he dared anyone to challenge him. He nodded toward the woman's body and simply stated, 'Bolsheviks,' before he spit on the ground, as if this one word could justify the blood that now ran between the cobblestones and my purple beets, which had been smashed by the soldiers' boots."

Anke returned to the present, looking between us. "And that is how I met Edsel, the butcher's son." She released her brother's hands. "We have been seeing each other quietly ever since."

"Oh Anke," Lucas groaned, then leaned over and hugged her deeply. I couldn't help myself—I had to join in on this hug, until the three of us had squeezed ourselves into one, as Lucas and I tried to press the sadness out of Anke.

We resettled ourselves back onto the ground and spent the rest of the afternoon admiring the sky and asking Anke all about Edsel, never mentioning the bookshop or Bolsheviks again.

▼

LATER THAT EVENING, Lucas and I lay in bed, he with his book and me with my back toward him in thought.

"I really enjoyed today with you and Anke," I told him.

I felt him set his book down. "Me too."

He reached over and touched my arched hip atop of the covers. I flinched at his touch, then sat up.

"Do not worry . . ." Lucas whispered, leaning in toward my face.

My eyes began to close and my heart started to race, but as his lips came closer, I pulled away on instinct, breaking the mood and killing the moment.

"I'm sorry, I can't."

"What is it?" Lucas asked. "Is it me?"

The right words could not formulate in my mind, so I sat in silence.

He pondered it for a moment. "What happened to you before you came to live with us?"

I rolled back over again, showing him only my back.

"It is alright if you are not still ready to talk about it. I just thought . . . well," he muttered, "since you live here, you sleep in my bed, and now you also know about my parents, I thought that you might, maybe, feel like you could talk to me by now."

He lay down and rolled over so that his back was now to me. "But if you don't . . ." He sighed.

"I don't," I said feebly.

Lucas reached up and turned off the lamp.

"Okay. Good night then."

In the darkness and stillness that followed, only our breathing could be heard.

I sat back up in the bed, speaking bitterly into the absence of light. "What do you want to know, Lucas? About how my stepfather beat me? Or about how Marteen and his friends held me down . . ."

The light clicked back on, and Lucas rolled over to see my hot face and watering eyes.

"How they stripped off my clothes . . ." Spittle flew from my mouth as I wept out these words. "Or how they forced themselves on—no, in me, by the river?" I threw my hands over my face to hide my shame and sobbed, yelling into them, "Or how my own mother then abandoned me for the money of a furrier?"

His warm and tender hands lifted my own off of my mouth and from my eyes, away from the dripping of drool and tears.

"I am so sorry, Josef," he whispered. "I never imagined— I saw the blood on your pants, but . . ."

He put my hands into my lap and threw his arms around my neck, and I broke into more pieces than Sally's mirror at the Rote Schwein.

His words boiled with fury. "Who could do this to you? Who could harm someone so kind?" Unclasping my neck, he lifted my face up into his hands. "Someone . . . so beautiful." His voice simmered into a husky passion.

He came in slowly, and this time I did not resist his efforts as his lips touched mine. The wetness of his mouth met my own. I leaned into him and let our tongues entwine. With each hot and measured heave, I felt the pains of the past recede from my mind.

Lucas clasped the back of my neck with one hand while his other began to trail along my chest. He squeezed my body, pulling me in closer.

I moaned with delight as his hand began to trail toward my stomach. Suddenly, he had landed beneath my cotton pants, and I writhed with heavy breaths as he pulled the garment down from my legs and freed me from my clothes.

We kissed with heated passion as he removed his own clothing.

Now we were entangled, flesh pressed against flesh, and we rolled atop of the sheets, pressing our bodies together, exploring each other's mouths with our tongues.

Lucas maneuvered his body on top of mine, then lifted my legs into the air until they were over his shoulders.

I felt a moment of panicked fear, as thoughts of the River Spree returned to my mind. But Lucas's touch was tender and reaffirming. There was passion in his eyes and gentleness on his lips so I pushed those fear aside and trusted myself to Lucas's care.

Lucas leaned in to kiss me deeply as his hands worked to guide his swollen shaft into me, where I was nervous yet eager and pulsating. As he entered, I bit his lower lip and cried out in both discomfort and excitement. The pain was not the same as when Tielo had forced himself upon me—this time it was welcomed and wanted. My body opened to this intrusion and felt freedom in the joining of our forms.

Our bodies moved in rhythm, slowly at first, as we discovered each other's flow. Lucas reached down and grasped my own member at last, pulling it in time with the rest of our gyrations until our dance grew more and more heated. Finally, we both screamed out and released our passion, his deep into my body and mine out onto his chest.

Once we were finished, Lucas rolled off of me, and we lay there holding hands until we drifted off to sleep.

FOR THE NEXT FEW WEEKS, I spent my days stitching and sewing with Anke. My evenings were spent watching Lucas and Sally perform at the Rote Schwein, where I was becoming fast friends with Wolfe and many of the bar's patrons. But it was my nights that were the most special, as I spent those in Lucas's arms.

One afternoon, I was finishing a hem on some trousers when a knock sounded on the door. I dropped my task onto the sofa.

I swung it open and started to ask "May I help you?" but never was able to get all the words out of my mouth, as I was stopped by the sight before me.

A handsome man who looked to be in his midtwenties and stood over six feet tall was there with flowers in his hand and a smile. The bouquet of deeply blue cornflowers surrounded by the gleaming white of a small handful of edelweiss could not distract from this man's blond hair and gray eyes, or the perfect lips that parted just enough to reveal a smile of glinting teeth.

I recovered myself as he asked, "Is Anke at home?"

"And who may I say is calling?" I looked him over from biceps to calf muscles, which I could make out beneath the pale linen suit that hugged his body.

"Edsel. My name is Edsel."

I urged him inside the flat and shut the door. "Oh, you are Edsel?" I asked through batted eyes.

"Yes, um— Yes, I am." He chuckled at me, clearly sensing my ridiculous attraction.

"One moment, Edsel," I said, unable to keep a hint of seduction out of my voice. I sashayed to the kitchen, looking back over my shoulder to see if his eyes were following me.

When I reached the steps, I yelled toward Anke's bedroom a little too excitedly, "Anke, you have company!"

Anke stormed down the steps in a flurry of yellow polka dots, tying a white scarf around her neck. She scolded me. "Josef, I told you I needed fifteen minutes to—" She stopped at the entrance to the kitchen and turned quickly into a lump of giggles.

"Oh, Edsel." She covered her mouth with one hand and tilted her eyes downward, as coquettish a look as I had ever seen. "What are you doing here?"

I thought to myself that she looked quite dashing and put together— with this yellow, figure-framing dress that ran to her midcalf—for someone who was suddenly acting so surprised that she had a visitor.

Edsel's face scrunched in confusion. "It's Tuesday. I told you I would pick you up for the best pig's ankle over at Scheiners on Tuesday."

After a moment of awkward silence, Anke lowered her hand from her face and laughed. "I know you did. I just wanted to make you sweat a little."

The two shared amused winks and snickers, and he declared her his "little devil" while Anke threw her arm into his and they sat down onto the couch together. I faded into nonexistence and recognized that I was no longer needed, or wanted, here.

I walked toward the hooks for my coat, feeling ridiculously alone in this room. "Speaking of pigs," I said softly to no one, "I promised Lucas that I would meet him at the Rote Schwein in a bit. Miss Sauerkraut has a new song that she's debuting tonight."

The walls ignored me as effectively as Edsel and Anke, who were lost in each other and did not hear me speaking at all, so I plopped a hat on my head as well and aimed for the door.

"I'm leaving," I announced loudly. I glanced back at Edsel, but he was facing Anke and the two were in a fit of flirtatious laughter. "Goodbye," I said as I opened the door.

Not even an acknowledgement? I wondered to myself, then slammed the door shut so loudly that my own teeth rattled. *That will teach Anke to bring home someone who looks like that then distract him from me with the perfect dress so that he completely ignores me.* I huffed and pouted my way toward the Rote Schwein.

"Oh well," I consoled myself with a laugh, "I still have Lucas."

When I arrived at the Rote Schwein, the place was dark and nearly empty. Wolfe was behind the bar, using a towel to dry bier steins and glasses shaped like boots. With each wipe, he would place the cleaned glass above his head in an open cabinet. He looked up at me, motioned with his head toward the stage, and rolled his eyes. I followed his glance toward the piano, where Lucas sat on the stool, while Sally, sans makeup and any semblance of womanhood, towered over him.

"*Macht schnell,*" she growled. "Mama doesn't have all night for you to make a decision on the tempo. Maximillian expects supper sometime before the return of Christ." She put one hand on her hip and the other raised, pointing into Lucas's determined face. "And if you have not learned by now it is your job to follow *my* lead, then I will have to retrain you as if you were ein Schüler im Kindergarten all over again!"

"Kindergarten!" Lucas howled. "What would you know about that when you're one step away from a complete loss of hearing, you old goat . . ."

A small snicker left my mouth as I continued right past them. No need for me to get involved in their lighthearted artistic squabble. The sounds of their comedic barbs turned into a barely audible jumble once I entered Sally's backstage area.

Taking advantage of the solitude, I walked around and inspected her scattered items of beauty. I picked up a hair clip in gold and ran my finger over the deep blue butterflies, cut from some kind of precious-looking metal that was soldered to the clip so that they became one object, both hard and beautiful.

I moved on to a hairpiece in ebony, lifting it off its perch. I pulled it onto my head and walked toward Sally's cracked mirror. A cry of laughter escaped my lips as I admired how it was short at my neck, with perfectly straight bangs over my eyes but long strands of hair that ran past my ears and toward my shoulders.

In the mirror's reflection, a dress on the wall behind me caught my eye, so I turned and pulled it off a hook. It was a pale champagne satin sleeveless dress that plunged dramatically at the breast. The hips were cut so that the bottom flared in every direction, while the hem was lined with large ostrich feathers dyed in the same shade as the fabric.

I pulled the dress up toward my body and admired myself once again in the mirror, posing as dramatically as the dress demanded. I giggled at my reflection.

A small cough that sounded like pebbles in a paper bag startled me. The reflection in the shattered glass was no longer just my own, but Sally's as well.

I gasped in embarrassment and pulled the dress down from my body, tossing it into a heap of clothes that sat atop a nearby table.

"Oh goodness, I am so sorry," I stammered. "I was just—"

Sally reached out one of her large hands and dropped it on my shoulder to stop me from speaking.

"Forget it, darling," she said gruffly. "I knew you were a doll from the second you stepped in here months ago."

"Me?" I laughed nervously.

Sally began to circle me closely, measuring me with her eyes. "A couple of minor adjustments here"—she nodded—"and hmm, ole Sally'll have to worry about keeping her job here at the Rote Schwein in no time with *dieses kleine Mädchen.*"

She pointed to the stool in front of the mirror. "Now sit."

When Sally barked, you moved.

She turned me around so that my back was to the fractured shards. The small table on which the mirror sat was covered in a muted yellow cloth with tiny flowers in pink, white, orange, and green. All over the table were little bowls of creams that lay between tiny brushes with caked-on foundation and shadows from years of use.

Sally pulled the wig off my head and threw it across the room. She snapped her fingers and said to herself, "I know exactly what will work." Then she pulled out a small glass bottle that was labeled "Covermark Concealer." She opened it with her rough hands and began to dollop a few drops onto spots on my cheeks and forehead. The cream felt cold, and I giggled. "What are you doing?"

She hushed me. "Our lives are just like applying makeup. First, we start with *der concealer*," she explained, as she fanned the concoction out evenly across my face with a cotton pad, applying what was almost a new layer of skin in a beautiful shade of soft peach. As she did, she continued to instruct me. "We spend the beginning of our lives hiding who we are from ourselves and others. In our youth, we cower from fear in order to persevere and survive."

She lifted up a tiny cup filled with *lidschatten* in the deepest shade of pink I had ever seen. It dazzled and sparkled as she dipped her index finger inside. "Close your eyes," she commanded.

"Next, we come alive and flower." I felt her finger brush over my eyelids, one at a time.

She picked up a charcoal pencil that she ran over each of my eyebrows. I felt its sharpness as it pressed closely against my upper and lower lids at the lash and water lines. "At this stage, we learn, we grow, we begin to add color to our lives. Slowly, we reveal who we are in all its beauty."

A puff of soft wind hit my face, and I could feel powder flying through the air as I inhaled its faint perfume of lilac and rose.

"Now pucker your lips out, *mein sohn*—or I should now say *meine tochter*, as I think I am at last the mother of a newborn girl." A wet smudge swept across my lips. "I always wanted a daughter, to be honest, but there never was anyone who I felt I could present as my own . . . until now."

She slapped both hands onto my shoulders. "Now, open your eyes!"

I turned around to face the mirror and found staring back at me from one of the large fragments of glass the face of a soft and beautiful young woman.

I leaned forward and looked in disbelief. "This seems . . . so strange," I stammered.

"Something tells me you always felt strange in your own skin."

I reached a hand out to touch the mirror. "I guess that is true."

Sally started to fumble through a bag on the floor and came up with a soft pink scarf, which she proceeded to wrap around my head.

"You will have to grow your hair out, darling, but for now, scarfs will do. That black mop you had on earlier is definitely not suited for you. That's the look of a woman who worked at the factory all day and rolled in for a *wodka* and a screw at night. But that's not your look, meine tochter—your look is youth and beauty."

"My mother always insisted I have short hair, though." I touched the scarf with my fingers.

"You have a new mother now, and Mama says you can only wear headpieces for the moment, but they do lose their drama if they are overused, so no more barber for you for a long time." She stopped to look me over fully from head to toe one more time.

My face crinkled. "Sally, I thought you said there were three parts to life and makeup. There is the concealer, then the eyeshadows, but is lipstick the third?"

"Oh!" she gasped coarsely. "I forgot the most important thing."

She leaned back down toward the bag and came back up with a small compact case and a long, angled brush.

"Now suck in your cheeks," she ordered. "Like this." Sally pulled both cheeks in and held her head high, modeling the pose she wanted me to strike.

I followed her lead as she dabbed the brush into some thick red powder, which she began to run up and down over one of my cheekbones.

"That tickles," I said, laughing.

"Relax, my darling. It is only rouge."

"What is it for?"

She dipped the brush again and then began to apply it to the other side of my face, moving it in a line from the corner of my mouth at an angle upward toward the tippy-top of my ear.

"It contours your face and gives your cheeks definition. This is the third and most important part of all, my child. *Das rouge* is power. When you arrive at this part of your life, you finally and unapologetically take the reins."

She stepped back and looked down at me.

"No matter how little makeup you have with you, remember this— there is absolutely no excuse not to put on your cheeks, darling. It is the difference between a regular Mädchen off the streets, and a doll. There, there," she approved to herself, as she examined me fully. "See what Mama has taught you about life?"

I stared at myself in disbelief.

Sally continued, "It's quite simple, to be honest, but this is the secret to everything, my darling daughter. Life is just like makeup—first you cower, then you flower, until at last you claim your power."

"Is that really me?" My voice cracked as I opened my eyes wider, surveying myself more closely to take in the full effects of Sally's new addition.

The young lady who looked back at me was no less than stunning.

"You truly are only seeing yourself for the first time," Sally mused.

I stared at myself for a few seconds before Sally abruptly shoved a wet rag in my face.

"Now wash it off!" she barked.

"Why?" I cried, not wanting to break free from whatever spell she had cast upon my face.

She pushed her hand toward me again, more firmly.

"What did I say about listening to Mama?"

I sighed, then took the small towel and began to rub the beauty off of my face.

Sally stood over me. "I want you to come to the bar an hour before Lucas does on each day. I have a wonderful little idea for the two of us to surprise him with a duet a week from next Tuesday. What do you think?" she asked, a twinkle in her clouding eyes.

"A duet? I wouldn't even know how to—"

Sally put a finger up to my lips.

"That's why you have me, my darling daughter. Just continue to study me, the way you have already been doing." She winked.

THE NEXT EVENING, Anke and I were sewing in silence, she on the couch, me on a kitchen chair. After I passed a loop through a blouse, I looked up at a small hardwood clock on the wall that read five o'clock.

"That is all for today," I said as I cut the needle from the thread and placed it in a bright red pin cushion that looked like a ripe tomato. "I promised Sally that I would meet her at the Rote Schwein early."

"From what I have heard about her, you do not want to be late." Anke laughed as I folded the white blouse with little blue flowers onto the table.

Walking to the coats, I grabbed one and headed toward the door. "Auf Wiedersehen!" I waved with the hand I had just pulled through my jacket sleeve.

"Aren't you going to wait for Luc—" Anke's voice cut off as I closed the door and practically skipped down the street.

It was delicious cooking up this little surprise for Lucas. For once, hiding something about myself didn't feel quite so painful.

The normally twenty-minute walk felt like seconds and I rapped on the bar's door so musically that even the normally frightening Captain Blue-Beard looked on at me with delight when I flitted into the Rote Schwein.

I bowed to Wolfe before lauding him with a howl, and then I headed back into Sally's dressing room.

She was already there, tapping the floor with a dancer's cane.

"But I'm not even late," I whined as I made my way over to her cowering glare and kissed her on each cheek.

She softened. "I know. I just never want you to lose your deference for your mama."

We soon both found ourselves laughing.

It was rare that Sally let down that gruff exterior, except for when she was performing, so I knew we were sharing a special trust, and it left me feeling warm inside.

She cleared a spot on a wooden trunk for me to sit by swiping a white feather boa onto the floor with a sweep of her cane.

For hours, we sat there going over the words to the song we were to perform together.

"It's *love* like the loss from war," she would exhort as she slammed her stick into the floor, "not *love* like a virgin girl running through a field of wheat. You have to feel the pain and then make sure it hurts the audience even more than it hurts you."

Word by word, Sally would dissect and rebuild my elocution and my personhood at the same time. It was clear how seriously she took my education. I could not remember a time in my life that anyone had shown such devotion to an endeavor I had been a part of. Because of this, I doubled my commitment to see this through—not just for Sally, but because I wanted this surprise for Lucas to be a way of thanking him for his gift of this new life. One where I finally felt fully safe.

When we were not rehearsing, Sally stood over me in the mirror, where she meticulously instructed me on how to paint each lash so that it curled upward, beckoning the onlooker to fall deeper into my eyes.

We would always end our routine practicing and then practicing yet again, the application of rouge onto my cheeks I would paint with a brushing action to create deep hues so that my face looked high-angled and regal. To Sally's point, the other makeup gave life to my face, but the rouge defined me and turned me from ein junge with makeup into a force of nature with high value, judgment, and maybe even power.

This continued for almost two weeks. I had to steal time wherever I could, but mostly it meant I had to skip supper with Anke and Lucas, which for some reason made Lucas endearingly full of suspicion for my unaccounted hours.

One late afternoon, as I prepared to leave the flat, I could hear Lucas downstairs in a whispered conversation with Anke where he insisted that I must be seeing another man or even multiple men. I stood at the top of the steps and listened to his jealous rant and found it adorably full of devotion. *He must really love me to be this incensed*, I thought to myself.

Lucas moaned to his sister, "It makes me wonder if I unlocked the beast within and now he prowls for other lovers each night."

Anke replied with a chuckle, "I was not aware that your prowess as a partner was so intoxicating that it could be the cause of an insatiable need."

"I'm being serious," Lucas insisted. "I am worried I will not be enough for Josef. He is incredibly attractive, you know. I see all of the other men at the Rote Schwein who stare at him, and some have even started to make their move."

"Have a little faith in Josef," Anke said with care, and I noticed her hand patting his arm as I ran down the stairs, pretending not to have heard any of their conversation.

His suspicions made me giggle to myself, as I stole off into the dusk— not to sleep with other men but to become a woman.

THAT NIGHT, when I returned home, Lucas would not even talk to me. As he sat in his bed, he pretended to be completely absorbed in his book for ten solid minutes, never once turning the page.

In between his heavy breaths of annoyance, I could feel his eyes aflame with jealousy as he looked up over the top of the book at me undressing.

"Where have you been?" he barked at last.

I laughed as I pulled a sleep shirt over my head and walked toward the bed.

Climbing in, I leaned over and kissed his spectacles, smudging his right lens with the imprint of my lips.

Lucas slammed his book down in his lap. "Being cutesy is not an explanation." He pulled his glasses off his face and began to wipe them with the hem of a sheet.

"Oh, Lucas," I said with exasperation, "it's the same answer I had the night before, and the night before that."

I settled into the bed.

"You will find out soon enough," we both said at the same time, though his tone held an annoyed mimic.

"I just hope my finding out doesn't break my heart," he added softly.

I rolled back over and began to stroke his nearest arm, running my fingers through its light blond hairs.

"Do not be ridiculous," I assured him before rolling over to go to sleep. "There could be no one else for me but you, Lucas Strechburg."

I yawned, then slipped into dreams of b flats and low necklines.

AT LAST, THE DAY Sally and I had worked so hard to prepare for had finally come. Finished with my work, I begged Anke, "I know this is early, but I promise today will be the last day I rush off to meet Sally. We have been working on something special for Lucas, and tonight I will finally give him my gift."

"Go, Josef." She nodded, not even looking up from her own work. "Whatever this surprise is, I am glad it has finally arrived, as I don't think I could take one more sulking dinner with my brother, nor one more minute of your secretive elation."

I ran over and kissed Anke on her cheek, then rushed out of the flat, just as I had been doing for many days past.

When I got to the Rote Schwein, I found myself alone in Sally's dressing room. I used the few minutes I had to spare before she came marching in like a major general and commanded me to my war post to examine in greater detail the beauty of the wardrobe that she kept here.

The long dress in chartreuse with purple feathers that flowered along the hemline at the ankles was particularly delightful. I pulled it out and held it up to me, noting the way the light danced off of the center and how the neckline forced one's eyes toward the breasts.

One day, maybe Sally would let me try it on, though I wouldn't dare without her permission. I laughed to myself.

After a few minutes, I sat on a chair and waited. It was one of the first moments I'd had to just simply relax in weeks, so I wasn't disappointed that Sally was uncharacteristically late. My eyes lowered as I thought about the song we had rehearsed and were at last prepared to perform that night. Nerves bubbled in my belly, but my greatest feeling was of happiness at this opportunity that Sally had given to me. "Maybe she isn't so *sauer* after all." I chuckled before I began to drift into unconsciousness.

I MUST HAVE BEEN snoring when I was startled awake midsnort by a foot kicking on the leg of the chair I lounged in.

"Where is Sally?" Lucas asked.

I surveyed the room with waking eyes that slowly focused on his face. "I don't know," I said, fighting back an audible yawn. "What time is it?" I asked through sleepy eyes.

"Half eight." Lucas said with some concern.

I shot upright. "Half eight? She was supposed to meet me here at six o'clock."

"It's not like her," Lucas said. "Usually she is the early bird waiting on others to arrive."

"No kidding," I chuckled.

"I'm serious. Let's go check with Wolfe—maybe he knows where she is."

I pulled myself out of the chair and followed after Lucas into the main room and directly over to the bar, where Wolfe poured bier into glasses for the scattered patrons who had already arrived for the evening.

"Have you seen Sally?" Lucas asked.

"Is she not in the back?" Wolfe replied, stacking his glasses of various sizes.

The look of concern on Lucas's face deepened. "No. In fact, she was supposed to meet Josef here over two hours ago, and now she's late for our rehearsal."

Wolfe stopped what he was doing. "Now that is very unlike Miss Sauerkraut. If she is anything, she is prompt, so that she can remind us all that we are not." He ended with a smile. "I am sure she is okay, as I believe Maximillian was coming back to town today after a business trip. She will probably be here and bitter any minute now." He shrugged.

Just then, BlueBeard let a dapper old man into the bar. He was dressed like a dandy in a black-and-white-checkered wool suit, complete with a pocket square of solid pink. The stylish gentleman in his late sixties trembled and shook as he stumbled toward the bar.

"Maximillian?" Lucas gasped, running to his side. He then guided the old man onto a bar stool.

"What happened?" Wolfe begged across the bar. "Where is Sally?"

The old man's hands shook as he lifted one toward his mouth, almost covering it but not before he cried out with terror. "They took her!"

"What do you mean?" Lucas asked. When Maximillian did not reply, he said more sternly, "What do you mean, Maximillian? Who took her?"

Finally, he grabbed the man's shoulders and clenched them, almost yelling into his face. "Who took Sally?"

The old man began to weep, and his body shook.

"One minute she was there"—he lifted his head toward Lucas—"and the next . . ."

He lowered it again, then Maximillian fainted. His body began to slip off of the stool and toward the floor. I rushed to help Lucas save him from the fall. Together we brought his body back upright, and Lucas gently slapped Maximillian's cheeks to help him regain consciousness.

Wolfe took down a bottle of whiskey and pulled out a small glass. He filled it and pushed it toward Maximillian's body. Lucas pressed it into Maximillian's hand, then helped the gentleman lift the glass to his lips, forcing him to swallow some of the calming potion.

Once he had taken a few sips, Lucas gently pushed him, "Now then. Slowly tell us everything."

Maximillian swallowed both the whiskey and his fear, and began. "She had just left our flat to come here. I had only just gotten back to Berlin this afternoon, but she insisted she needed to leave earlier than usual as she was to meet someone here."

He started to tremble again, so Lucas helped Maximillian to take another sip.

"No sooner had I heard her footsteps fade from our stairwell than there was shouting outside on our street. I rushed to the windowsill to see what was happening down below when . . ."

Maximillian dropped the tumbler, sending both the glass and whiskey spilling onto Lucas's legs as well as my shoes. A cry that sounded like a sacrificial lamb being bled broke from Maximillian's throat, and then he continued his story through agonizing sobs. "It was a gang of them...the *Sturmabteilungen!*"

I began to rub this man's back, who until a moment ago had been a complete stranger but was now someone I could not help but feel a great need to comfort.

"Stormtroopers?" Wolfe choked.

Lucas looked in my eyes. "Sounds just like the ones Anke saw shoot the bookseller." His brows grew worried. "But I don't get it, Sally is not a Bolshevik—is she, Maximillian?"

75

Maximillian had stopped his crying and now just stared vacantly across the bar. He shook his head at Lucas's question, then continued quietly. "All the same, they were shouting at her. Before I could even pull myself away from the window to run down to her aid, it was over."

He sat there in silence as Wolfe, Lucas, and I exchanged looks, unsure what exactly Maximillian meant by "over."

A single tear welled up in the man's vacant eyes. "A wagon pulled up, and they threw Sally inside." His voice began to fade. "They drove off into the night with Sally, and I do not know if I may ever see her again . . ."

Lucas joined me now in consoling the poor man, rubbing the other side of Maximillian's back.

"Well that's it," Wolfe declared. "The rumors are true."

We looked at the bartender in confusion. "It's no longer just the socialists and the trade unionists they are after," he continued. "First they closed the bars, but they left us alone so long as we remained in the shadows, but now . . ." His unfinished words left us all to think on the whisperings that blew through the streets of Berlin like a cold wind. Stories about all types of people who'd disappeared or were taken away to no one knew where.

Wolfe called out to his trusty young barback, "Johan, come over here will you."

Johan, who was retrieving mugs from tables, dropped his ware onto the bar and approached.

"Johan here will help you to my flat, Maximillian," Wolfe announced.

The young man nodded, then came up beside Lucas and me. We were still holding Maximillian in place to prevent him from slipping toward the floor again.

"You can stay with me for the evening," Wolfe continued. "I have a cousin in the bureau, and I will make inquiries for us in the morning about Sally."

Johan put one of Maximillian's arms around his shoulders, and the three of us hoisted him up. As Johan made his way toward a door behind the bar that must have led to Wolfe's apartment above or behind the Rote Schwein, Wolfe came out from behind the bar and put his hands on his hips.

"Listen up, all," he said loudly, quieting the murmurs that had been rolling since Maximilian entered the Rote Schwein. "There is no point in us staying open this evening!" he shouted. "Perhaps any evening." He mumbled these words under his breath. "It is just a matter of time before . . ."

76

Maximillian, who had been allowing Johan to drag him away while he silently cried, threw the man's arm off his shoulder and marched sternly toward Wolfe.

"What?" he asked with great indignation. "You can do no such thing!"

He turned to the bar's customers and then back to Wolfe. "Sally would not hear of it. The Rote Schwein means everything to her, and she would insist you carry on."

With his declaration spoken, he turned back to Johan. "You may escort me to my seat, young man," he directed. "I will not be going home, whether that be to Wolfe's, my own, or anywhere else, until a night is had, for Sally's sake. That is what she would want."

The audience broke into rounds of applause and hollers. Maximillian walked over to a small round table, where a middle-aged man sat alone with his bier. Maximilian grabbed it out of his hands.

"For Sally!" He held up the glass and toasted with verve.

"For Sally!" echoed as glasses were raised and clinked together around the Rote Schwein.

"Wherever she is . . ." Maximillian said to himself, before he chugged the man's drink.

Wolfe grunted, somewhere between a scoff of disgusted disbelief at the group's recklessness and admiration for their determination in the face of the unknown. He slowly walked back behind the bar, then leaned across it toward Lucas and me.

"Drink and be merry?" he asked. "I don't know how we can do this without Sally."

He began to wipe the counter off with a towel. "Who will give us laughter? Who will give us glamour, however twisted it was from ole Miss Sauerkraut?" He laughed to lighten his own mood.

A long, sad pause followed as he wiped the countertop back and forth, then back and forth again. We stood in melancholy for at least a minute before I stepped forward and slammed my fist down onto the counter, causing the glasses on either end to jump up before settling back down in a rattle.

"I will," I stated.

Lucas, Wolf, Johan, and the other bar patrons all stopped to look at me like I was crazy.

"Josef, what are you talking about?" Lucas asked. He sounded annoyed by my attempt to help in any way.

Everyone looked on as I began to explain, "I'm the reason that Sally was on her way here early tonight. She and I were going to perform together."

Gasps came from across the bar, but none looked more surprised than Lucas, whose lower jaw fell open.

I grabbed his arm. "It was the surprise I've been hiding for these past weeks."

"But . . ." he stammered. "You mean you were here with Sally each evening?"

His sheepish tone was both apologetic and full of self-chastisement.

"That is no longer important, Lucas." I squeezed his arm to reassure him that his suspicions, while ridiculous, were already forgotten. "What is important is that I will do the number alone, just like Sally taught me."

"You do not have to do this," Lucas said sternly.

"Yes, I do."

I turned to the small crowd. "We have to show that the Rote Schwein will be here waiting for Sally when she returns!"

One of the bar's patrons stood up on his chair and shouted, "To hell with the Nazis!"

The rest of the bar returned his call, thundering the words in return, as people stomped, clapped, drank, and shouted their defiance.

Determined to see through what Sally and I had worked so hard on, I took the determination of the Rote Schwein and its customers with me as I marched across the bar into Sally's dressing room.

Once inside, the enormity of the task, and of her absence, hit me. I leaned against the wall just inside the entrance, where no one could see me, and let a shiver run through my body. "What in the darkest pits of hell was I thinking saying that I could do this on my own?" I asked myself aloud.

Somewhere in my mind, though, I heard Sally answer me back, telling me to just do everything Mama had taught me, that it would all work out fine . . . or else she would boil me in hot oil if I embarrassed her.

The thought of her gravelly growl gave me the strength I needed, so I walked myself over to the mirror, removed my shirt, and slowly began to paint my face the way Sally had shown me so many times over these last few weeks.

I smeared myself first with the Max Factor foundation Sally had recently received as a gift from Maximillian, smoothing it across my cheeks, forehead, and neck. My skin already began to soften into more of a delicate, even tone with each layering of this base. When I was through with the concealer, I wiped my hands onto a rag, then dipped my index finger into the bold blue shadow Sally had insisted was the perfect shade for my eyes. "It's sapphire, darling, and the men will swoon from the jeweled glint it brings out in your own blue eyes." I slid it across both lids until they sparkled.

With the darkest of coal pencil sticks, I lined my eyes until they almost popped out of my head.

Reaching into a small bag on the table, I pulled out a tube of lipstick in the shade of pink tulips and rubbed it across my lips, then smacked them together to spread the cream out evenly.

I reached down into a pile of clothes on the floor and came up with a black piece of fabric, which I wrapped around my head like a scarf.

After this, I pulled back from the mirror and gazed with wonder. Who was this woman who stared back at me from amidst these fractured shards of glass?

When I was finished admiring my own doing, I started to get up from the chair in front of the mirror—and then something hit me.

"I cannot forget my cheeks," I declared aloud. "I could fall while on stage or forget the lyrics, but Sally would never forgive me if I went out on the stage without rouge on my cheeks." I laughed, opening a small round container of crimson powder, which I dabbed a thin-tipped makeup brush into. Once it was covered, I ran it up and down from the top of my ear to the corner of my mouth as I sucked in both of my cheeks. I repeated the action on my other side.

"Now I am ready!" I said to myself. I pushed the chair up from the table and headed toward Sally's rack of dresses.

The bar was full by the time I left the dressing room. Whispered and animated conversations alike ricocheted off the walls. Words were exchanged in some corners of the room in sadness over Sally, while others reverberated in hushed tones colored with fear for what this all meant for each of us.

Lucas, who was lightly tinkling on the piano, stopped abruptly when I entered the room. His cessation began a hush of silence that swept like a wave from the front of the bar to the very back, where BlueBeard could barely be seen between smoke and shadows.

I approached the piano, at first with great trepidation, as I looked into Lucas's gawping mouth and bulging eyes.

After a few seconds, he recovered himself and turned his stare into a smile of wonderment, his eyes never leaving my approaching figure. His fingers began to run lightly across the keys, which settled the crowd and pulled them in so that their bodies seemed to lean toward us.

My dress of deep blue sequins hugged my body. It was floor length, though it cut from my mid left hip, opening my legs for view all the way so that my black heels with their ribbons of silver bounced off the light.

I had placed a shimmering necklace of Sally's around my neck, falling from the nape into the plunging cleavage that the cobalt sparkles revealed. Having seen myself only in the broken mirror before I stepped out into the view of all, I could only imagine the image that my entire ensemble produced for the crowd of gawking patrons and bar staff. All I could do was hope that everything Sally had taught me and everything that I did tonight would make her proud.

The music from Lucas's fingers rippled and rolled as even I became lured into the moment, no longer myself but a creature of design, birthed from the imagination of Ms. Sauerkraut's and onto her stage.

A dramatic pause in Lucas's playing gave me the entrance I had been waiting for my whole life. With a tremor in my voice, I closed my eyes and let loose my first notes, no longer as Josef, but as some yet-unnamed siren.

"*Love found but lost was never love at all,*" I trilled with dramatic effect. I looked across the room at a wistful Maximillian, whose teary eyes let me know this decision was the right one.

"*Like winter to spring then summer to fall,*" I continued, pulling the crowd in ever closer with my roiling vibrato.

"*A flower does grow but it returns to the ground,*" I warbled, "*withered, decayed, its cycle is bound.*" My voice haunted like an abandoned old barn whose thatched roof had fallen in and collapsed from the weight of years of weather and wear.

Lucas swelled the music to a great crescendo, then stopped at the tip-piest of tops before he pulled it softly back as I cried through the final notes: "*Love found but lost was never love at all.*"

As I finished the last note, the hall was quiet. Even Lucas sat with his hands at his sides, soaking in the loud silence left in the wake of my song and Sally's absence.

A man in the middle of the bar began to clap slowly and was soon joined by customers throughout the cabaret; some people jumped to their feet and howled while others fell into each other's arms and embraced in tears.

Whatever had happened to Sally, and whatever might happen to any of us, in this moment we were alive, and we stood our ground.

Lucas made his way around the piano. He grabbed both of my hands in his and looked deeply into my eyes. "That," he said with breathless wonder, "was truly mesmerizing."

I tilted my head in shy thanks.

"And you," he continued with great emphasis, "are unbelievably beautiful."

A surge of love and pride swelled up in my breast, and I threw my arms around Lucas. How could this man I had only known for months have brought more goodness to my life than I had known for the entirety of my existence before him?

Lucas led me by one hand through the crowd, while many stopped to thank me multiple times along the way, applauding both my performance and my bravery.

At last we reached Sally's dressing room, where Lucas sat me down and began to slowly help me undress. He removed my headscarf with great tenderness, never once breaking the captivating look he held me in.

Bit by bit, he denuded me of my outer being until at last all that stood before him once again was Josef. No dress, no shoes—not even makeup, as he had washed it all off for me.

"You are just as beautiful like this as you were when you performed," he said to me, leaning in and drawing my lips toward him as if by a magnetic force.

I closed my eyes and became lost in his kisses. When I opened them again, Lucas had swept me up into his arms so that my body now sat in his lap, my legs wrapped around his back, our lips touching with a smoldering fire.

I reached down and unbuttoned Lucas's manhood, freeing it to enter me while I sat on top of him. We rocked in rapturous movement until we could no longer bear it.

"I love you," I yelled out, spilling my heart as well as my seed onto Lucas's shirt.

He slowed his movements, now freed from his own release, then pulled me closer to him and said the words back to me that I had waited forever to hear from someone who truly meant it. "I love you too, Josef Dietrick."

I let the words and the substance from his organ sit within me for a moment of quiet thoughtfulness, before I unattached myself from his body and stood upright. I reached my hand down and helped Lucas to his feet, both of us smiling.

After a moment, I grabbed a towel from among Sally's things.

"Goodness," I said, as I began to wipe myself off of Lucas's shirt. "You can't go back out there with that on you." I giggled.

Once he was fully presentable, I slipped on the trousers I'd arrived in, what seemed like years ago now, and dressed myself till I was ready to return to the bar. Then I grabbed Lucas's hand and led him out.

As we entered the main room of the Rote Schwein, I knew in my heart that this day had been transcendental for me. I could never be the same again. Both Sally and Lucas had played a direct part, but I was no longer Josef of Treptow. I was now *die blaue blume*, the blue flower of Schöneberg. The author Novalis himself could not have painted with words a bloom more beautiful to behold in his novel *Heinrich von Ofterdingen*, according to those who knew me by this title going forward. For so long, I had lived dormant and unseen. A seed under humus and dirt that the feet of others trod upon while I lay silent. Now, all at once I had pushed up through the soil and claimed my place with bold color and a demand for attention and for admiration.

▼

WEEKS, THEN MONTHS WENT BY, but Sally never returned. From sunup until sundown, Anke and I continued to work furiously at our sewing and mending. In between our paid labor, Anke would show me how she designed and crafted her own dresses, which she would then sell at the market for extra *geld*.

Dusk until midnight, these hours were spent at the Rote Schwein, where I filled in as the resident doll during Sally's continued absence. My confidence had grown as long as my hair. No longer was I an unsure boy but the prize rose of the red pig's garden. I used the skill I had gained from Anke to turn Sally's wardrobe into my own, taking extra fabric in or letting it out so that her dresses now hugged me better or accentuated my own features more than they did for their original owner.

Twilight into dawn, Lucas repeatedly demonstrated that behind his kind and unassuming eyes was a deceptively skilled man when it came to lovemaking, and I was delighted to be the recipient of his learning.

One increasingly rare evening, Anke, Lucas, and I ate dinner at the table together. It had been so long since all three of us had been together at once, and we laughed with delight at the tales the others shared as we enjoyed the simple company of our trio.

Lucas and I were hard at work filling our mouths with hot soup when Anke stood up. "I have something to share," she stated, which caused Lucas's spoon to clank down hard into his ceramic bowl.

Having gotten our attention, we waited for Anke to continue, but she nervously shuffled her body from one foot to the other.

"What is it, *meine schwester*?" Lucas asked, "You are making me nervous—you are not usually one to hold your tongue."

"I have loved every minute of us being together," she continued. "The three of us," she said as she made her way behind us and put an arm on each of our shoulders.

"Time changes things, always. First Lucas and I had parents, then none. We were alone, then Josef came into our lives and our family grew," she said with emotion as she squeezed my shoulder.

There was a knock at the door. My back stiffened.

"I can get it," I said, beginning to push my chair back.

"No!" Anke declared. "It is for me."

She made her way to the door, opening it to reveal a beaming Edsel holding a basket of eggs.

"And now there are four—or rather, two and two."

Edsel rushed in and swept Anke up into his arms, holding out the basket with care so as not to crush its occupants.

Lucas stood up. "Does this mean . . ."

His words faded in disbelief.

Anke grabbed the eggs from Edsel's hands and beamed, "Yes, we are engaged to be married!"

We howled with delight. Lucas rushed to hug Anke, while I happily shook Edsel's hand until his arm nearly fell off. We all switched, and the joy continued.

The rest of the night we celebrated with the traditional scrambled eggs, and talk of the wedding and where they would live once married. It seemed like life had fallen into a pattern of happiness. Day, evening, night—each brought its own equal contentment and joy.

THE NEXT MORNING, I decided I would use the money Wolfe had been slipping me in an envelope each evening for my performances at the Rote Schwein to buy a gift for dear Anke on her engagement.

I snuck out at first light, not wanting to give my plans away to either Anke or Lucas, and I made my way toward the gendarmenmarkt. There was an eerie stillness in the air, like the morning after fireworks, when sound is still muffled and the smell of used gunpowder, now wet with dew, suffuses the air.

When I rounded Pfarrstraße, I began to notice bits of glass strewn along the sidewalk. It wasn't until I was in front of the shops on the corner that I saw the many storefronts whose windows had been smashed.

Men and women skulked along the street and examined the storefronts, with great big holes through the glass, as if rocks or rifle butts had smashed them to smithereens.

As I passed two women, I heard one say, "Kristallnacht," and I paused to examine a gigantic yellow star painted on the broken door of the apothecary.

I continued to walk as the sound of my feet grinding crushed bits of glass deeper into the cobblestones pierced something in my stomach. Hastening my steps, I finally arrived at the small store owned by Herr Schmitt.

Practically running inside, I closed the door behind me, and Herr Schmitt came out at once to assist me.

"How can I help you?" the shopkeeper inquired.

"I am here to buy that machine in the window," I said, pointing to the black hand crank sewing machine that sat welded to a beautiful piece of polished cherrywood. I was desperate to do anything but think about what I had witnessed outside and what it must have meant for the people who owned and worked at those stores.

Herr Schmitt went to the window to remove the Dürkopp-Lowenstein from display.

"An excellent choice," he said, sounding unnervingly chipper for one of the few shops on the street whose store was still remarkably intact. "Though I imagine you may want to paint over the name as soon as you get it home." He bent down to search a shelf for the box the machine came in among the many items lying around the store.

"What do you mean?" I asked with confusion. "Why would I paint the name off of a brand-new sewing machine?"

Herr Schmitt stopped his search then looked up. "Because Lowenstein is a Jewish name, of course." He went back to searching for a second, then stood up with the box in his hands, taking it over to a counter.

He began to place the machine inside while, continuing as calmly and without emotion as if the box itself were speaking. "After last night, I would think most Germans would follow their government's lead and erase anything with a trace of Jew on it."

He closed the box, then stuck out his hand. "Eighty Reichsmarks."

I reached into my trouser pockets and pulled out the bills, placing them into Herr Schmitt's cold palm.

After I paid, I rushed from the store and decided to walk a different way home, bypassing the main road for Jahnstraße. I was not halfway home when I heard some people inside a flat cheering and saying Germany was finally dealing with their real problems. Some neighbors were out on the streets, clapping and singing songs about the fatherland like, "Deutschlandlied" and other anthems of glory.

In other places along the roads I passed on my way home, there was silence. I could see curtains being pulled closed tightly to block out the morning sun that they had likely only just opened to let it inside. Some flats screamed with silence, while others swelled with joy.

I considered my own actions, or lack thereof. "Was I just as complicit as those who had harmed the Jewish shop owners?" I pondered. A push and pull settled into my intestines as I contemplated the fact that lack of action was an action in itself. What could I do to help others when I was often a victim myself? Yet how I had wished others would have stood up for me on the many occasions when I was on the receiving end of brutality.

When I finally made it home, the joy and anticipation of sharing my gift with Anke had faded from the intense internal grappling my walk had entailed. It now seemed almost silly and self-indulgent to give someone such a materialistic gift when others were being singled out and targeted with such vitriol and violence.

Not wanting to ruin it for Anke, though, I perked myself up before I burst into the flat and presented the box to my completely shocked and thrilled sister and friend.

"Oh Josef," she exclaimed, pulling the machine out of the box with wonder. "How could you have afforded to pay for such a luxury item?" she asked, stroking the black metal with a care that showed it would be treated as if it were her newborn.

"I've been saving here and there—and besides, you will need it to make your wedding dress!"

She clasped her hands in the air in joy.

"If I left you to hand sew it, it would probably be another decade until you made it to the wedding bed!" I laughed with effort as she hugged my neck and thanked me repeatedly.

The deed finished, I confessed a headache, then headed up to the bedroom and lay down. Perhaps the joy of Anke and Edsel's wedding would help temporarily distract from what was happening all around us. For now, though, I was not emotionally prepared to deal with anything else, so I shut my eyes, taking for granted that luxury of sleeping safely in my own comfortable bed.

▼

LUCAS AND I HAD A RARE afternoon to ourselves one day, so we decided to go to the cinema and see Helmut Käutner's *Kitty and the World Conference*. The film was a rare comedy at a time when we needed a light-hearted lift, so we strolled briskly to arrive in time to laugh the waning hours of the day away in our faux Hollywood fantasyland. Of course, the newsreel at the start of the film announcing the Third Reich's war on Poland was a far cry from the humor of the film's content that followed, but we tried to ignore this reel as best we could, the way we'd ignored a lot of goings-on around our city these last few months. Like the cinema, on the surface our lives seemed to go on like they had before, full of heady stories and laughter, but scratch too deeply and you found this was a world of illusion and shadow.

When the film was over, we decided to take a slow walk toward the Rote Schwein, though we were not due there for a few more hours. As we passed a bank of flats, three women wearing Jewish stars were being surrounded by a group of Nazi soldiers. One of the women held a baby in her arms, which a soldier appeared to be trying to take from her. We made our way over to hear what was being said, but before we had crossed the street to get closer, a single shot rang out, and the mother lay on the street. The other women cried out but did not resist, following their captors into a waiting vehicle. The baby was simply tossed to the ground next to its mother and stomped on by the soldier until it was nothing but pulp and mash.

An older woman leaned out her window on the second floor and cheered for the soldiers, while I put my hand up over my mouth to stifle my own screams, as I knew that drawing attention to ourselves would not bring the baby or its mother back to life.

Lucas grabbed my arm and led me quickly away until we found ourselves in an alley. I threw my body up against a wall and sobbed. Unable to stop myself, I hurled violently onto the ground, spitting up acid and bile.

"Why?" I cried out, unable to make sense of the horror I had just witnessed. I did not know what had affected me more—the image of the dead mother's face or the baby's brains mashed into the pavement like a squash that had been beaten and blended for soup. Perhaps it was simply the woman in the window who raised her arm into the air and gnashed her teeth in delight over the death of these other human beings she considered to be vermin.

Lucas held me close in that darkened space until I recovered enough to walk, and then we stumbled our way to the bar.

Once we were inside, I realized that the heavy door and the menacing frame of BlueBeard no longer seemed like much protection at all against the world.

While it was difficult, I forced myself to perform that night and many others afterward, emoting both the resilience of hope and the inevitability of the darkness that was creeping up, slowly encircling us all. The Rote Schwein, which at its height was the toast of the Berlin doll bar community, was slowly becoming a graveyard. The once-jostling crowds, where finding a table was a near impossibility unless one arrived hours before the dolls came out to sing, were now gradually thinning, leaving gray pockets of emptiness and silence. Some customers stayed away out of fear, while others were simply there one day and then heard from no more. Traces of their existence evaporated like the cigarette smoke that swirled around the lights above Lucas's piano.

My own appearance continued to change, as I'd stopped cutting my hair and my nails ages ago, allowing both to grow out. While I considered it a small protest against our nation and its ever-increasing eyes, glaring into the darkest corners of our lives, it was also an act of liberation for my own identity.

I simply liked being die blaue blume. There was a freedom in transformation, and it seemed to lift from me all self-doubt and victimization. Never again would I be that weak boy, beaten, abused, violated, and unloved, I told myself each night right before I came out to perform, reminding myself what I had come from and who I was now. She, and by this I meant me, was someone who could stand on her feet and say yes when I meant yes, and no when I meant no, because I mattered. I was important. I was seen.

When I stepped in front of the piano, I felt it was my job to share that same feeling of self-love with the others in the room. Whether there was a crowd of one hundred, or just two people, I knew what it was like to be the person who felt alone, and my songs were for them. They could be strong because I had learned to become strong. We could do this for each other.

There was increasing disturbance at the whisperings of work camps for dissidents and deviants. No one really knew what was true and what was embellished gossip, or just even Nazi war propaganda, so most of us tried to go on with our lives as normal. Yet the reality was, whatever was happening, the city moved slower, as if ash were settling over our lives. An unseen but blackened substance stuck to our limbs so that even simple tasks like buying potatoes at the market felt laborious and strainful to the limbs.

But life buds even in darkness, and so at last, Anke and Edsel's special day arrived. Anke had worked on her dress for countless hours, and as she came down from her bedroom, she was a sight to behold. The gown was a deep crème ivory in a glossy satin that hugged her frame from the waist, displaying her well-proportioned body and full bosom that nearly burst out from the whalebone corset she had sewn in underneath. At the hips the dress flared out like a bell, the satin dancing with a cascade of tiny glimmering stones that ran like a waterfall from one hip to the floor. The dress was finished with long sleeves and tiny buttons that started at the wrists and ran up to the elbows, giving it an air of nobility.

"Twirl around the room for us," I insisted, as Lucas and I clapped and cheered at her radiant vision.

Anke threw back her head in delight when Edsel entered the apartment dressed in a suit of black. The jacket was long and ran to his knees, where his strong hands rested, holding a large black satin top hat.

Lucas and I each wore simple suits, mine gray and his a brown the color of tree bark.

Together the four of us walked to the fine home of Edsel's parents, where a priest married the two of them in the living room while a small group of Edsel's family joined us in watching the ceremony.

We then moved to a dining room, which was fitted with a long table in dark walnut that Edsel's grandmother had imported from the Balkans decades ago. Anke and Edsel sat at the head, followed by Edsel's parents, Lucas, me, and a handful of aunts and uncles. A smattering of small children ran around the table while chewing on dark pieces of bread that Edsel's mother gave to them to stop their fussing.

As soon as we sat down, big steaming bowls of *Hochzeitssuppe,* a rich broth with chunks of chicken, meatballs, and asparagus, appeared in front of our faces, and we lapped at the potion with spoons of polished silver.

Next, trays of cold *Tafelspitz* were brought out. The steak was already sliced, so we ate it off of little plates with gherkins and sliced onions.

This went on and on for several courses, where we inhaled large volumes of *Grööner Hein* with slabs of hot bacon mixed with pears and potatoes followed by grilled pork covered with an herb sauce in the deepest shade of green.

Finally, when our bodies could take no more, the *Baumkuchen* was brought out with glasses of sparkling *Sekt* and *kaffee.*

When the honey and almond cake was finished, at last we all got up from the table and wobbled to the door to wave our goodbyes to Anke and Edsel, who gleamed with hope for the future as they headed for the train and a short honeymoon to the country house of Edsel's family in Lübben in Brandenburg.

Lucas and I thanked our gracious hosts, then headed back to the flat, where we would no longer be a trio but a quiet couple living in the intoxicated bliss of privacy.

We were barely in the door when Lucas spun me around and kissed me deeply. He then led me to the couch, where we fell into a fury of limbs and saliva. Lucas pulled his face away from mine and looked deeply into my eyes as his hands began to unbuckle my belt and unzip my suit trousers.

As he pulled my pants down and tore them off my legs, he gave me a sneaky smile before he descended, his mouth finding my flesh and causing my eyes to roll back in my head from the sensation that every time felt excitingly like it was my first experience with oral gratification.

Lucas sucked and pulled at my phallus until I was overwhelmed by the moment. I threw my head back as I flooded his mouth with my love.

When we were finished, Lucas held me in his arms and we lay there on the couch for hours.

Sometime in the night, as I lay between the waking and sleeping worlds, he kissed me on my forehead and whispered, "If I could, I would marry you today, Josef Dietrick."

I smiled at his words and teased, "Would you? I would have to think about it, personally, as I'm not sure how I feel about you yet, if I were to be perfectly honest."

He responded by tickling me under my arms until we were both in hysterics. Once we resettled, Lucas began again. "I would marry you, Josef. But, since that is not possible by any law here, what I can do is tell you today that just like when I found you in the Lohmulenstraß alleyway, I will always do my best to take care of and protect you. Always."

He lifted my chin and brought my face close to his. "I love you," he whispered. Then we kissed gently and lay back to fall into a contented sleep, enveloped in clouds of uncontracted matrimony.

IT WASN'T LONG AFTERWARD before Lucas proved his declaration of protection to be true.

It was a quiet Tuesday morning, and I had gone out early to the bakery for a loaf of bread. I had just purchased a Berliner rye and was walking home holding the bag close to my nose to take in the heavy scent of the fresh warm loaf when I felt something hit my back. I turned to find a young man in a white shirt and suspenders that held up his navy-blue trousers, which stopped an inch above his ankles, standing there with rocks in both of his hands. He gave me an intense stare from a short distance away.

Noticing what he held, I looked down to see a stone about the size of a quail egg at my feet and realized I had just been pelted with it by this stranger.

"Why did you do that?" I yelled.

He responded by throwing another, straight at my chest. It hit me with such force that I dropped the rye loaf.

Another stone whizzed past my head.

Not willing to take any chances or risk further delay by speaking to this young man, I started to run down the street, as I was not far from our flat.

Behind me, I could hear the echoes of his running feet in pursuit.

As I neared our home, I slammed into our door only to find it locked shut. Lucas must have turned the key when I left by force of habit.

My hands entered my pockets, groping frantically to find my own key, as a rock ricocheted off my calf. It was followed by a handful of pebbles that sprayed across the back of my neck and onto the door.

That sound must have piqued Lucas's interest, as within seconds he opened the door only for me to spill in just as another stone hit my shoulder and landed on our floor.

Lucas ran out of the flat, his arms flailing in the air like a man gone completely mental, yelling and screaming after the young man, who turned and sped away.

He returned a few minutes later, panting and huffing, and asked me between breaths what had happened.

"I do not know. I only went to buy bread and found myself being stoned by a stranger."

He shut the door.

"What is it about me that no matter where I go, violence seems to follow?" I asked aloud, though mostly to myself.

We walked over and sat down at our table with this and many more questions left unasked and unanswered in our heads. No more words were spoken aloud.

ANKE WAS SHOWING within months of her wedding to Edsel. We had all settled into a new routine where Anke and her ever-expanding pouch would come to the flat in the morning to stitch and sew with me until midday, when Edsel would take a break from the butcher's shop to walk his pregnant wife home.

I spent the rest of the afternoons alone, taking advantage of the solitude to teach myself how to use the Dürkopp I had bought for Anke, which could not fit in her and Edsel's new flat. Lucas had surprised me one afternoon with a bolt of light blue fabric, the color of the azure skies Anke, he, and I used to look up at and gaze upon for hours while we tried to guess the shapes of the clouds from the Volkspark. I cut that fabric with the gentlest of care, edging the sewing scissors around each outlined pattern I had measured and remeasured to ensure perfection within a millimeter of the feathery crepe.

By the time I had completed the dress, Anke had dropped twins from her womb, and my quiet days alone were soon filled with crying babies and a frantic mother dashing from sewing to feedings all day long.

Lucas spent more and more time with Frau Anderson's bratty son, preparing him for a recital. Apparently sausage fingers could play Brahms, especially if their mutter's money said they could. In this case, the Frau's funds meant that Lucas was to personally ensure Tomás Anderson was ready for his own special premiere performance of "Wiegenlied," to be held at the Heinbreitzhalle the following week. Tomás's mother planned to showcase her son's alleged talent if it took every last Reichsmark she had to do so.

The preparations left Lucas uncharacteristically on edge. Trying to create talent where there was none was one thing when you were simply teaching someone to play in their living room. It was another thing altogether when many of Berlin's wealthiest and most connected were coming together with one aim—to watch your student demonstrate the mastery of their learned instrument. It was an even more bitter pill to swallow when you yourself actually did possess great talent and longed for the opportunity to play at such a fine hall as Heinbreitz, but you did not have the means to showcase it like the Andersons.

The stress of lack of privilege combined with the pressure of the ticking clock meant Lucas spent much of his days over at the Anderson's, where he moodily drilled Tomás on finger routines.

Meanwhile, Edsel's butcher shop was overflowing with orders, or so he said. Somehow, both he and Lucas had managed to find ways to escape the fury of the near-constant bawling of the twin boys and their sleep-deprived mother. I, however, was left with Anke's bloodshot eyes and hair-trigger temper.

When I shared with Anke what had happened with the stranger throwing rocks, she responded curtly, "It's no wonder you are a target, Josef, with your hair now longer than mine."

I had expected a little more sympathy, but I recognized that Anke was in over her head with the twins, so I remained silent.

AT LAST, IT WAS TIME for Tomás's recital. I arrived at Heinbreitzhalle to support Lucas in a suit of dark navy wool. As I would not have time after the performance to prepare myself fully at the Rote Schwein, I had plucked my eyebrows into high arches and styled my hair into loose curls. My kohl-lined eyes widened when I entered the main hall, which was ornately cavernous, to find dozens of people sipping on glasses of champagne. Waiters in black suits dashed to and fro while they carried trays of bubbles and nibbles. When one passed me by, I reached out to grab a glass of my own. I looked up to admire the ceilings, which were painted with scenes of angels, awash in dramatic light as they defeated demonic foes in deep shadows.

A bell rang out, and we all followed a guide into a smaller room filled with chairs lined up in neat rows. The walls were white, with intricate gilded molding that ran up to the ceilings, where three large crystal chandeliers hung suspended, casting twinkling light down onto the now-seated throng.

Lucas was at the front of the room, receiving what appeared to be stern instructions from Frau Anderson. The Frau's blond curls, piled high on her head, shook as she pointed a white-gloved finger toward Lucas, with what I assumed were last-minute directives for the performance.

When she was finished, she gathered up the hem of her large golden gown and took a seat in the front row.

I sipped my champagne, finding a seat at the end of the last row. I had barely sat down when the audience rose to their feet to applaud the introduction of Tomás, who entered the room in black tails. His stomach nearly burst through the twills of his white shirt. I concluded that Frau Anderson must have bought him a size smaller than his actual wide frame; she was likely as delusional about his size as she was about her son's musical abilities.

The fabric of Tomás's suit stretched across his large backside as he sat down at the piano. Lucas stood beside him, his fingers on the pages of sheet music, prepared to turn for his student at the appropriate time.

Tomás's fingers hit the keys, and he began Brahm's lullaby in the key of F major. The first notes were soft yet solid, but when the first expected b flat went sharp, it caused a number of tensely false smiles to appear on people's faces. It was quickly clear this was going to be a painful evening.

Yet suddenly, out of nowhere, swept in the most luminous vision. A stately woman in a crimson gown approached the piano and on cue began to sing.

Guten Abend, gut' Nacht,
mit Rosen bedacht . . .

Her rich soprano bounced off the geometric pattern of the inlaid wooden floors and echoed toward the cavernous, vaulted ceilings and their handpainted scenes of Adam and Eve. The room's acoustics gave her already full voice a fleshed-out tone that poured into every inch of the space.

With cloves adorned,
slip under the covers.
Tomorrow morning, if God wills,
you will wake once again.

She continued, leading us along with her clear timbre until we at last found paradise. By the time she had finished the final lush verse, we were all lost in a land of dreams, and none could remember a single one of the sour notes that had emanated from the pianist.

We rose to our feet and applauded this experience that Frau Anderson had masterfully put together. Her son was not humiliated for his lack of talent, but cleverly covered over, and in doing so, the Frau was lauded as a mother all would wish to have.

At the conclusion of the event, I made my way over to Lucas to congratulate him. Tomás, who was still seated on the piano stool, began to make faces at me and laugh under his breath.

"Is there something wrong with that child?" I asked Lucas loudly, making sure Tomás could hear me emphasize the word child.

Lucas hushed me, grabbing one of my arms. "I told you before, this is a very spoiled but powerful family." He looked over my face. "And why did you come here with makeup on your eyes? Did you not think about who might be here?"

As he spoke to me, Frau Anderson approached menacingly. "Is there a problem?" she asked, raising a brow when she saw me closely.

"Not at all," Lucas rushed to say. "May I introduce my sister Anke's friend, Josef," he announced, surprising me with his lie.

I reached out my hand to shake the Frau's, but she rebuffed me.

"In fact, Josef is an actor," he continued suddenly, and my eyes widened at his introduction.

"Charmed," she said coldly before she turned her back and walked over to her son. The two of them whispered back and forth before she took his hand and led him into the crowd who fawned over this bloated prince.

"Friend of your sister?" I said, as I twisted my lips.

"Sorry," Lucas sighed. "It just came out, and I do not want any problem with the Frau, as I need her continued employment and support, so I couldn't have any issues here tonight."

My face softened. "Fair enough—but an actor, really? Besides, both she and her child seem obnoxious." I chuckled.

"Let me just say my goodbyes, and I'll meet you out front in a few minutes," Lucas said to me, so I followed his instructions and turned to leave the enchanting Baroque stylings to the crowd. As I was exiting the room, I caught from the corner of my eye the Frau standing in the corner, pointing toward me while she talked with an unknown man.

"She really is a cunt," I said to myself, then went outside, where Lucas met me.

We walked to the Rote Schwein together, insulting the Andersons and the company they kept the entire way.

When we arrived, I quickly changed into the gown of midday blue that I had been working on for months. It seemed only fitting to wear it on the one-year anniversary of Sally's disappearance. Maximillian did not attend, as he had moved away to Leipzig after Wolfe's calls to his cousin went unanswered.

As I stood alongside the piano, I remembered the day we said goodbye to Maximillian. He pressed a folded note into Wolfe's hand and said, "If Sally does ever return here, give her this." Then he turned to me and whispered, "I waited as long as I could bear, but I'm old, and I'm afraid that sitting here night after night on a barstool, hoping Sally will walk through the door, is proving to be too much for me to bear any longer."

He pushed a black-and-white wool hat onto his head with one hand and held a small brown case in his other, as he crept toward the door.

We would never hear from Maximillian again.

The pain of continued loss came out through my tone as I trembled the notes to the song I had written in memory and honor of the night that Sally was taken from us.

There once was a bird; an eagle she was.
And a great wind lifted her and carried her off above the mountains.
We wait for her return.
But the seasons changed and yet her cry is no longer heard,
nor are the shadow of her wings seen
like they were when she flew over our heads.

Come back to us, mother eagle,
and grace us with your call
and your beautiful flight
once more.

I emoted these words melodically as I shook my shoulder-length locks with fury at the last notes.

I may not have been the soprano in Heinbreitz Hall with a voice from God singing for hundreds of people. Here, there were no more than a dozen random characters left sitting in this audience, but I trilled for them like they were a thousand and as if we were standing together in the Opernhaus in Vienna.

When the night was over, Lucas and I made our way back to the flat and fell asleep somewhere around midnight. It was still dark when I rolled over to find that he was not in the bed. Downstairs, in the kitchen I heard a muffled conversation. My hazy eyes focused on the small hand that pointed to the number five, while my ears picked up rapid mumbles that sounded like Anke's voice speaking. With a few more hours left until we normally began our work, I swung my legs off of the bed and threw on some loose pants and a shirt.

I stumbled down the stairs to find her at the kitchen table, sitting across from Lucas.

"It is very early," I said with a tone dryer than my morning mouth was.

The two sat in silence, so I walked to the stove, picked up our blue ceramic pot, and filled it with water that at first sputtered out of the faucet before settling into a quiet stream. After placing the pot back, I opened a drawer and took out a box of matches, striking one, which I then used to touch the burner. Blue flames jumped up to dance around the circle.

The silence persisted, so I took three rust-orange mugs off of a shelf and placed one in front of them each. As I reached my own seat, I placed the cup down and instructed Anke, "Go ahead and tell us all about what happened between you and Edsel."

"Edsel?" she asked with great confusion.

"This lover's quarrel must have been *verrückt*, or why else would you be here at five in the morning looking like your mama just slapped your *arsch*?" I let out a drowsy tee-hee.

The teapot whistled, so I got up and lifted it from the stove. I walked over and poured some steaming liquid into my cup. When I looked up, I realized that neither Anke nor Lucas had responded to my silly question, so I froze with unease at their tense expressions.

"Wait. What *did* happen?" I asked as I placed the pot quickly back on the stove. "And where are the boys?"

"The boys are fine," Anke said briskly, tapping her palm on the table, summoning me to sit. Now fully awake and realizing the seriousness of the mood, I obeyed.

"Anke was just starting to tell me something important, Josef," Lucas informed me with a look of concern.

"Edsel had just come home last night and sat down to a late supper. I'd kept the boys awake, as he has been so busy he doesn't ever get to see them." Her tone was heavy. "I made carp and fried potatoes because I knew he had to be sick of beef, cutting and weighing it all day." Her pitch and pace heightened. "But he had not even gotten in a bite yet when they knocked on the door!"

"Who knocked on the door?" I asked.

"Gestapo," she said, and that one word hung heavy in the air.

We all feared the Staatspolizei, as they were known to act first and ask questions later. One did not get a visit from the secret police unless they were already sentenced.

"They saluted and heiled and then said they wanted to talk to us about somebody." Anke's body shook.

"Who were they coming for?" I leaned over the table and asked with great worry, "Not Edsel?"

Anke just looked at me with eyes filled with tears. She shook her head. "No, not Edsel, Josef. You."

My dry throat crackled like autumn leaves beneath feet. "Me?"

"One of the Staatspolizei stood with his back to me and thrust a photo into Edsel's face. I ran over and picked the boys up into my arms—they had been lying on the floor—while I heard Edsel reply to him calmly that he did not know much about you, besides you being a paying tenant of my brother."

Her lower lip began to tremble as she continued, "Another soldier then came up from behind me. I did not see him, but he took one of my boys right out of my hands . . ."

Lucas's fists hit the table. "Oh my god! They didn't do anything to the twins, did they?"

She shook her head and continued. "I was paralyzed with fear, but Edsel kept calm and answered all of their questions. They seemed to think you and I were personal friends, Josef. Not that we are not, but they seemed convinced that you and I knew something together; perhaps we were even engaged in some kind of criminal behavior."

We all shrugged at the thought of my being a criminal.

"When they showed me your picture, I told the Stoßtruppen that I knew you only generally as a quiet tenant, but I believed you were about to move to Dusseldorf any day now to go live with some family," she explained, as if quietly imploring me to consider following through with this.

"At that point, Edsel came and took the baby back from the soldier's arms. He stood beside me and laughed at their questions, saying we had been too busy making blue-eyed babies to pay any attention to anything our brother's boarder was doing.

"This seemed to be enough to satisfy them, but as they left, they turned back and said to me that I may want to warn my own brother that Josef was said to be an unsavory sort and that they would be paying Lucas a visit of their own shortly. I waited until just before light to come and warn you," she finished.

At that, Anke got up. "I really should get back. I do not know if they are watching us. They could have followed me here," she said with some measure of hysteria.

Lucas ran over to hug his sister, looking at me over her shoulder with grave concern.

I joined their hug and thanked her for her warning.

Anke straightened and spoke directly to me. "It's not too late, Josef. I would go and cut your hair right now."

She stepped back and addressed us both. "And neither of you are to go back to the Rote Schwein, starting immediately. You cannot afford to be associated with anything suspicious right now."

"But I have to go tonight! I at least have to say my goodbyes one final time," I countered, while thinking to myself that I was not sure that staying away after tonight would even be an option for me.

"Josef!" Lucas stamped his foot while Anke's face hardened.

"You are both to go and prepare my old room as soon as I leave here, so it looks like the two of you sleep separately." She pointed toward the stairs as she spoke. "And for the love of me and those boys, please promise me you will be subtle, lowkey, and stay safe." Her voice trembled as she lowered her finger. "Deny everything if it comes to it, and do not give them any reason to question you further."

At that, she ran to Lucas and hugged him again. She choked back tears. "Oh Lucas, I have to go back because of Edsel and the boys, but I feel terrible leaving you."

His face was now wet from his own tears, and his sister's body began to shake with great heaves. "I have tried all of these years since our parents' passing to take care of you as if you were my own child, but now I feel helpless and scared."

"It's alright, Anke," Lucas assured her. "Nothing is going to happen—to either of us." He looked at me. "We will stay indoors and not make a spectacle of ourselves until this all blows over."

With that, Anke released her brother from her arms, and ran toward the front door. She turned back to say, "Ich liebe dich."

"We love you too." Lucas waved to her as the door softly closed.

THE REST OF THE MORNING lay heavy, as if a wet cloth had been wrung out then placed damp over our apartment.

Lucas and I seemed to dance around each other, never staying in the same room long enough to discuss what Anke had shared. Both of us frequently looked up toward the door at any sound that might signal we were about to have Nazi visitors.

Finally, somewhere around three in the afternoon, both exhausted from fearful anticipation, we landed with sunken shoulders in the same spot, seated at the kitchen table.

Lucas let out a long sigh. "Maybe they are not coming. Perhaps they have decided against it—they likely would have been here by now."

I shrugged and shook my head. "When I was leaving the recital yesterday, I saw Frau Anderson pointing at me and speaking with some man."

Lucas pinched his face up. "Scheiße! I was hoping your interaction yesterday with Tomás and his mutter was brief enough to avoid any issues. Had I thought about the risks, I might have told you not to come at all."

"Why should I have to stay behind because someone else is unhappy about the way I look or the way I feel?" I countered. I could sense the anger rising up inside me.

He ignored me. "That is why they went to Anke last night, because I told her you were my sister's friend." He slapped his head with an open palm.

"Who cares?" I scoffed as I sucked my teeth in. "We have done nothing wrong to warrant Stoßtruppen descending on Anke!" I exclaimed.

"You don't have to do anything wrong, Josef." Lucas said as he pushed his hands down onto the table. "Sally, die Juden—hell, the book shop owner—none of these people did anything wrong, Josef. They just existed, and that was enough."

"Well I am tired of it, Lucas." I jumped up, knocking my chair to floor. As it bounced off the tile, I moved toward the wall. "My whole life I have tried to hide so that others wouldn't—no, couldn't see me for who I am, and I am nauseous from it."

I grabbed my coat off the wall.

"Where are you going?" Lucas cried out, rising from his own chair. "You can't go outside . . . They could be waiting for you."

"Let them come, but I need to get some air before tonight's performance."

Lucas ran toward me and grabbed me by the shoulders, "You cannot go to the Rote Schwein tonight, Josef—you cannot!" He shook me sternly. "And you certainly cannot perform!"

"I will just as soon eat horse shit before I will stand here in the shadows again for anyone, let alone some ficken Nazi Stoßtruppen." I broke free from his grip.

Lucas stood back in disbelief as I tore out of the flat, slamming the door behind me.

▼

I WALKED FOR THE REST of the afternoon. Only occasionally I would throw a glance over my shoulders to see if anyone was following.

Eventually I found myself on Leipziger Straße and entered the ground floor of the Hertie Department store. I made my way to the center, then rode the escalator up to the second floor, where I began to peruse the garments in the women's section of the posh establishment.

My hands brushed over fine fabrics and dresses of various lengths and shades. My eyes widened at the sight of the wispy chiffon dress in a light

brown with green leaves and little orange flowers. It was so beautifully delicate that my mood became as light as its weight.

No sooner had the exquisite flowers began to dance in my vision than
it was disrupted by the sight of Herr Karg, who watched me over racks of
ladies' undergarments. His face was round as a wheel of yellow Rachelete
cheese right before it is melted and spread out on toast, but it had the tone
of off-white creamed curds that had gone bad.

I ignored him and walked toward the skirts, which hung neatly on a
rack, but his narrow green eyes, which lent him the air of a lizard ready to
lap out his tongue to catch a fly, followed my movements. I admired a pink
blouse in a semi-sheer made of batiste, and he peered at me from behind
some boots on a low-lying rack.

"What a *schwantz*," I muttered under my breath. It felt like all of Berlin
was somehow always watching my every move, waiting for an opportunity
to snuff me out.

Having had enough, I glared at Herr Karg as I marched past his plump
stomach and took the escalator down and stormed out of the store.

It was now dark out, so I started my way down streets and backroads
toward the Rote Schwein, but not before I first stopped in one dark alleyway
to pull a garment out from under my shirt that I had tucked up in there,
over my belly, on my way out of the shop. The chiffon felt even better in my
hands as I pulled it to freedom knowing I'd nicked it from right under that
fat fuck Karg's nose.

I laughed to myself at the thought of this being a fitting piece to wear
tonight as I made my way toward what was likely to be my final performance for a while, at least if Lucas had anything to say about it.

The narrow roads were nearly silent, so the constant shuffling of a set
of feet behind me did not go unnoticed.

I turned to see the shadowy outline of a figure a number of yards
behind me, so I quickly turned a corner and dashed down a small road.
Echoes from someone's shoes on the stones rattled near me, and it became
clear that I was being followed.

The click-clack of these shoes matched the pounding of my heart, and
I picked up my pace. I turned here and there as I rushed down streets and
alleys that I was not fully familiar with.

Was it the Stoßtruppen, just as Anke had warned? If so, I needed to
lead them as far away from the Rote Schwein as possible before I lost them.

Or perhaps was it Herr Karg seeking his merchandise that I had lifted from Herties?

At one point, it seemed like the stranger was upon me, as the noise from their running seemed to rattle my teeth, so I made a quick jag sideways and found a dark, empty doorframe that I pressed my body up against.

The footsteps receded into the distance.

I waited several minutes, until I was certain that I had lost them, before I stepped out from the doorway and slammed directly into my pursuer.

"Scheiße!" I screamed out as we both fell a few steps back from the impact of our bodies and the smell of gardenias spilled out into the night air.

"Shhhh," came the response. "Quiet, Josef, and do not say such curse words!"

The voice and smell both brought back an odd mixture of confusion and lost chances.

"We don't need to attract any more attention to us," this person insisted, as they led me by the arm into darker shadows.

"Helena?" I asked incredulously. "What are you doing here?"

My mother wrapped her arm into mine and began to walk with me gently down a quiet road. The familiar scent of Fleurs de Rocaille hit my nose like a fisted punch.

"Walk with me, Josef. No one will think twice about a mother strolling along with her son."

"How did you find me? Where did you even begin, and . . ." I was full of questions, but she cut me off quickly.

"How hard can it be to find a boy who prances around on stage like a showgirl?"

I stopped abruptly and pushed her arm off. "It is good to see you have not changed at all in these years, *Mutter*." The words spat out of me, with years of disappointment baked in then broiled hard.

"And what about that boy you are with?" she asked, sounding gravely concerned.

"Lucas rescued me when my own mother threw me out, so do not even think of speaking badly about him," I started to fume. I stopped speaking, though, and shook my head, as curiosity still nipped at my heels. "Wait, I still do not understand. How did you find me?"

Helena put her hands on both sides of her wide hips, "Do you really think the Gestapo has any trick a mother didn't already invent?" she asked through a sneer.

I considered her answer, then volleyed back another question. "Then why exactly are you here in Schöneberg? Why now?"

She shook her head and let out a hiss of air in frustration.

"You always were too absorbed with yourself and your dramatics to pay attention to what was happening around you."

I returned her serve. "One might say it's hereditary."

After a pause she continued, "They took Mr. Füchs and Marteen six months ago, and I've been searching for you ever since."

I heard her words, but for some reason I could not quite understand them. "Mr. Füchs and Marteen?" The words came out slowly.

My mother looked both ways down the quiet street to make sure we were alone. Then she pulled me closer and lowered her voice. "I had known all along that Mr. Füchs was a Jew, but he was rich, so what did I care?" She shrugged with no outward evidence of emotion at his seizure. "We made an agreement if they ever came for him, though, that I would pretend he tricked me into marriage. This way, I could keep the furrier shop and his house for him until he could return."

Her voice began to trail as she concluded her story wistfully. "I am not sure he ever will though, now."

There was a silence deeper than the night air for before Helena grabbed both of my upper arms with her hands.

"I need you to come home now, Josef," she said sadly but with resolve. "I am all alone."

For a moment, we stared into each other's eyes, and I thought I saw something resembling regret and what they elusively called a mother's love. That faded quickly when she looked up at my head, then reached up a hand to grab a lock of my hair.

"This will have to come off immediately, though." She scoffed, and it broke the veneer of devotion like a plate shattering onto the concrete. "From this day forward, you will be as if you were invisible, Josef, not constantly drawing attention to yourself."

As she spat her last words out, I pushed her away from me and felt exhaustion land heavily on my chest.

"You mean like all the years I was invisible growing up?" The words hung in the air.

"Josef!" she exclaimed, "I cannot run the furrier shop on my own!"

As she started to ramble, I held up my hand to stop her from speaking. "One would think you would have looked for me three years ago." I began to tremble, as years of pent-up anger at her behavior toward me finally broke loose. "Any mother would have gotten down on their knees and cried out to their son, even begged them for forgiveness that they had made a terrible mistake when they turned them away and let them go." My volume was increasing by the syllable.

"Instead, not one single word until now, when the very tormentors you forced me to live with are hustled off to who knows where—probably a death camp," I hissed, raising my finger and pointing it directly in her face. "And even then, you come to me not out of love, guilt, or even concern for my or their safety but so that I could help ensure your continued comfort?"

It was part question and part clear acceptance that I was and continued to be nothing of any emotional worth to Helena, as frankly I had never been.

"Oh Josef," she whined.

"'Oh Josef' nothing, Helena. There's no point in going with you and pretending to be invisible. To you, I always have been."

A sad stillness filled the space between us. At last, she begged, "How will I live without your help?"

I reached into my trouser pockets and came back out with a handful of coins. I tossed them at her feet, and they fell with the weight of a judge's hammer onto the stones. "This should feed you for a day or two."

Helena's eyes narrowed at my gesture. Before she could respond, I pulled off the woolen coat I was wearing and deposited it directly on top of the money. "Oh, and I'll just tell Lucas that you stole it."

I turned and left my mother in silence, standing alone on the barren street. The sound of my own footsteps now faded from her hearing forever.

WHEN I MADE IT to the Rote Schwein, it was all but empty—only Wolfe, Johan, who was now opening the door as BlueBeard had left to sail the seven seas, and a small handful of patrons.

I rushed to the dressing room, the venom from Helena's visit still pumping through my veins.

As I stood before the cracked mirror, I looked at myself closely. I moved my profile from side to side, then reached up to touch my hair.

"After tonight, you actually will have to go away for a while," I said wistfully to my sandy mass, just as the glimpse of something in the far corner of the room caught my eye.

I turned and walked to a mannequin head made of canvas that had a bright blond bob pinned to it.

"Why have I never worn a wig before?" I said, as I unplucked the pins and pulled the wig off of the false head.

"Ah that's right, Sally said wigs like this were for dolls who were part street tramp," I remembered laughingly, as I took it to the mirror and pulled it over my own locks. I tucked my excess strands underneath the bob with my index finger.

"I'll give Sally this, this is definitely something you wear when you want to make some kind of statement. I think I will wear it for tonight actually," I declared, sitting down on the stool to begin my transformation.

By the time Lucas arrived, I was in full doll regalia, sitting at the bar and sipping on some kind of libation whose name I did not know or care to know.

As I grew lost in thoughts of my mother, Herr Karg, and Anke's close call, the liquid loosened my shoulders, and helped me clear each of them off of my mind the more I swallowed.

Lucas approached me sternly and spoke in a staccato, emphasizing the seriousness of the matter. "Anke said you have stormtroopers following you." His voice clapped with each syllable.

When my only response was another sip of the peaceful potion, he grabbed my arm.

"It is not safe here any longer!"

I waved to Wolfe for another refill. He leaned over the bar toward us as he poured. "Lucas is right," he said sadly. "There was always a possibility, really more of a certainty, that this day would come. We have managed in secret at great risk to stay around when all the other establishments have long closed up." He topped off the glass and stood back upright.

"You see? Even Wolfe agrees." Lucas scolded me. "It is settled then."

He put an arm around my shoulder and guided me up off of the stool.

"Take all of that off, quickly," he commanded, repositioning my body to face the dressing room. "We will go and pack, and I will leave with you for Dusseldorf first thing in the morning, until things become settled."

I couldn't move. I looked around the Rote Schwein and considered all that this place had meant to me since Lucas found me in Schöneberg. A tear gathered in the corner of my eye as I looked back at Wolfe, then scanned the premises. I settled my eyes on the large and peeling red pig on the wall. How could I walk away from a place that had been the catalyst for so much good in my life?

I looked at Lucas's face. Here was a man who'd rescued me, more than once. A man who was once again willing to put himself on the line, this time by offering to leave his own secure home to move with me to the unknown.

A tear shook loose, and I became more determined than ever that for that night, at least for that one night, I could honor the love that I had for both.

"Okay, my love." I hiccupped. "If this is the case, then let us make sure that this one last performance here tonight creates a memory none of us will soon forget."

One last dance of defiance before we faded away did not seem like much to ask.

Yet Lucas shook his head.

"This is not a good idea. You should not risk this. Think of the people here." He pointed out to the dispersed imbibers. "Staying here any longer would put even them in danger, and for what? One last moment of glory?"

His determination to flee only strengthened my resolve to fight. I leaned back into the bar and downed the drink Wolfe had poured me only a moment ago, then tapped the glass for more.

Wolfe sighed, but he poured.

The full effects of the brew now pulsated through my veins and pushed my judgment farther away from my head and toward my feet. Clumsily, I grabbed the glass and took an uneasy step forward.

"Enough!" I exclaimed. "For these people here tonight, for this place that has been like another home"—I motioned around the room—"and yes, for glory, as glory is all that is left in a world that has been shrunken each day until there is nothing but fear hidden behind doors in dark alleys."

With the cocktail in one inebriated hand, I placed the other on Lucas's steady shoulder. "I will perform this last time to give them something to hold on to in the uncertain days and nights that lie ahead for us all."

Once I had swallowed the remainder of my drink, hard, I turned and marched toward the piano.

With arms raised in the air, I quieted the entire Rote Schwein and addressed the small crowd. "Dearest friends," I began, as I looked out on the uneasy faces of the men who still bravely skulked their way to this establishment night after night. Those most basic human needs—to be seen and to be loved unconditionally—can motivate one to stare down even the most frightening of terrors. The Nazis may have been committed to eliminating us, but even words like "prison" and "death" could not stop a seedling from reaching toward the sun.

"We have become like family over these years," I continued. "Unfortunately, though, tonight we must be separated."

Chins hung low, and tears of resignation flowed down cheeks. Lucas at last recognized that I would not be stopped, so he made his way to the piano and began to play what was now my signature song.

Empowered by the clarity and assurance that only comes from too much alcohol, I called out over the notes. "This is not goodbye, as we will all meet here again someday."

Lucas played more beautifully than I had ever heard him play before. Each note belied a sense of uncertainty for our futures. He rolled across the keys, and his music seemed to speak as if it were the Holy Spirit interceding between our souls and the Almighty through words that were made of spirit and thus just beyond the full reach of our comprehension.

Caught up in his music, I let the words and the vodka carry me to new heights.

Love may come.
Love may go.
New love is like the falling of fresh white snow.
One minute it is there
and then it melts and goes.
But the memories fill your heart
till it overflows.
Love may come.
Love may go.

The final note hung in the air for a few moments after I had stopped my singing. It was as if it were fingers desperately clinging to the sides of a life raft before it slipped away with the current.

Suddenly, a loud explosion rocked the Rote Schwein. The seemingly impenetrable heavy wooden door that BlueBeard had once menacingly guarded scattered like dust on the wind. Wooden shards and pieces of Johan's body, who had been standing nearest to the door when some kind of a device was detonated, lay scattered and strewn across the room.

The muffled sounds of screams barely broke through the ringing in my ears as Hitler's secret police, rushed in through the smoky hole that stood where the door to the Rote Schwein had protected us from the outside world.

Patrons were being dragged out of the bar by officers. To my left, I saw Wolfe disappear to the floor, two Staatspolizei standing over him, swinging their batons.

The blast had sobered me fully, so I turned around, frantic, to search for Lucas by the piano.

Through the haze, we found one another, and just as we reached out and grasped each other's hands, we both found ourselves being pulled apart by the arms of the Staatspolizei. I was slapped forcefully across the face before my arms were yanked and twisted until they were both behind my body. Someone then kicked me hard behind my knees, and the force compelled me to move as they guided me toward the exit.

I shuddered as I stepped over what appeared to be a part of Johan's forearm.

Once outside, I felt a mixture of immense fear and comfort. Yes, we were being handed over to Sturmtruppen by the Staatspolizei. This meant we were not to be gunned down in the alley, but it also meant we were likely fated to something far worse than immediate death.

"Take these homosexuals to the train," I heard an officer command his troops, and we were herded toward two trucks that appeared to be some type of mobile prison.

Relief flooded me when Lucas and I were both placed on the same transport vehicle. Once we were seated inside, the metal door at the back of the truck slammed shut, and we pressed our legs and shoulders together to let one another know in the darkness that we were still present. As the wheels rattled through the dark streets of the city, I took small solace in knowing that Lucas and I were both not only alive but thankfully together.

PART III

Das Blut Rouge

Dachau

T he train slowed to a stop. Inside, I could hear the heavy breathing of what was now over a hundred of us jammed into this cattle car. We had picked up a handful of men at each stop between Friedrich-shain-Kreuzberg and wherever it was we were at this morning. Only, at this location, there appeared to be stirrings that we had not heard at any station prior to today.

A biting wind blew through the cracks in the wood, bringing with it the sounds of dogs, boots, and iron. The unease that swept in on this breeze caused murmurs and moans to ripple throughout the car. We were many, but we were rundown, hungry, and thirsty. It is hard to muster much beyond fear when you have been dehumanized, transported like chattel but treated worse. Cattle you sell or butcher for food. What use to others were a hundred weakened men who were already outcasts to the society at large? We were Jews, Poles, Bolsheviks, gypsies, homosexuals, and criminals. Who would ransom this lot? There were no rich farmers waiting at the end of these tracks to take us home.

"Something is different," I said nervously, the white puffs of my breath dissipating into the air as I spoke. Lucas reached over and grabbed my hand tightly to reassure me.

"We are still together," he said, and it brought comfort to my uneasy spirit.

When the door to the cargo train screamed open a final time, we were met with a half dozen snarling German Shepherds on short leashes held by the hands of sneering Nazis.

A handful of *Sturmabteilungen* rushed inside the car and began shouting, "*Bewegt eure ärsche*" and "*Sich beeilen*," demanding that we get out of the train in quick succession.

The men immediately in front of me were being sternly pushed from behind with gun barrels that poked menacingly into their backs. Lucas and I locked our fingers together and pressed hard one last time before we too were forced out of the door and into the bright light.

It took a moment for my eyes to adjust to the midmorning sun after days of living in near total darkness. Once my pupils undilated, they looked out on a concrete train platform where the train tracks ended. There was no journey beyond this location; one simply arrived and never moved forward. On the platform, many soldiers marched in different directions. Some walked their dogs and others forced our ragtag group of men forward toward a series of administrative buildings just inside a tall black metal gate. Here the soldiers officially handed us off to *Schutzstaffel*, the dreaded prison guards.

Directly over the gate hung words shaped from the same cold black metal that read, "*Arbeit Macht Frei*." Work sets you free. As I took in their dark meaning, in front of me I heard someone whisper, "Dachau," and another followed closely behind with terror in their voice as they muttered, "Work camp," and then a third cried out "Death!" A stale smell of smoke hung on the air as if fire and flesh had become one. I crossed under the sign and knew instantly that these guards were in fact Charon leading us this last distance across the River Styx. We were now in hell.

As our group of men entered the gate, we were organized into a straight line, where each person was forced to approach a long table, one at a time. Seated at this table were two *Schutzstaffel*, one who appeared to be something of a low-level officer and the other his aide. Each time a new man from our group approached these two, the prisoner stated his name. The officer then nodded to either his left or his right. Other guards of lower rank would step over and escort the prisoner toward the declared location.

It took very little time to realize that those who were sent to the right were older, weaker, and infirm. It was clear that they were headed toward something more unpleasant than those on the left, if you could consider any part of being assigned a position in the underworld as more or less unpleasant.

The organized line moved fairly quickly. There was an eerie efficiency that the guards here had perfected in order to sort men out right and left, as if they were wheat and chaff. As Lucas and I got closer to the table our-selves, I could feel fear rising up the back of my neck.

A loud whistle rang out, and I turned to see that one of the men in our group—a short, squat Pole who looked to be in his forties—had broken free and was running back up the tracks toward what he hoped was his freedom.

Two dogs were released from their leashes, and they caught up to the breakaway in mere seconds. They toppled him to the ground in a fury of teeth and blood. His voice was carried back to us on the wind as he cried out in Polish for help—*"Pomóż mi, pomóż mi!"*

That help came in the form of a bullet, which caused the dogs to back away from their prey. The hunt was over.

The man in front of us was forced up next, and he stepped forward feebly to give his name to the officer and his aide. The aide looked for the old man's name in a large book, searching until he found something that made him point, then whispered into the officer's ear. Hades studied the prisoner before nodding to the right, deciding this man's fate.

"No," the old man screamed out. He fell to his knees and began to cry. "Please, I beg you! I am still healthy and virile. I can do much work!"

The officer's face darkened, and he nodded to the right again.

When the man did not get up off of his knees and stop his begging, another guard ran in from the side with a fresh German Shepherd, who growled and snapped at his prostrate form. The old man had seen what happened when the last dogs were turned loose, and he did not want to suf-fer the same fate. Though initially unwilling, and now with great effort, he arose from the ground only to be chased off in the required direction, the dog snarling behind him the entire way. As he approached the door to a red brick building nearby, a guard kicked the old man, who then fell through the doorway to the laughter of all the gathered Staatspolizei.

There was no time to feel any empathy for this poor soul, for as soon as he was gone, Lucas was beckoned forward.

My own hands shook as I watched with great trepidation.

"Name?" the aide asked in a crisp tone.

"Lucas Strechburg," he replied obediently.

"City?" the aide continued without looking up.

"Berlin."

The aide's finger ran through pages in his book before it settled on the appropriate line, where he wrote something down.

The officer eyed Lucas over and quickly nodded to his left.

A rush of relief flooded through my body, as I watched my lover follow a guard to join the men lined up to the left, who had also been saved from whatever fate the old man had just been assigned.

When Lucas was almost in position with the others, he slowed his pace and turned back, catching my eyes before I was the next to be prodded forward.

As I approached the table, the officer's eyes widened. He stood up from his chair and came around to get a closer look at me. By now, my dress had been shredded. Most of the fabric below my knees and from its sleeves had been ripped off and used as various forms of bandage or as toilet cloth along the journey. My makeup was all but gone, except for faint traces of kohl around my eyes and a few sole splotches of crusty concealer. Of all the people who faced judgment at this table in Dachau, I was certain I was the most curious of creatures.

"What is this?" the officer asked incredulously. "I thought this train was only bringing men today."

He studied me up and down. We were of even height, me in my bare feet as my heels had long since disappeared, and him in his polished Nazi work boots.

"Name?" the aide called out with great interest.

"Josef Dietrick," I replied in almost a whisper.

At the sound of the name of Josef, the officer clicked his teeth together in disapproval, as the fact that I was male registered across his disgusted face. He barely waited a second before he nodded his head to the right.

I gasped in horror. I turned back to Lucas, whose pained expression was crushing to my soul because I knew it meant that he could protect me no longer. These were to be our final seconds, and we were separated by meters filled with guards, rifles, canines, and regret. Had I only gone to Dusseldorf with Lucas that night like he had requested instead of insisting that I perform.

As I slunk off slowly toward the red building where the older man had been sent, another officer in a different uniform approached the table.

"Wait a moment," I heard. "I have information that this prisoner is skilled at sewing. We have need of his type at the uniform factory."

The table officer deferred to what must have been his senior, as both he and his aide saluted.

Before I knew what was happening, I was being moved away from the building toward the right in order to join Lucas with the other group on the left. I was saved.

▼

ONCE ALL OF THE OTHER men had been sifted one by one, those of us who remained were ushered to a different large red building on the opposite side of the area from the one where the elderly and sickly man had disappeared into.

As we entered, we were herded into a door on the right, which led us immediately to a large, empty room.

"Strip down everything!" a guard yelled out from the front. We all began to look around at each other nervously, certain we had misheard the directive being given to us. The voice screamed out again, harsher. "Strip down now! Take everything off, leave not a stitch!"

Two dogs barked at the doorway where we had entered. Their following growls led us all to slowly disrobe. I slipped the remains of the dress over my head and pulled down my knickers. Sheepishly, I tried to cover my manhood with the chiffon rags as I shook with a chill from the state of my undress.

"You will fold your clothes, then bring your items one at a time over here," a man directed as he pointed toward a hole in the wall where two men with more books stood ready to collect our belongings and sort them in some kind of storage room behind them.

Eyes darted back and forth as we stood there in full nakedness, pushed up against each other in the space. My feet scraped against the cold cement as I was herded forward to hand off my bedraggled clothing. Once the small pile was torn from my hands, I was ushered into yet another room with the rest of the men. This one was covered in slick yellow tiles that were wet to the touch of my toes.

We were barely inside when I heard the door slam shut behind us and lock. Our bodies were pushed up even harder against each other now, as someone's buttocks spread against my leg while another's penis brushed against my back. Yet, there was no time for concern, modesty, or embarrassment as a loud hissing sound was heard. The noise started a chain reaction of panic among the naked men.

"Oh God, we are about to be gassed to death!"

Someone else began to sing loudly in Hebrew, in a tone that echoed off the tiled walls and floors: "*Sh'ma Yisra'eil Adonai Eloheinu Adonai echad.*"

Another cried out for his mother in what sounded to be Russian.

This was followed by many fearful shouts, muttered prayers, and cries for mercy in various languages.

They were all silenced suddenly as I felt a thousand wet bullets landing hard against my skin from every direction. A strange relief washed over me as I realized we were being hosed down, not killed. The water from these shower spouts poured out violently from over our heads and all of the walls. I lost my footing from the enormous force, I was pressed so deeply in between the other men's bodies that I was unable to fall, so I stood there and let the water, which smelled faintly of lye and some type of chemical disinfectant, wash over my body.

When it stopped, a new door on the far end of the room opened, and once again we were forced to swarm out into some kind of formation. We found ourselves in yet another large room, where we stood for endless minutes in order to drip dry, surrounded by Schutzstaffel who were completely dressed and looked on at our naked bodies with sniggers and scowls.

One by one, we then came forward and were ordered to sit in chairs, where men in striped prisoner uniforms shaved our heads under surveillance, as if to remove any last vestige of our dignity. When I sat down, the prisoner grabbed my long locks and violently yanked my head backward before he denuded me fully of my doll identity. I may have arrived as die blaue blume of Schöneberg, but six jagged clips of the buzzer later, I was left with only a pale stem where I'd once flowered.

Finally, we were moved along once more, this time to a smaller room with benches, where we each received a stack of new clothing that consisted of thin gray pants with blue stripes and a matching shirt. We were told to put our new clothing on quickly, and as we did, we noticed that different-colored triangles were sewn into the coarse fabric of our shirts. Lucas and I both were emblazoned with upside-down triangles in a bright pink. The Schutzstaffel shouted that these now marked us as homosexuals. The man who had sung in Hebrew wore his upside-down triangle in red, which had an additional right-side-up triangle in yellow, and someone told him these signified him a Polish Jew. Underneath the triangles were numbers stitched into the fabric. A guard informed us that we were to memorize our numbers, as we would forever after be called only by these and not our names. We were no longer to be recognized as individual people, or as humans, but as digits under badges that ranked our worth—not only in this camp but within the entire Reich.

As we exited the room, a pair of brittle, dark leather clogs were handed to each of us. My new shoes looked old and worn, and I had the feeling that something terrible must have happened to the man who was their previous owner.

At last, we were pushed through doors and back out into the now-afternoon sunlight. Lucas, with his shorn hair, looked small and frightened. Our large group of men were divided into smaller groups by screams and shouts of numbers. Each of these newly formed clusters were then escorted away in different directions.

I threw my head back in relief as I realized Lucas and I were still together. Our group of about ten men began to march down a small dirt path. On each side of this path stood buildings that appeared to be some type of dormitories.

During our short march, we traveled by random lone men, if you could call them that, as they appeared more like skeletons—eyes sunken, skin that clung closely to their bones as if something here had eaten away at the layers of life between the derma and the soul. These pitiful beings were mostly doing mundane tasks such as sweeping or cleaning, and they looked up with blank faces to stare at our group as we rushed by. They had almost no emotion or life behind their eyes, until they saw the flashes of pink on my and Lucas's breasts. At that, the ghouls sneered and looked away, except for one who hissed, "*Es ist eine Sünde, lebensmittel an homosexuelle zu verschwenden.*" They didn't even want to waste food on us.

Most of the walk was empty of people, though. I would come to learn shortly that almost no one returned to camp before sundown unless it was to die.

Our small group began to thin as a guard would lead one or two of our number off at a time and deposit these men inside the front doors of one of the many dorms we passed, until at last only Lucas and I remained. We were finally led off to a small wooden building that stood about a hundred yards in front of a line of barbwire fencing that seemed to run the length of the camp.

Once we were inside the door of the building, the guard stated firmly, "Wait here. The others will be back soon, and they will tell you what to do." Then he shut the door behind him. The sound of his boots faded, leaving us to ourselves for the first time in probably well over a week.

Lucas and I moved away from the door and embraced.

"I am so sorry I did this to you," I cried.

"I thought you were gone forever," Lucas said through his own tears, holding me closely.

"I believed the same as well, but how did they know that I could sew, and who was that man who saved me?"

We unlocked our arms from each other's bodies. "I do not know, but clearly he is some kind of angel sent from *himmel*," Lucas responded with a smile, pointing toward the heavens.

"What do we do now?" I asked, looking around this space we found ourselves in. It was a rectangular room, the walls all rough-hewn boards of wood. There were as many cracks in between these planks as there had been on the train, so it was still the same temperature as it had been outside. Perhaps it was even colder, as we lacked the benefit of sunlight. Yet, even with air flowing through, the room had an unbearable stench, like a gymnasium full of sweaty feet.

Two rows of about twenty bunk beds each stood pushed against the walls. On top of every bed was a pile of brown rags that served as covers. There was little space between the rows.

We walked along, taking in our surroundings as we discussed our situation.

"I am worried about what comes next," I confessed.

Yet Lucas assured me with his soothing words. "It can't be any worse than what we endured on the train, now can it?" And as always, I found myself feeling safe in spite of everything so long as he was near.

After we determined that there was little more to see in this bunkhouse, I decided to sit down on one of the lower bunk beds until the others arrived and filled us in on our new lives, just as the guard had ordered.

As I pressed myself down onto the mattress, which felt as if it were filled with hard clumps of wet straw, an emaciated boy of about eight or nine shot up out of the ratty cloth covering.

"Who are—" I began to ask, partly from being startled and partly from the realization that I had just sat down on this thin critter's feet.

The boy lifted a bony finger and pressed it over my lips. "Shh!" he whispered, his voice hoarse. "They don't know I'm in here!"

"Who doesn't?" Lucas asked as he moved closer to the bed, alarmed at the boy's sudden appearance.

"The guards, dum-dum," he replied with a smile. "They sent me to the infirmary and I snuck back in here to hide instead."

"Why would you do that?" I asked him. "If you are sick, wouldn't you want to go where they could make you better?"

The boy's eyes widened as if he were talking to two idiots. He leaned over and coughed quietly into the covers, then turned back to us and explained, "One of the first things you need to know is when a person is sent to the infirmary, they do not ever come back."

"Why wouldn't they come back?"

The boy slapped his hand to his head. "Once you are so sick you cannot work, they simply kill you—or do even worse things." He shuddered.

"Worse than death?" I asked nervously.

"Yes. Unless you think it's better to be experimented on, like having your eyes injected with things or one of your legs cut off and then sewn back onto your arm. And those are the nicer things they do."

I stood there unable to process what was being told to me, but Lucas started to uncharacteristically peck at the boy. "Don't tell make-believe stories, little boy. We are worried enough just by being here."

He shrugged. "Suit yourself if you don't want to believe me."

"And won't they figure out that you are not in the infirmary and come looking for you here eventually?" Lucas continued. "Seems foolish, like you're going to get yourself caught and in more trouble." He huffed with annoyance at the child's words and presence.

I could only assume all of the pressure since the Rote Schwein had at last brought Lucas to a point of near emotional collapse and that this poor boy was in the right place and time to bear the brunt.

The boy did not seem to be intimidated though, as he simply stuck his tongue out as if Lucas were an older brother who had stolen his lollipop, not any kind of a threat. He rolled his eyes and he pointed at him, addressing me. "This one is a real humdinger, isn't he?"

I couldn't help but laugh as he turned back to Lucas. "No, you *lusche*. They had a new batch of incomers like you come in today so the guards got distracted."

"What's your name, kleiner junge?" I interjected to break this childish standoff.

"Adam," the boy said.

"That is Lucas"—I pointed—"and I am Josef." I started to twist my body around on the bed so that Adam and I could sit face-to-face, but as I did so, the boy's eyes landed on my shirt, and he recoiled and jumped back in the bed.

"Oh no, you're one of them," he exclaimed with a look of fright.

"Don't worry." I laughed at this innocent. "We will not hurt you." I giggled at his alarm over our identification.

The boy leaned closer to me and said in a hushed tone, "It's not that I'm afraid *of* you, it's that I'm afraid *for* you—because of what that triangle means and what happens to the people like you who wear that here."

This set Lucas off again, and he bent down closer to us. "What do you mean by what happens to us?"

With the truth of youth, he laid it all out to us plainly. "Well, your type doesn't usually last long around here, to be honest. Between the beatings and the fact that you will rarely be allowed to keep the food you are given each day, you will be lucky to last a few weeks at best." His face fell as he spoke. Then he looked up and stated as if this were all just a matter of fact, "Not to mention that no one will probably speak to either of you."

"Why you little lying shit!" Lucas exclaimed, reaching over to grab Adam by the shirt. Right then, the door to the bunkhouse crashed open, and the back of the door slammed hard against the wall.

An exceptionally loud guard entered with his rifle drawn, and he began to growl at us with a volume that made the floorboards groan. "Who are you two talking so loudly to in here?" he bellowed, stomping toward the bunk bed.

I glanced back at the covers and found that Adam had completely disappeared under them, his thin body barely noticeable under the rags.

"Just each other," I said nervously as the towering figure and his rifle approached.

"I thought I heard three voices in here, and I only count two people in this room," he boomed. He began to slam the butt of his gun into the various mattresses that he passed along his way toward us. "If you are hiding someone," he continued as he got down and looked underneath the beds, "it will mean both of your deaths right here and now, and in the most painful manner."

Lucas's eyes widened in terror, and he shot me a quick glance as if to say, *I'm not dying for anyone here today, let alone this sickly child.*

He stepped forward toward the guard. "Well, actually . . ."

I jumped up and cleared my throat, stepping in front of Lucas, "Yes, actually—the voice that sounded different was my own." I raised my voice an octave to match the pitch of Adam's prepubescent tone and continued, "You see, when I am nervous, I sometimes speak with a higher voice." I managed a nearly perfect boyish lilt.

The guard stopped his search and stood up straight. He came closer to me and looked down at me with great disdain. "I really do not know why we don't just kill all of *der schwule*! You effeminates are a complete waste of space!" He stepped back. "Fortunately for you both though, I am not in charge, or I would rip you apart this very minute with my bare hands. Instead, I have come to bring you your work assignments from the Labor Allocation Office."

The guard pulled a wad of paper out of his back pocket and looked it over before looking at us once more. He lifted his rifle in the air, gesturing toward Lucas, and shouted, "Hey, you there—spectacles."

Lucas was only a few feet away from the guard, so the almost unbeliev-ably loud voice made him jump back a few steps. He steadied himself and adjusted his glasses to look toward this man who was about to proclaim some kind of sentence on us both.

"Labor," the guard said dryly. The corners of his mouth lifted into a slight sneer as he looked at Lucas and laughed. "I think my bare hands won't be needed to pop your arms out of their sockets here after all, now that you have that particular work assignment." He started to shake with each guffaw. "I expect to see you broken and expired soon enough. *Seltsam* don't last long at manual work."

Lucas and I looked at each other in fear.

When he was done laughing, the guard glanced back at his papers, then growled toward me, "The princess here, on the other hand, has been assigned with the female seamstresses that go out to the uniform factory each morning."

He turned around and started to march off, but as he reached the door, he turned back to address Lucas directly. "Oh, and spectacles, it seems like someone likes your wifey too, or else she would be hauling bricks like all of you other weak fucking homos. So, you better take care that someone bigger doesn't try to snatch her away."

We looked at each other, terrified by those words, but he continued, "Pussy is always a premium at Dachau." He paused for a second to let those words sink in before he signed off with, "*Tschüssi*, sweet girls!"

The door slammed behind him, leaving us in silence.

After a moment, Adam's head crept out from under the thin rags.

"Thanks," he said softly.

"For what?" I asked, completely lost in his warning and in our work assignments. The meaning lay so heavy on me that I'd nearly forgotten that Adam was even with us.

"You could have turned me over to him." He sat fully upright. "You don't even know me, yet you risked your own life for me just now." The boy's face was locked in a combination of disbelief and appreciation.

Lucas walked over and put his hand around the back of my neck and squeezed. "Did you not hear one word that guard just said to us? We could have been killed for this little stranger!"

"But he's just a boy," I retorted.

At that, Lucas stepped back and pulled on the triangle on his chest. "We already have these, and we do not need to give them any other reasons to be suspicious of us, Josef!"

Incredulous, I pressed, "Even if it would have meant this boy's death?"

"As long as it was not our death, yes!"

Lucas was already changing, and we had barely been here for a few hours. I shook my head at him in disbelief. With plain disappointment, I muttered, "Well then I am just glad that the person who found me behind a slop bin only a few years ago didn't feel this way toward strangers at that time."

My words seemed to deflate whatever had built up in Lucas, like a pin releasing helium from a balloon. He let out a long sigh, then put his hands on his hips and lowered his head for a few seconds. When he lifted it back up, he turned to address the boy directly. "He's right, Adam. I am really sorry." Lucas began to pace the floor. "I'm just frightened, and have been ever since we were captured. It was a long journey here, and the unknown scares me, to be perfectly honest."

Adam rolled it off with the resilience of the young. "Hey, it's okay," he said with a smile. "I'm just glad the guard didn't find me."

After that, he lay back down on the bed and coughed violently, pushing his face into the mattress in an attempt to muffle the sound.

Lucas and I exchanged looks of pity at both Adam's health and our own situation.

The door to the bunkhouse was yanked open again, and we shot upright, assuming the loud guard had returned to check to see if we were actually still alone. Instead, a group of close to thirty-five men dragged through the door. They were of various heights, with all shades of stubble on their heads and faces, but each was covered in dust and dirt and possessed the same look of utter exhaustion.

As they filed in, each moved their way toward one of the limited bunk beds, which they began to climb into, mostly in pairs.

One thin man with dark eyes walked toward the bed that Adam was in. When he noticed Lucas and me, he stopped short at the sight of our shirts and growled violently, "Get away from that bed, you deviants!"

At those words, Adam popped out from the covers, and the man rushed to his side, where he leaned down to hug his boy. Then he stood back up and spat, "Stay away from my son!"

At that, most of the men got down from their beds and surrounded us in a circle. One huge man, whose Russian accent was as thick as his arms and neck, came to stand directly behind the man and his child, cracking his knuckles. "Do you want me to snap their necks, Rabbi?"

Adam crawled down from the bed and feebly made his way into the circle, placing himself between his father, the Russian, and Lucas and me with his arms and hands extended, warding them off.

"It's alright, Papa," he said weakly. "These two are good people." He turned around to look at us, then back to his father. "They protected me from the guard finding me earlier. I was sent to the infirmary today but I came in here to hide instead."

He stepped closer to his father, grabbing his hand. "These two saved my life."

The rabbi looked between us a few times before addressing us in an only slightly less unfriendly tone. "We don't always take kindly toward the pinks in this camp," he stated matter-of-factly.

Though the shift of tone was small, I saw an opening. I stepped forward with my hand extended in greeting, though it still shook from nervousness over the potential confrontation with the rest of the men of this bunkhouse. "I am Josef."

The rabbi looked down but did not offer his hand back. "My name is Rabbi Horowitz." He nodded to the bull of a man and said, "And this here is Vladimir." After a pause, he added, "He's from Russia," as if to warn us that while we might not be getting attacked as of yet, if we were planning to cross any red lines, thoughts of this Russian bear should give us pause.

Vladimir, whose triangle was the bright red reserved for political prisoners, looked at my hand as well and provided us with a short grunt. He walked off to one of the other beds and climbed in.

"Um, okay," I muttered to myself as I put my hand down. "And this is Lucas," I said, as pointed him out to Adam's father.

The rabbi finally relaxed his shoulders and unset his jaw. "Since you saved my boy today, you are welcome to share this bunk above Adam and me. There's two per bed," he explained as he walked over and slapped the top mattress. "Not that you two should mind," he muttered to himself as he looked up toward the heavens as if speaking directly to God himself.

Adam began to cough violently again, so his father put his arms around him and helped him back into the bed.

"I'm tired, Papa, and I need to sleep," he whispered through a hoarse yawn.

"Of course you do, my son." The rabbi gently tucked him in, pulling the covers up so that only Adam's nose and one of his closed eyes were visible. The man looked upward again and said, mostly to himself, "Why does a child like this suffer?" Then he stood and faced us directly, providing his own answer. "But who are we to know the mind of God?"

With a small shrug, Rabbi Horowitz announced to the bunk in its entirety, "I suggest we all rest now too if we hope to make it to the day of Exodus and then freedom in a land of milk and honey."

At his words, the rest of the men found their beds and climbed in with murmurs of agreement and sighs of goodnight. It was clear by the way they departed for their bunks at the rabbi's words, like the seas had for Moses, that this man held great sway in the building. His acceptance meant we were marginally safe inside these walls, at least in comparison to the others of our lot.

Completely wiped out from the anticipation of the train's destination, followed by all that had transpired since our arrival, Lucas and I climbed our way up onto our bunk and fell asleep on top of the thin covers within minutes.

▼

IT SEEMED I HAD barely closed my eyes when a stern man in brown clothes burst through the door with a torch. He did not wear the uniform of the guards, but he also did not wear our blue and white stripes. Yet this man had a green triangle on his clothing.

"Hurry up!" he snarled at the top of his lungs, kicking at the ends of each bunk as he worked his way down the floor.

At his insistence, the men jumped up and began to make their beds in a hurry.

The rabbi stood up and whispered to us, "That's the *Kapo*, Carl. Hurry up and tidy your bed, then stand at the front like Adam and me."

Lucas and I wasted no time in tidying, and it was only seconds before we were lined up like everyone else.

The Kapo paced the floor, inspecting the bunks with the look of a lion seeking a wounded animal, to tear at its neck and take it down to the ground. The man had a fierceness in his step, and I could feel the terror in the men to my left and right as he approached them, followed by their relief when he continued past without stopping.

Satisfied that everyone was ready, Carl announced that it was time for the latrines, and we all followed him outdoors to a building where other Kapos had their own charges lined up. There were several hundred of us waiting in the cold air. It was still dark, and there was almost no hint of the night sky lightening in the east.

"What exactly is a Kapo?" I whispered to Adam.

I was trying to distract him—his frail frame looked like it was about to fall into a fit of coughing.

He whispered a meek reply—Kapos were other prisoners, whom they put in charge of each house or unit. They were to make sure that we followed all of the commands of the camp.

Rabbi Horowitz added on that these men were usually chosen for their criminal backgrounds. They were known as the *Berufsverbrecher* and delighted in being especially cruel with their power, having earned their ferocious reputations in back alleys and regular prisons prior to their placement at camps like these. The more they were seen as vicious, the more they were fattened up with food by the Nazi guards for doing their job of keeping us in line for them. These were plush positions—the Kapos would be rewarded for their sadistic treatment of others.

"Carl has the added benefit of not being fully right in the head," the Rabbi shared. "He occasionally talks to his twin brother, whom some say Carl murdered over a woman and that's why he went to prison in the first place."

We were moving closer to it being our turn, so he concluded by advising us to stay clear of Carl and any of the Berufsverbrecher.

Finally, our bunkhouse made it to the latrines, where we found ten toilets for the several dozen of us with only a few minutes to make use of them. The horrible stench inside nearly knocked us over, as people pushed and pulled to get a moment's use on the feces-spattered porcelain bowls before they rushed to a half dozen sinks to splash water on their faces and over their bodies, then dashed yet again for the doors.

When we exited, our Kapo, Carl, waited on the other side of the exit in what was now the early light of dawn. He glared at Lucas and I when we exited and said aloud, as if he were speaking to someone next to him, though there was no one there, "These must be the new ones."

His invisible companion appeared to have replied, because Carl said, "Yes, I agree with you. We will have to make sure they learn quickly. But for now, you are right. Not yet . . . not yet."

Satisfied that both he and his unseen brother were in agreement, Carl marched our group to collect our breakfast.

As we passed an administrative building on our way, outside stood a Schutzstaffel watching our group go by. He held a leash in his hands, and at the end of the tether was no German Shepherd but a naked man on all fours. His eyes were pointed toward the ground so that he would not have to meet our gaze as we passed his humiliation.

"Steady, steady . . . good doggie," the soldier laughed. "Now show the boys daddy's little bitch." He cackled as he pulled the rope tighter, choking the man's head up until we all could fully see his face.

I caught his terrorized eyes and realized he had one of the same pink triangles that were sewn onto Lucas's and my uniforms, only this patch was sewn directly into the flesh of this poor naked man's right cheek.

"Now lift your leg and take your morning piss," he shouted with venom, and his creature obeyed. The man-dog hoisted a leg and sent a stream of pale yellow out of his flapping member, which trickled down and swirled into the dirt around his violently shaking hands.

I felt my body begin to shake from fear at this lack of humanity and not knowing how the man wound up in this horrific situation, so much worse than ours. Then someone muttered, "I would rather die than be subject to such humiliation."

To my great relief, Carl pushed us quickly forward, and we left the terrifying sight behind.

While the sad and frightening image of that poor man would haunt me for some time, there were worse horrors yet to come that would take up all of the space in my head. He was soon forgotten.

The cold ground crunched beneath us as we reached an open area in the camp with many wooden tables atop an area of grass mixed with patches of dirt, trampled by many feet. Along these grounds were several wooden stations, where prisoners stood behind giant pots of some kind of hot beige slop, which they scooped into bowls and handed out to lines of frail men who pushed each other to get their own bowls filled first. Once they had their food, the prisoners rushed to tables to eat it quickly before returning their empty vessels to the other side of the camp and depositing them into big bins. After this, they grabbed rough metal cups filled with watered-down coffee, barely even light brown, which they gurgled down in fits of dry relief.

As I approached the line to get my own bowl of food, I noticed a frail man starting to sit down at a table nearby. As this enfeebled being was mid-squat, a big, strong man stormed up to him and yanked the steaming bowl right out of his hands. Silence rippled across the nearest tables as other men sat up to see what would happen next.

The frail man was helpless, doing nothing as the strong man poured the entire bowl down his muscled throat in less than a second. Gone was this sad being's sustenance for this day. The strong man then stood over him with a look of death, daring him to say something. The frail man simply lowered his head.

This goliath glared at the gawping onlookers, offering them the same dare, but they too dropped their heads and returned to their own bowls. At this, the strong man slammed the empty bowl back onto the table and walked off, his chest pushed out in pride.

As I grabbed my own full dish, now filled to the brim with the hot slop, I started to walk past the sickly man. I looked down at my food with great longing. As hungry as I was, I stopped and handed my bowl to him instead. I could make it through this day without food, but I was not sure that this poor creature could.

The man held his hands out to me in tentative disbelief at my act, and his squinting eyes caught my own.

Something about those eyes looked so familiar—and then it hit me.

"Marteen?" I asked, in disbelief.

The emaciated man who sat before me surely could not be my step-brother and the personal torturer of my youth. Yet he was. Gone was the trickster who resembled a weasel, though—this Marteen looked more like a starved and nearly-drowned rat.

Upon hearing his name, Marteen looked at me more closely, as if I were something from a forgotten dream, until at last recognition came across his face.

He struggled to get to his feet, asking repeatedly, "Josef? Could this really be you?"

Noticing his struggle, I insisted Marteen sit back down, and I walked around the table and helped him to do so.

"Eat this food, Marteen. No need for you to get up. You need it. Now eat," I insisted.

Tears formed in Marteen's eyes. In between spoonfuls of the slop, he cried, "Josef, my brother. I am so sorry for the way I treated you."

The only things I felt in my soul at that moment was mercy and pity. Marteen may have been a horrible stepbrother, he may have even participated in the worst moments of my life, but I took no joy in seeing him in this current state. There was no comfort to be found in his discomfort, no happiness in his condition.

"If only I had known how cruel the world was when I was younger, Josef. I would have shown kindness to you the way you show it to me now, in spite of my mistakes," he sobbed.

Finished with the food already, Marteen clutched my arm tightly.

"It's alright, Marteen," I reassured him. "Hearing what you say now brings us both healing."

He dried his tears and then leaned closer and spoke in a much more somber tone, "I must warn you, then . . ." Marteen stopped to look around. He glanced in each direction and over each shoulder before he turned back to me. "He is here," he whispered.

"Who?" I asked, confused by his alarmed tone.

"I don't know what he will do to you when he finds out, but he *is* here!" Marteen repeated again.

Before I could get further clarity, Lucas approached the table with the full bowl of food that he had finally retrieved, and he chided me sternly. "We cannot afford to keep helping people!" he insisted.

"This is no stranger, Lucas. This person is family," I explained.

Lucas looked at Marteen, then rolled his eyes to me, assuming I meant this frail man was another homosexual that I was feeding. "The only family you can afford to help here, Josef, is me!"

I replied calmly, "I mean actual family. Lucas, meet my stepbrother, Marteen." I waved my hand toward him in an act of introduction.

Lucas looked back and forth between Marteen and me with his lips pursed tightly and his fingers clutching his bowl as if he were about to pull it apart. At last he muttered, "You mean . . . from Treptow?" His question faded into the morning air as the brief battle that had played out behind Lucas's eyes to no one's awareness but my own had quickly been decided. The momentary struggle where he asked himself if he would pummel this man, who as a boy had treated me so poorly. But Marteen's condition was clearly so bad that it would be almost as horrible to make him pay for his crimes now as it was for him to have perpetrated them.

"Yes, and Marteen was just telling me that the furrier, Herr Füchs, is here as well." I realized that the only "he" Marteen could have been referring to was his father.

Marteen's eyes widened, and he had just started to say something to me when a Schutzstaffel's whistle blew loudly, signaling that breakfast was over. One of the other bunkhouse's Kapos stood up and yelled, "Paper factory, here!"

Many men ran from their various tables and began to line up in front of him in perfect formation.

Another whistle blew, and from across the grounds a different Kapo yelled, "Munitions!"

More men ran to him to form up.

At last, Carl yelled, "Labor!"

This time, the men who slunk their way over moved at a far slower pace. Each of them looked more ragged and worn down than the next.

Lucas turned to me with fear in his eyes. "I better go now. I will see you tonight," he said, then muttered, "God willing" under his breath.

"That's my group as well," Marteen said softly, rising slowly. He looked down at the bowl I had given him, then back at me with eyes that were wide open for the first time that I could remember in our lives. "Thank you, Josef. You were my only friend when I needed one."

He began to limp his way toward the group of men assembled for Labor duties.

About halfway there, he collapsed to the ground. No one moved to help him up, not even me—I just stood there in shock.

In that brief moment of indecision, Carl came over and kicked Marteen with enormous force in his stomach. But Marteen did not move. He just lay there on the ground motionless, and I knew.

Marteen was dead.

The Schutzstaffel with the whistle stormed up and called some other guards over to fetch Marteen's body.

"Take him to the infirmary," I heard the guard with the whistle order.

Silence stretched across the yard. The Schutzstaffel looked out at the many men who stared blankly at Marteen. His lifeless body was now being dragged by his legs by two prisoners whom one of the guards had mustered up to perform this unsavory task.

"He is the first for today," the Schutzstaffel warned loudly to the assembled men. "Does anyone else want to join him?"

Each head turned away.

I was frozen in a mixture of time and space. Images of Treptow passed through my mind each time Marteen's lifeless body bounced off of the cold, hard ground as he was yanked onward until at last he was out of sight.

When Marteen was gone, I turned one last time to catch Lucas's face, as his group marched off led by Carl toward a day of hard labor.

I realized at last that truly none of us had any power here. How could we? Our body movements, even our bowel movements, happened at the command of others.

"Uniforms!"

The announcement that came from the mouth of yet another Kapo brought me back to my own present state, and I found my body had begun to move without thought into a line of one. Why were there no other men from Dachau headed to work on uniforms other than me? It was a curious question that did not go unnoticed, and more than a few sneers came my way as I was led past the men who remained.

I was marched through the camp until the Kapo handed me off to an angry-looking guard at the gate, but not before he muttered an insult. This new guard then brought me to a formation of about twenty women, who all wore the same blue-and-white-striped clothing as the male prisoners. I joined the back of their lines, and we all walked silently down empty industrial roads outside of the perimeter of the Dachau concentration camp.

We were led by a small team, consisting of the lone angry male and two female Schutzstaffel. When we had made it about a mile or so away, I saw a large factory looming on the horizon at the end of what looked like a hauntingly barren street. The factory was a deep red brick and dotted with two rows of large windows on the front, two stories tall. Along the sides of the building were smaller windows, likely for the offices of industry. On top of this mammoth sat eight chimneys of various widths and lengths.

All around the perimeter of the factory was the same barbed wire that had surrounded the camp. Outside of this wire, the fields of corn had already been harvested. Dried-up, withered stalks stood where golden plants once grew strong in the sun. I took in the large piles of rigid rock that stood on the east side of the building before our party was led through two large doors under a sign that simply read, "*Uniformen.*"

Inside, I found myself directly on the floor of the factory. The morning sunlight poured in from the large windows, shining brightly onto rows of sewing machines, dutifully lined up like prisoners waiting for the latrines.

Behind the sewing machines were three large tables that held many bolts of the gray-and-white fabric with the stripes we all wore. A machine with a large blade stood at the front of one of these tables, and the other two had what looked like canisters with scissors the size of my head standing upright in each. This area, I could tell, was where the large bolts of fabric were cut down to size in mass.

The women all walked swiftly to their assigned machines, and the loud whir of motors and needles poking in and out of cloth followed closely behind.

A pale, prune-faced woman, with long black hair that rested atop her head in some sort of bun resembling a butter danish, approached me with a stony look. Her long nostrils flared on her beak as she inspected me in the same manner I inspected her, though I hoped I was less obvious.

On this female guard's uniform was a patch with simple block lettering that read "Vogel" and I laughed to myself at how closely she did resemble a bird, particularly the barnacle geese that would hatch their goslings on the River Spree each spring. The hens would swim up and down the bank, ever on the lookout for any creature from air, land, or sea that might move against their babes. In this same manner she seemed to hover over the factory floor, ready to pounce on any movement she deemed to be personally against her country and her cause.

"You will report to this station immediately," she informed me, pointing to an empty space about a third of the way down along the first row of machines.

As she escorted me to my place, she rattled off the expectations of my servitude. "You are to stitch the seams on twenty pairs of trousers each day. If you break a needle on the machine, you are docked five pairs of trousers from your daily quota."

I listened on in silence, as the women we passed behind each tensed their shoulders at Vogel's proximity to them.

"It makes best sense then to aim for forty pairs every day, as the needles can and will break often," she said with a smirk as we stopped in front of my station.

"What happens if we do not meet our daily quota?" I asked innocently.

Around me, the gasps from the other women were louder than their machines.

Vogel honked loudly so that all in the vicinity could hear her response. "Talking is only permitted when permission is granted!" She looked around to make sure that everyone was back at work but also that they were well aware of her preparedness to mete out punishment. "That will cost you five pairs right at the start," she addressed me directly.

On the floor to the side of every machine lay piles of flat trouser legs that had been cut from a pattern.

"Here are your materials—now get to work," she commanded. "I am assuming you know how to use one of these." She leaned over and patted one of the sewing machines with her palm. "Otherwise, what need would they have for someone like you to come here each day with female prisoners?"

She raised an eyebrow. This was the same question I knew must have been on everyone else's mind as well, including my fellow seamstresses. It was on my mind too, but I had no response other than to nod and take my position in front of my sewing station.

"I will leave you to it," Vogel said as she turned to leave me. "You are already behind if you plan to make your quota for today."

Her thick, matronly ankles pressed the heels of her heavy shoes into the factory floor as she marched off to inspect each woman's work.

I looked around my little station to familiarize myself with the setup. Before me was a machine not too different from the one I had gifted to Anke back in Schöneberg, only this one had the name "Köhler" written across its cast iron arm.

I took a spool of blue thread and placed it onto the spool pin, then carried some through the thread guide. I pulled it around the tension dial and the spring, then back through the front thread guide.

As I did so, I could see the women on either side of me cast curious glances in between carrying on with their own work. To the right of me was an older woman who appeared to be in her early fifties. She was short, with dark brown hair that peeked out from under a piece of the blue and gray uniform fabric that she had used to create a headscarf. Her looks were grim and full of judgment, and she cast them from dark brown, suspicious eyes that matched the color of her hair.

To the left of me was a fair woman with the most porcelain skin I had ever seen. She appeared to be in her early twenties, and she had a similar hair scarf that could not control her bushy red curls, which had been allowed to grow back wild after her initial intake shaving. Though she was in an internment camp, she smiled while she sewed, as if she were spinning golden threads on a machine in the throne room of the Black Forest for the faerie queen, Frau Holle, herself.

Without formal instructions beyond "make trousers," I needed to study what each of these women was doing in order to complete my assigned task. It was my first day on the job, and I did not want to lose what was obviously a plum position when put up against the hard labor Lucas had been assigned to endure for the day. I quickly surmised the need to use the machine to stitch together legs, which were then joined together at the seat. These were next placed in a pile for the end-of-the-day quota count. Later I learned these trousers were then picked up and brought down the line to be stacked for a small group of older women who sat in chairs and hand-sewed strings into the extra fabric that they folded around the waist to hold the pants up when they were worn.

After I had completed the first five pairs with some effort, my machine jammed. I looked closely and found that its cheap *Klasse* needle was warped—it really did not fit this model of machine. The dark-haired woman near me rolled her eyes and turned the other way. The redhead happily pointed me to a box of replacement needles that stood between her and me.

"You will have to put the broken one on top of the bobbin cases at the end of the day," she instructed with a breathy, somewhat French timbre. "Vogel will then count your trousers and will be looking for the additional five for each one." She paused to get some air. "Since you were already docked five, that makes you ten behind, and it's not even lunch" She giggled as she ran the numbers through her head, as if she had just solved Mohammad bin Musa Al-Khwarismi's quadratic equation. There was something so childlike and warm about her that I could not help but smile back.

The rest of the morning passed by in a blur of whirring noise and lost thoughts. I could not help myself from worrying about how Lucas was making out.

I had just finished my twelfth pair when Vogel blew a whistle from over by the doorway in which we had entered in the morning. Each of the women filed out from behind their machines and formed lines in front of the guard. We were then led back outside into the courtyard of the facility, where a set of portable stations were set up similar to the breakfast layout in the camp earlier that morning, only much smaller. Here, at one table, a prisoner handed us each a hard-boiled egg and a chunk of bread. At the other table, another gave us a tin cup of that same watery coffee that we had received in the morning.

The ladies moved to various parts of the yard in couples or small groups. As I was handed my fare, I looked around and found myself back at the Berlin Jungen der Schule, with no one in sight having any interest in spending their few minutes of lunchtime with me.

I was walking toward an empty space in the dirt near the factory's perimeter fence when the breathy woman from my left called out to me, "Over here." She waved her hand and smiled.

Surprised by the invitation, I scurried over to her small group, which included the dark-haired woman who had been casting rude glances at me all morning, and another woman in her thirties whose eyes widened at my incoming figure. All of the women wore yellow on their breasts, so it was clear that at least this small group of ladies were Jewish.

In her French accent, she began to make introductions. "I'm Alma, and this is Matya," she said as she pointed to my sewing machine neighbor from the other side. "Oh, and this is Edna over here, who works behind us on the bolt cutting."

Edna, who I recognized from having stood at the machines behind the rows of seamstresses, nodded and said, "Hallo," while Matya looked at Alma with annoyance.

"Why are you here?" Alma asked innocently.

Matya stepped forward and flicked her fingers at my breast, hitting the badge as she spat, "For this, you dummes Mädchen."

"No, not here." Alma lifted her hands up and moved around to signify the entire camp. "I mean here!" She pointed toward the factory and then down at my feet.

"I worked for a seamstress in Berlin before we were picked up, so I can only assume that they decided that my skills were better put to use than killed off."

Alma shrugged and smiled. "Oui. Well, I'm glad you are working next to me."

I smiled back. Matya turned and walked away, grabbing the unsure Edna's arm and dragging her to another group.

"Oh, don't mind her," Alma reassured me. "She is just mad because no man ever looked at her, and here you are with that *belle* face. She knows any . . . what do they say in Jewish? Oh, mensch. Any mensch in his right mind would rather schtup you than her angry *vagin* any day."

We both giggled at her bawdy explanation, dipped in Yiddish and lusty française, and it felt good to laugh, for it had been ages.

"You are French?" I asked, then shook my head at my silly question.

But to my surprise, Alma responded, "Actually, I am not."

Over our eggs and bread, she shared her personal story. Before she'd been taken here, to Dachau, Alma was a happy young lady who lived with her widowed father in the city of Antwerp in Belgium. Her father was a clockmaker, but Alma spent her days working for a local dressmaker in hopes of one day creating her own fashion line.

"I wanted to be more well-known than Madeleine Vionnet"—the famous revolutionary Parisian female designer and Alma's hero. In fact, Alma had secured a job at Vionnet's couture house on the Rue de Rivoli but the growing antisemitism in Antwerp in the leadup to the German occupation made her hesitate, as she did not want to leave her father alone in Belgium. In the end, she shared how both of them had been swept up and deported by the Germans, him to Auschwitz and her to Dachau.

"They stole my dreams," she continued before sharing how this had caused her to make a decision when she arrived at Dachau. As she got off the train, she declared that in spite of the Nazis' inhumanity, she would smile every day, no matter what happened around her, no matter what she saw or heard. Alma insisted that "they can take everything from me but my smile, because I own that until I am dead. So I choose to wear it at all times in an act of defiance."

I saw clearly that Alma was no simple happy fool, but a woman with deep thoughts hidden behind kind eyes. Her one little act was meant to neutralize an entire movement without so much as lifting an arm.

After lunch, we hurried back to our machines, and I worked like a mad horse to ensure that I hit my first-day quota, which was twenty plus the five for talking aloud and the additional five for having bent one needle.

At the end of the day, we stepped away from our machines and Vogel came around with a young girl of around ten, whose job it was to count each of our piles. If she miscounted, she was whipped on the back with a long ruler that was meant to measure the bolts of fabric. Vogel clearly delighted at the girl's cries at each stroke, so she made it a point to count correctly the first time and spare her back the lashings by wood.

Satisfied that everyone had met their quota, Vogel announced that we had done well for such a load of embarrassing trash and that it was time for us to return to the camp until the next day.

We headed back the same way we had arrived earlier that day, though it seemed like it had been far longer than ten hours. When we entered the main gate, the women all broke off to the right and I was escorted back to my bunkhouse by a guard.

At the dormitory, someone handed me a single boiled potato as I went inside. I was glad to see that Lucas was already sitting on top of our bunk. He gobbled down his food by shoving it into his mouth with both hands. It was gone by the time I had crossed the room.

"I'm in horrible pain," he said as I got closer.

"Where does it hurt?" I asked, and Lucas lifted up his feet. I removed each clog and began to rub them, which brought us a look of intense dislike from Vladimir in the next bed.

I glared back at him. Though I was unaccustomed to being the one to take care of Lucas, who normally saw to my needs, I was not to be dissuaded from attending to him this day no matter how uncomfortable Vladimir, or anyone else, was.

My potato was placed on the bed as I rubbed his poor feet, and Lucas looked at it with great longing. "I'm terribly hungry, too," he moaned.

"Well then eat half of this, and tomorrow, you will take half of my breakfast as well." I pulled the potato into two pieces and offered the bigger of them to Lucas. "You obviously need more energy than I do to stand in front of a sewing machine all day," I continued with something just short of pity in my eyes and my voice.

"No!" Lucas insisted, unwilling to trade our traditional roles of protector and protectee. "I will not take your food."

He lay down on his back, muttering, "There's no point anyway. The way I feel right now, I'm not sure that I will even survive long enough for it to matter."

I was frightened by Lucas's words, as this was only the first day, and he was normally much more optimistic.

"Let's not talk like that," I told him. I glanced back over toward Vladimir, who still cast a menacing scowl in our direction.

"It is clear that neither of us can survive here without the other," I said plainly, pulling myself up onto the bed and settling next to Lucas. "Let us make a promise that no matter what, we survive for each other."

"Okay, Josef," Lucas responded, but there wasn't much strength in his voice.

"It's settled, then. You take the food—if not for your sake, then for mine."

"I'm too tired to talk," he replied.

"Sleep then, Lucas. But know this. I will do anything to protect you, the way you have always done so for me." I looked at what was left of my potato. *No matter what the cost to myself.*

Lucas began to snore, so I popped the last of the food into my mouth and then lay back and closed my own eyes.

AT BREAKFAST THE FOLLOWING MORNING, Lucas and Adam continued with what had now become their brotherly routine of having a go at each other.

"Hey Pinky?" Adam called out between wheezes to Lucas.

"Yes, my little angel of death?" he playfully asked back.

The rabbi had become more than fine with us interacting with Adam; he saw it as both innocent and healing for the boy, who needed any uplifting of the spirit to battle back against whatever was attacking him inside of his chest.

"How come you look so crap? Have you never actually had to work a day in your life before the Labor group?" the boy joked.

"Even worse than that, I had to teach a little piss-pot kleiner junge, who was almost as annoying as you, how to play the piano." Lucas jabbed back, poking Adam in the ribs and eliciting a laugh.

"Piss pot? This coming from someone who likes to put his mouth where piss comes out of other men."

And they both carried on, taking bites out of each other through laughter, but never in anything but good fun, as Adam had quickly become as dear to Lucas as if he were now his own *bruder*. I wondered if having Adam filled some kind of hole left in Lucas's heart that Anke had once stood in. After all, they had spent their whole lives relying solely upon each other, and then in the blink of an eye they were separated.

If these doings were hard on us grown people, how much harder on our youth? It suddenly came to my mind that I had not seen any other young boys within the men's camp besides Adam.

"Where are all of the other children?" I asked the rabbi, who was seated on the bench at the wooden table along with us, Vladimir, and a few other men from our bunkhouse.

Everyone slowed and then stopped their eating. Something strange had been loosed into the air at my words. Unsure if it was sadness, anger, jealousy that Adam was present, or a little bit of them all, I pressed on, determined to understand what had happened.

"Surely, there must be some reason in this small sea of adults that only one child is present."

The other men returned to their food, remaining silent.

"Boy children do not live at Dachau," the rabbi said simply before he got up. "Let us get some coffee," he directed Adam, who swung his legs out from under the table and followed after his father. "Coffee is always good at opening the lungs when you have a bit of asthma," I heard him explaining, his voice fading away.

Once they were out of earshot, Vladimir turned to me and in a thick Russian accent said, "Stupid question."

"Why, though?" I pushed back.

"When the transports arrive, all children, but especially the boys, are taken to the ovens."

The other men one by one got up from the table in order to remove themselves from this conversation.

"Your question is stupid not for what you ask," Vladimir continued, "but for how it makes the others feel."

I at last began to understand their awkward silence.

"Theirs is sadness for their loss, but also for the question they hold in their hearts—why their children, especially their boys, were not allowed to live, but Adam was."

He continued on, first emphasizing that these men loved Adam as if he were their own. My questions had simply opened a strange wound given what had been stolen from them—along with a strong need to protect this one remaining child at any cost.

"I am still left wondering, though, why Adam is here then, where the others are not?"

"The rabbi and his family came from inside the great city of München, in the mountains of Bayern. There, Rabbi Horowitz was a respected spiritual leader—his father and his father's father before him were Rabbis at the main synagogue. As such, Horowitz was no ordinary rabbi living and instructing in the Jewish villages. No, he was an important member of the community. Adam was the fifth of his and his wife, Sarai's, children. The three elder girls had already been married off and moved in with their own husbands. The older boy was sent away to Frankfurt to study at the great yeshiva, Torah Lehranstalt. Since there was already a rabbi-to-be in the family, Adam was freed to become something different.

"When things began to fall apart for the Jews of München, Rabbi Horowitz's long term relationship with one of the former Bürgermeisters, Herr Scharnagl, allowed for him to get Adam assigned to work in Scharnagl's household as an apprentice accountant. This took place while the other Jewish children of the city were being shipped off to ghettos with their parents."

The guard with his whistle arrived on the scene, but Vladimir pressed on with the story. "Finally, Scharnagl could help the Horowitz's no more, for he was killed by his successor, Karl Fiehler, during Fiehler's crackdown on all political dissidents, meaning anyone who did not follow the Nationalsozialistische Deutsche Arbeiterpartei. I myself was swept up in one of Fiehler's raids as I had moved to München as part of the underground Kommunistische Partei Deutschlands, attempting to reestablish a foothold for communism in the city for the time when the Nazi party would fall and a new political vacuum would allow Marxism to flourish—but that's another story."

The first whistle blew, and some of the men on the ground began to line up.

"The members of Scharnagl's household were sent here to Dachau, but by then, Adam, though incredibly young, had already established a reputation for being something of a genius with numbers."

Another whistle rang out, and Vladimir began to rise from the table. He finished in a hurry. "Not wanting to waste a job counting numbers on any of the guards when they already had a perfectly good accountant in a small frame, there was a rare exception made here, and Adam was assigned to work for the officers, where he accounts for the rations of food and the transportation of prisoners." He began to walk away. "That boy slaves away for one of the high commanders each day but returns to his father in the evenings. Jews might be on their way to extermination here in Germany, but even Nazis are not stupid enough to pass up on free brainpower—until, of course, he is of no more use to them. Why do you think they have not killed him like all of the other boys already in spite of his wheezing?"

"What about the girls?" I asked, but Vladimir was already gone.

THE NEXT FEW DAYS passed in a very similar fashion. I went off to the uniform factory while Lucas was taken for Labor. Each night, he returned looking half as alive as the day before. It was a terribly alarming situation; he was fading so quickly, and I was helpless to do anything about it.

One morning, we arrived at the factory in what was now the usual fashion. As we began to work at our machines, Vogel approached, this time with a new young girl. The one from the previous days was nowhere to be seen. Alongside Vogel were two male guards who stood straight and waited for instructions.

They stopped right behind Alma, and Vogel tapped the smiling seamstress on her shoulder, interrupting her work.

"Number 61725, you failed to meet the quota yesterday," she barked at Alma.

The smile on Alma's face began to falter, replaced quickly by a look of confusion.

"I counted multiples times," she began, stuttering. "There was a problem at one point with my machine, but that didn't . . ."

"Silence!" Vogel screamed, and Alma's red curls seemed to blow away from her face in the squall.

"There are no excuses, 61725! And the fact that you can stand here before me now and lie about your laziness makes you a worse animal than I already thought you beasts were. They told me never to trust any of you, and I keep learning this lesson over and over again. You truly are not humans but some kind of devils."

Most of the women in the factory stopped their sewing and stared at the scene.

"That little Juden bitch child yesterday thought she could cover for your mistake. She'll never do that again," Vogel spit, "because thanks to you, I had them pluck out both of her eyeballs so that those eyes of hers can fail her again no more."

The pronouncement of the young girl's fate hung in the air. Not only had she lost her sight, but there was no way the guards at the camp would allow her to live long without her vision to help her. In fact, she was likely already headed toward her fate, if she had not already met it.

As tears began to form in Alma's eyes, Vogel sicced the male guards on her, commanding them to "take her away!"

Off Alma went, with the men on each of her sides. They hoisted her by the elbows so that her feet barely had time to touch the ground with each step. Then they took her out through the front door and slammed it shut.

Vogel turned to the rest of us. "There will be no lunch today since you wasted so much time listening in on my conversation with 61725! In fact, your quota for today is thirty each—now get back to work you fucking *ungeziefer* vermin!"

The machines began to whirl loudly once more.

Matya leaned over from her area and said to me above the noise, "This is all your fault."

"Mine?" I asked with genuine surprise.

"If she wasn't so fascinated with a queer in our company these past few days, she might have paid better attention to her work." The woman turned back to her work, her feet as well as her instruments of industry moving more loudly and angrily for the remainder of the day.

When the light in the factory began to fade, Vogel blew her whistle, and we all assembled at the door once the new young girl had correctly counted our daily batches.

As we departed through the doorway, everyone gasped. We were led past Alma, who was completely naked. The guards seemed to delight in shaming and debasing us with the removal of our clothes. The only thing Alma wore now was a frown.

Her arms hung from a pole, and the tips of her feet barely touched the ground. There were gasps from our group as her body spun around and it was revealed that the flesh on her back was purple and torn, with marks the size and shape of Vogel's measuring ruler. Alma moaned slightly—she was alive. She spun once more and looked up at us weakly.

"Move," Vogel yelled, and we rushed toward the guards who regularly escorted us to and from the factory each day. Alma remained behind in her state of suspension.

When I made it back to the camp, Carl was in a fury, yelling at all of the inhabitants of our unit.

"They will never make me *blockältester* if the members of my own house that I supervise are as lazy as pregnant women!"

I stood at the doorway, unsure of what to do as Carl continued to rail at all of the others, who stood in front of their bunks at attention.

"There will be no food tonight for this group, and you will all clean the latrines," he announced. The already-exhausted faces of the men fell in disbelief and defeat.

"Now form up and get ready to scrub until your mother could eat off of those shit pots. As a matter of fact, I just might have one or two of your mothers brought over here to do exactly that." He smiled at his witty idea while the others rushed to the door.

I joined them in their line, where I fell in behind a dragging Lucas. He was trailing a wheezing Adam and his father. Even the strapping Vladimir looked to be pulling himself along unwillingly. There was not much left in our group to give, yet we were faced with this arduous task.

In the latrine, we were given buckets, which we filled with murky water from the washbasins. Our task was to scrub everything from top to bottom, including the walls, with disinfectant and brushes. Carl informed us that we had one hour to clean these filthy toilets but that the one *schmutzige Polacke* who lived in our bunk was to first stick his head into each toilet and hold it there for five minutes before anyone could clean that particular bowl. That left little time to clean the toilets with how long we would be waiting on his disgusting humiliation.

Lucas and I worked close to each other, and whenever Carl would turn away, I would stop Lucas from working, insisting that he rest while I doubled my efforts. Stroke by stroke we washed, the putrid water splashing onto the floors, mixing with urine and moist dirt.

At one point, poor Adam looked like he was falling asleep, so I rushed over to where he and his father were washing and helped them complete their task. This did not go unnoticed by the other men of the bunkhouse, and I received more than one smile from the exhausted faces as they turned to nod in approval at my assistance.

At last, the hour concluded and we were marched back to our bunks, much worse for the wear, as not only was everyone beyond exhausted, but we all stank to high heaven.

▼

THE NEXT DAY, I watched with great concern as Lucas lined up once again for Labor. We had only been at the camp for a couple of weeks, and already he had dropped so much weight from his ever-thin frame. What I wouldn't give to save him from this daily hell that was robbing my great love of both his dignity and of his life force. It appeared to be ebbing away before my helpless eyes. I had little time to contemplate further, though, as the begging cries of Rabbi Horowitz caught my ears.

I turned around to see Carl pulling the wheezing young Adam out of the rabbi's arms as the dreaded pronouncement of "infirmary" came from the lips of the Schutzstaffel who blew the whistle for duty each morning.

Adam tried feebly to hold on to his father, but the two were at last separated. The rabbi was pummeled until he fell in line, sobbing, for his work at the munitions factory, where he would be forced to create munitions for the Nazi war while his son was removed from this world. A father did not have the luxury of mourning a child who died at Dachau. There was only the choice between one's own death or work and a silent prayer that you would one day make it home to take care of the rest of your children.

My eyes watered freely as I returned to the uniform factory along with the formation of women to find that Alma was no longer there suspended. The pole remained, but her body was nowhere in sight.

We all silently entered the facility and took to our machines, quietly mourning the happy redhead who was almost certainly no longer with us.

After about five minutes, two doors in the back of the factory opened, and the guards who had taken Alma from her station the day before marched her back the same way she had left, each on one side propping her flailing body up.

When Alma was deposited in front of her machine, Vogel announced, "61725 confessed her sin and took her punishment. She will make thirty pairs of trousers today instead of twenty to atone for her misdeeds."

Vogel continued, gazing into the eyes of those nearest to her one by one. "Should 61725 fail to meet her quota today, I have instructed these

Schutzstaffel"—she pointed to the male guards—"to chop off each of her titten and serve them to you all for lunch tomorrow."

There was a nervous silence as our eyes looked to each other's in disbelief.

"You animals only understand firmness, and I can be as firm as necessary." With that, Vogel turned on her heels and left us all to our sewing.

It felt like everyone in my small world was suffering. While I had only been here for weeks, the horrors of our minute-to-minute existence made it feel like it had been years. I felt the pain of each of the people I had come to know, as if everything happening to them was happening to my own body. Yet, in order to survive the long term, I knew it was necessary to harden myself and retreat from my emotions. Fortunately, I had a lifetime of masking my true feelings. Wherever I could, though, I vowed to find ways to help those nearest to me, as it became clear to me that little acts, like sharing food or a smile, could be the thing that saved someone from giving up that day—that saved them from their death.

As the morning wore on, I worked my machine double. I guided the coarse fabric through the foot of the machine and hit the pedal with resolute intent. Every third pair I completed I slipped quietly into Alma's pile, for I was determined that she would make her quota that day even if I had to break five needles and make up the difference for each myself.

Matya caught me as I put the second pair on Alma's side, and she shot me a look of consternation. I could almost hear her sucking her teeth between the movements of the machine's motor. However, about thirty minutes later, she shot me a new look, this one of defiance, and she followed it up with a quick wink. She turned to make sure that Vogel was not in sight, then snuck a pair of completed trousers into my pile and motioned for me to move it on over to Alma's.

I smiled at Matya, whose humanity couldn't help but peek out from under her until-now permanent scowl.

A few hours later, it was lunch, and we all sat around on the ground, offering Alma encouragement. We told her how strong she was for enduring what they'd done to her and that she was already halfway through the day.

"Before you know it, you will be back in the bunk, getting some rest," Edna consoled, while Alma moved her back around in agony. We watched with sullen faces as she tried to give us one of her usual happy glances, but the corners of her mouth refused to turn upward no matter how hard she tried.

Matya chewed on a dark piece of bread as she leaned over to me with her mouth full and said with an irksome tone, "That was completely *meshuggeneh* . . ." She smiled. "And brave."

She cupped her free hand and stated, "That took *beytsim*" while mimicking a descending male ballsack. "I don't care whether you're a queer or not. What you did makes you what we call a real *gever*, and that's what being a true man really is all about. Standing up, even when you put yourself at risk."

After that, Matya was as friendly to me as Alma had been from our first interaction. As the woman softened, I learned her story, and it showed me how she was truly as rough-and-tumble on the inside as she presented herself to be.

Having come most recently from the Czechoslovakian ghetto in Theresienstadt. Matya told me how she had first escaped her home in Terezín, where she refused to wear the Jewish star. "Instead, I ran off with a small group of Jews and we hid in the rocky overhangs in the canyons near the Dobřeň region." There among the caves, they lived for months, eating only what they could kill or harvest from nature, until at last they were discovered and Nazis showed up and began to hunt them, picking them off with rifles for sport, one by one.

"When at last the men and women were gathered together, I was captured," she said, but then she told of how she jumped off a cliff into a river below in one last attempt to evade placement in the Jewish settlement.

Matya might have been in her fifties, but she was as tough as any twenty-five-year-old man, ready to roll on the ground with fists with anyone if she thought it was necessary. I became increasingly glad that she was now somewhat of a friend, as toughness was an admirable quality in a place where each minute was a fight for survival.

My eyes would well up whenever I heard the stories of what the other women had endured. Theirs were but a few, yet they rippled across a pond of millions of lives that were being rooted out and destroyed one by one, all because of hatred and man's need to feel superior over others.

Each day, someone would tell me something new—sometimes their own story or one of the most horrifying of tales that they had heard from other women back at the camp. Each day, they would ask me my own story, and I would repeatedly decline. "It is nothing too interesting," I would say, as how does one tell others who have suffered the most horrible of indignities at the direction of an insane political dictator of their own account? My mother's abandonment, the rape, Herr Füchs, the Rote Schwein and their dolls—all of these things existed outside of the Nazis, and they somehow felt far less harrowing than what each of these women had been through, as if degradation had levels of horror.

One afternoon when we were through with our food and conversations, we returned quietly to our stations for the afternoon work. While the sun was still bright, Vogel and the two male guards approached us behind our backs. Alma looked as though she was going to pass out once they neared her, especially after what had happened the last time this group came up behind her, but it was me that they wanted this time instead.

Nervously, I stopped my sewing and turned around to face whatever unpleasant fate awaited me. It was obvious that I had either been caught or turned in by someone for helping Alma several days back, and I knew the penalty was bound to be particularly severe, since I was the only man assigned to the uniform factory.

"The officer would like to see you. Whatever it is you did, it must be bad, as even I was not informed of the details," Vogel pronounced, as the two men came to either side of me.

My legs began to shake, but I followed along with them as they walked me through the front row of the machines, back past the second row and the tables where the fabric was cut by Edna and the others. Once we reached the very back, the guards motioned for me to go up a set of stairs, as the rest of the seamstresses looked on in silence.

They all faded from my view as I ascended, and I found myself in a long hallway dotted with office doors.

"You are going to the last door at the end," one of the guards instructed, prodding me down the hall.

At the end, we stopped at the office door. It was a dark wood with no window, so there was no telling what awaited me on the other side. I knew it was going to be something fearsome, so I steeled myself.

I gulped hard as one of the officers knocked. A strong voice replied back, "Send the prisoner in," and then one of the two guards pushed the door open and shoved me.

The door shut firmly behind me, and he stood there, right in front of me. It was the face of my nightmares, the one with the scar above his lip that I had hoped to never see again in the waking world.

"Hello, Josefina," the deep baritone voice of a now-matured Tielo Tiegel rang in my ears. I felt in that moment a panicked scream that released forth from the deepest part of my soul.

Tielo moved forward to press his hand over my mouth, silencing me. Then he leaned in, and I could feel his stubble brush roughly across my cheek as he whispered into my ear, "It's been a long time."

Though I was completely paralyzed in fear, my right eye began to twitch uncontrollably.

Tielo released his hand and stepped back.

With a sly smile, he spoke again. "When I saw the list of incoming names from the transport a few weeks back, I could not help but take note of yours."

My heart raced as he paced around me in a circle, licking his lips and eyeing me up and down.

"Lucky for you, I am an officer at Dachau, or you would already be ashes," he sniggered. When Tielo reached my other ear, he stopped and leaned in again, this time to whisper, "Even luckier for us both, you will remain alive so long as you do exactly what I say."

Chills ran up and down my body, as the man who had stolen my innocence and assaulted my body was now the officer of my fate.

With a coolness that only evil possesses, Tielo stepped away from me and walked the length of the room, approaching one of its two windows. He stood there for a moment, staring out, and then he urged me toward him.

"Come here, Josef." It was a gentle command, but a command nonetheless.

My legs wanted to remain in place, but they moved forward, and I soon found myself standing alongside him. I looked at his chiseled face as he closed his eyes for a moment to bask in the afternoon sunlight that came in from over the western fields. How could such beauty be so hideous?

"Good little girl," he said. "Now take your delicate eyes and look down."

I obeyed and followed his own gaze to where a group of thin prisoners were stacking bricks. One by one, the men took the red blocks from a pile and formed what appeared to be the beginnings of a new wall.

"Well, what do you see?" he asked in a manner that seemed to mimic a predator playing with its food before consuming it raw.

"Men working . . ." I replied tentatively.

In an instant, Tielo grabbed my head between his two bare hands with great strength, and he forced my gaze so that it focused on one lone, bedraggled man who approached the others, pushing a wheelbarrow that was overfilled with the red bricks.

The man struggled with the weight of the contents, and I gasped as the wheelbarrow tipped over and spilled its contents onto the dusty ground. An Oberkapo, the foreman of this work group, ran over and punched the man twice in the head. I gasped even louder when the prisoner stood up, picked up a handful of the bricks that had fallen, and turned toward the window. As he placed the blocks back into the wheelbarrow, I saw that the face I looked down upon belonged to Lucas.

Tielo pushed my head forward, almost slamming me into the window, before he released me from his grasp.

"You will do what I say not just for your own sake, Josefina, but for the sake of your lover outside as well."

I watched in horror as Tielo unbuckled his belt and dropped his pants to the floor, revealing his swollen member.

"Get down on your knees now, and I will make sure that your precious pink man is moved from the Labor unit to the gardens. There he will tend to vegetables and herbs along with the elderly and idiots, all but ensuring he lives many days longer than he would if he were to continue to do that back-breaking work."

At a crossroad, I looked down at Lucas, then back at Tielo.

In front of me stood the person who had violated me, who had stripped away my dignity and left me forever changed. Behind me stood the one person who had healed me from this ruin and who loved me with a selflessness that I experienced from no other.

"If not," Tielo chuckled, "I am fairly certain your man outside won't make it much longer than a few more days hauling those bricks and stones."

There was only a second to decide. I sank to my knees with great sadness and opened my mouth.

Tielo stepped forward and mounted me. I closed my eyes, squeezing them tight in an attempt to stop the tears from flowing out.

When I opened them again, Tielo was grinning down at me. "It is so good to see you again, Josef."

In between soft moans, he closed his own eyes and whispered, "I hope we can be even closer now than we were as young schoolmates."

He finished himself quickly, then drew up his pants and rehooked the buckle, while I remained on my knees. The image of Alma's bloodied and bruised back flashed in my mind, as my insides felt the way her swollen and beaten flesh had appeared the day she was hung on the pole.

"Return to work, or the others will begin to wonder why you have been away so long," Tielo barked.

I rose from the floor and floated toward the door like a ghost who was neither in this world or the next.

"We will resume our conversation tomorrow," he informed me as I turned the knob and exited. I shut the door softly behind me. I was numb.

I DID NOT MAKE any conversation for the rest of the afternoon, completing my quota lost in a haze of disgust and disbelief. The others did not ask what had happened, and I did not tell them, as I could not speak.

On the march back to the camp, I struggled with what I would say to Lucas. It was unclear to me if I should be upfront and let him know the terrible dilemma the return of Tielo posed. It would only ensure that Lucas would absolutely refuse the move to the gardens, hastening his inevitable death from the manual labor on little food or sleep, which was something that I could not allow.

I only became resolute in my decision at the final moment I arrived back at the bunkhouse. Lost in my own problems, I had completely forgotten what had happened at the roll call following our breakfast that morning.

When I entered, I found Rabbi Horowitz, who stood still over his empty bed with a face of smooth stone.

"A man should not live to see their own child die," the rabbi said plainly, "especially one as full of life as my Adam."

Lucas sat on the floor. He stared at the rabbi, and it was clear that he was as struck by the boy's absence as his father, for Lucas had come to cherish the banter-filled interactions with the brotherly child.

After a moment of silence, Rabbit Horowitz began to recite Kaddish, the Hebrew mourning prayer for the dead.

"*Yit'gaddal v'yit'kadash sh'mei raba . . .*"

All of the men got down from their beds to gather around the rabbi and the empty place where Adam used to sleep. We lowered our heads and paid our respects to our fallen child—another life swallowed up by this insatiable abyss.

That night, Lucas and I lay there quietly until the Rabbi stopped weeping. Certain he had fallen asleep, Lucas finally moaned in the darkness for his own pain, though it was not just emotional, but physical.

He took my hands in his so that I could feel his swollen fingers, pocked with broken blisters and deep cuts.

"I don't think these fingers will ever play the piano again," he whispered with the resignation of one who had just been read his last rites by the priest. "I fear I will be with Adam again shortly."

"Don't say that," I insisted. "Tomorrow, things will get better—I can feel it."

"How?" Lucas asked with a soft laugh.

"They just will. Now go to sleep while you still can."

Lucas was snoring in seconds, and I was left to stare out into the darkness, contemplating if things could get any worse than today.

THE NEXT MORNING, we were finishing the last of our bowls of mush when the whistle blew.

"Labor!" the call came, as it did every morning.

When Lucas got up to go join the line, I put my hand up and tugged on the bottom of his shirt to stop him. "No, not you," I said plainly.

"What are you talking about?"

"You won't have to go to Labor today," I informed him.

With the bitterness that had set in from the thought of another terribly exhausting day, Lucas bit at me, "I hardly think that just because you decide I shouldn't have to go to Labor, they will suddenly release—"

He hadn't even finished his sentence before Carl came up quickly and kicked Lucas in his behind.

"Why are you not in line?" He screamed. "Labor has already been called!"

"I—" Lucas stammered as he looked down at me helplessly.

"There must be a mistake," I said to Carl, knowing that in doing so I was putting Lucas and me both at risk, but Tielo had made that terrible promise to me, so I continued. "Lucas has been transferred."

Carl leaned over to me and boxed my ears hard. "First, princess, I do not know anyone named Lucas. I know 75921 here, and that number remains on the list for Labor."

"But the transfer?" I weakly asked. "I was told—"

"Who gives a shit what you were told." His spittle flew into my eyes before he turned back to Lucas and pointed to the Labor formation. "Now get your ass in line or I'll gladly call in the dogs!"

There was nothing left that either of us could do, so Lucas lumbered his way over to the Labor line helplessly. Off their Kapo marched them for another day, while I looked on with confusion as Lucas, at the back of the formation, walked away looking pitiful.

I was seething the entire journey to the uniform factory. When we arrived, I got right to work on my quota, my foot slamming repeatedly on the pedal. I loudly dropped my completed garments down onto my pile.

Matya and Alma both looked up at me from time to time, unsure of how to help me. At one point, Matya did lean over and scold with a kind of motherly love, "Whatever has made you upset this morning, perhaps be a little less loud about it." She looked over her shoulders to emphasize her point and continued, "There is no need to draw the attention of bird face in our direction."

Her words made me giggle, and I began to be less obvious in my anger until whispers that the officer was on the floor doing inspections began to sweep across the machines in hushed tones. I could see from the corner of my eyes Tielo, followed by Vogel and her guards, as he walked from machine to machine and conducted some kind of audit. Whenever Tielo said something aloud, Vogel would hurriedly write it down on a pad that she carried with her.

When the quartet arrived at Alma, Tielo left Vogel to inspect her machine while he leaned over my shoulder to look at mine.

"You promised!" I hissed so that only he could hear.

Pretending to examine my work, Tielo leaned down and thumbed through the completed trousers that I had sewn thus far.

"You just keep doing what I ask," he whispered back. The back of his hand brushed against my calf, and I recoiled with a jerk. Tielo looked up at me from below. "In time, it will all be handled. Just watch and wait."

He stood back up.

"What time? He will be dead if you don't act soon!" I pressed in a hushed tone, as I leaned over to alter the thread on the spool.

Through gritted teeth, Tielo bit back, "Then you had better keep behaving."

Vogel walked closer. "Is everything alright over here, Officer Tiegel?" she inquired, with the hopes of one who longed for blood.

"Yes," Tielo stated, and Vogel's face fell. "I was just looking over this prisoner's work. Send him to my office in one hour," he instructed her. "I need to discuss his productivity."

Tielo then walked off, leaving the confused woman in his wake.

She looked at me, then rushed to catch up to the officer, following behind like a puppy with her notebook and pencil in hand.

RIGHT BEFORE LUNCH, Vogel and her guards came to get me. Once more I traveled up the stairs and down the hall to Tielo's office. It was odd to be called to the officer's room at all, much less twice in two days. The looks on the faces of both the workers and the guards were curious and questioning.

The door was hardly shut before Tielo ordered me to strip fully and bend over his desk. The sadistic delight he took in watching me slowly undress and approach the desk sent chills down my spine. I was close to running out of the room completely naked when flashes of the incident alongside the River Spree burst from my subconsciousness. How could he be doing this to me again, but this time with my own permission?

I hesitated too long, which gave Tielo the impetus to grab my body and throw my stomach down onto the desk. It was clear it was not just the act of sex but the thrill of forcing it upon me that excited him, then and now.

He muffled my cry with his hands, wrapping them around my face and mouth as he entered me from behind with great force.

His fingers then shoved into my mouth, and I tasted the salt of his hands and resisted my urge to bite one of his digits off. I imagined the saliva that spilled from my mouth was his blood, and this helped me remove my mind from what was happening to my body.

Between grunts, he admitted that this was far more enjoyable to him than when the Bishop would fuck him in place of rent so that he and his alcoholic father could live for free in the room provided by the church back in the Neukölln neighborhood.

Once he completed his act of control, he fell onto my back and whispered, "I always thought you were so beautiful." It was an odd statement from someone who'd humiliated me repeatedly in my youth and now with this in my present. As he lay there, still inside of me, his act and declaration caused vomit to form in the back of my throat. I pushed him off of me in a rush and threw up repeatedly into a wastebasket alongside his desk. Tielo readjusted his clothes, watching and laughing.

When the last button on his shirt was reset, he sat in his desk chair and opened up a drawer. From inside, he removed a cigarette case. He took one out and smacked the bottom of it on the desk, then popped it into his mouth.

"See you tomorrow," he said dismissively as he struck a match and inhaled deep. His head threw back into the chair, and he exhaled a long white trail of smoke up toward the ceiling.

I stepped into my own clothes and left, pushing my head back against the door after I'd shut it behind me. There was no time for tears; I had to return and make my quota. Tears would only bring more questions, so I hobbled down the hallway, sore from his attack but determined to enter the factory floor looking as fit as I had left it.

The others were at lunch, so I pulled myself together and joined them in the yard. After I collected my food, which unfortunately consisted of a sausage and coffee, I went and stood by the women and talked to them as if it were just another day and I had not been sexually assaulted by my life-long predator mere moments before.

"What did the officer want this time?" Alma asked, her smile starting to return once more to her face.

"I have specialized experience in the garment industry," I lied, "so he is picking my brain to learn the ins and outs of that experience."

"That probably means the putz is going to change how we do things around here just when most of us have gotten a rhythm going," Matya remarked with a frown.

Luckily, they seemed satisfied with the explanation I had given, and the rest of this lunch time was spent hearing Edna's tale rather than talking about Tielo. I listened in numb silence, unable to react, though hers was the hardest of all of the stories to digest.

Edna shared how her moments of normality had ended the day she was forced to peer out from behind the curtains of her window as her husband was choked to death by the goyim of the little town that she and her family had lived in for centuries.

"My husband, Metzel, having been well off, was sitting down to tea when the entire town's population showed up to loot and carry off our home's prized belongings," she began.

At first, Edna said she and Metzel stood there in disbelief and looked on in helpless horror as the people she had known all their lives, and had even counted as friends, walked off with their clocks, the fine paintings, and even their clothes.

When Metzel could take it no longer, he at last protested—"because a woman, my own next-door neighbor, carried off the heirloom silverware my Metzel's grandparents had given to us on our wedding day!"

My face remained devoid of any emotion.

The town's priest had dragged Edna's husband out of the house by his collar, then one by one, a circle of the other town folk took their turns wrapping their hands around Metzel's neck. They danced in delight and cheered each other on while his eyes bulged out of his head from lack of oxygen.

"When Metzel was dead, they laughed and shouted about the need to kill off all of the Jewish rats of the world." We all shook our heads at these words—even me.

Edna told us how she hid behind the long dark cotton curtains of her parlor, where with one eye stealthily peeking out, she bore witness to her husband's murder, and about how she cried silently so as to not be caught until they all had gone away. It was not long after this that she was picked up on a road, walking aimlessly from village to village in search of help.

We all worked diligently throughout the afternoon, as I thought about how I had been mistaken earlier in regards to the women and myself. Edna's events made it clear to me that we as people do whatever it is that we have to do in order to survive. Give up our dreams of being Parisian designers, jump over cliffs, watch our husbands choke, and allow ourselves to be raped. I was no different.

At last, we were taken back to our respective dormitories for another evening.

▼

THE NEXT DAY, when the whistle blew for Labor, Lucas, who by now had deep circles under his eyes, limped toward the line. I looked on as at last he was waved away by the Kapo, who told him, "Not you, *homosexuell*, you have been reassigned to *die Plantage*."

The Labor group marched off and left a bewildered Lucas behind. He looked over to me as his tired face broke forth with a grin of disbelief just as the Plantage group was called to formation.

Lucas zipped along on his blistered toes with a newfound pep, joining a small line of old men. As they walked away, my own formation was called, and I headed out of the camp, knowing for the first time in two days that I'd made the right decision, though my sore body and aching self-worth begged to differ.

That evening, I returned to find Lucas in a far different state than all of the other evenings before. I sat and listened to him in the bed as he heartily explained everything about what the Plantage looked like, how its buildings were laid out, and the type of assignments the prisoners were given there.

"There still is some hard work, but nothing like the labor I was doing before," he explained to me, sounding almost excited. "I have been given two main tasks, one working with the bees to collect the honey each day—imagine, honey! Not that we can have any. They already told me if I get caught tasting any, I will be drowned in a vat of it. But the other task is that I will be taught how to tend to the herbs and pick them when they are ready to be sold to the local populations in the Plantage's market at the front of the farm."

He lay down with a smile. "So not just honey, but a market too!"

Just as we had finally fallen into a deep sleep, we were awoken to the bright light of a *taschenlampe* that glared in our faces.

"One of the sergeants has asked to see you." I heard a voice behind the flashlight and I recognized it instantly as Tielo's.

"Now?"

Lucas became quite afraid and pressed me, "Where? Why does a sergeant want to see you in the middle of the night, Josef?"

I began to climb down from the bunk and assured Lucas that all would be fine.

"How can you know?" he pushed, with great terror in his voice. He must have thought I would not return.

"I just do," I explained, patting him on the legs. "Trust me. Go back to sleep and I will return shortly."

I turned around and followed Tielo out of the building. We walked across the camp in silence, as giant searchlights darted back and forth from atop large guard towers. Their light cut through the darkness and demonstrated that there was no place to hide in this hellhole. We were always under surveillance. No moment and no minute granted any privacy or any escape.

After a few yards, we approached a building that I had never seen nor entered before. Inside were long halls with doors, each one with a sign that bore the name of a guard or leader. When we approached the one marked "Tiegel," Tielo opened it and rushed me inside.

It was a small room with a bed, a tall chest for storage, and a single sink for washing.

"It is my turn to be on call for the guards this evening," he explained as he began to undress himself. "Since I must be awake in case I am needed for any emergency, why should I be alone?" he asked, now standing before me stark naked.

I noted to myself that when Tielo had placed his clothing on the floor, it included his belt, which holstered a black steel pistol.

Tielo walked over to his bed and pulled back the covers.

"Get undressed and climb in," he ordered. "If there is a knock on the door, you are to hide in the storage chest over there." He pointed. "Is this understood?"

I nodded as I began to remove my own clothing.

"Good," he said, satisfied with my obedience as he rolled onto the mattress and left space for me to roll in alongside him.

I got into the bed and lay there lifeless. As Tielo used me, every few seconds my head rolled back to take another look at the gun lying on the floor only a few feet from me. With each thrust, I imagined myself grabbing it and releasing its trigger before Tielo even knew what had happened.

The only release was his, and within seconds after, Tielo lay next to me snoring.

I lay there motionless for a few brief additional minutes before I made the decision it was time to make my move.

Careful not to wake him, I lowered my body from the bed and got up onto my feet. Inch by inch, I slid my feet across the cold floor until at last the pistol lay holstered at my feet.

I can end this all now, I thought to myself. Perhaps if I ran fast enough I could make it out of the officer's unit before anyone even knew it was me. If not, would being killed be any worse than having this man on top of me day after day?

"No!" I whispered aloud. I would not allow him to continue to degrade me a second longer.

I reached down and unsnapped the holster that held the pistol in place on the belt. My hand shook as I lifted the gun into the air and pointed it directly at Tielo's head.

The thought of poor Lucas being left here alone flitted through my head as my finger slid down toward the trigger.

A tear gathered in the corner of my eye as I recounted all that Tielo had stolen from me, and that tear became acid as the anger inside of me grew. My face turned to stone as I relished in the knowledge that at last I would make this brutal villain pay for all I had suffered at his hands.

My finger began to apply more pressure to the trigger, and I knew that at any moment this would all be over. It made me smile with a fierceness I did not know I had in me.

Just as I was about to shoot, a loud knock came at the door.

"Officer Tiegel?" a guard asked through the wood as Tielo opened his eyes to find the barrel of his own gun pointed in his direction.

Tielo's eyes widened, then narrowed in anger.

"What is it?" he asked the guard as he lifted his head off of the pillow.

"Sergeant Himmel is making rounds and has asked you to meet him at the east tower in five minutes, sir," the voice from the other side replied.

In an instant, Tielo leapt from the bed and gripped my neck and body in a full nelson, his arms under my own and his hands wrapped around the back of my neck.

"Thank you," Tielo grunted to the guard. "You can inform the sergeant that I am on my way," he said through pants and grunts, as the footsteps of the guard's retreat faded away.

Confident that the man was gone, Tielo violently flung me across the room and onto the bed. He had regained possession of the gun in his quick attack during my moment's hesitation, and I knew my time to neutralize this abscess had passed.

"I will not forget this," he said with gritted teeth. "And I will make damn sure you will not forget it either!"

Tielo began to pull his clothes on, and once he was fully dressed, he commanded me to throw my uniform on as well.

We approached his door. He opened it and stuck his head out to look both ways. "Quietly now. I will deposit you near the bunkhouse door on my way to the tower."

More quickly than we had arrived, we departed, and I found myself walking back into the bunkhouse in minutes only to find Lucas sitting there awake, waiting for me.

I climbed up into the bed and the two of us hugged each other strongly. We were still together after everything we had been through, and each of us knew right now how lucky we were for that. No words were needed, no questions asked or answered. Just physically holding on to the fact that the other was there. That was enough, and we lay holding one another until the early morning.

▼

FOR ALMOST A WEEK, nothing happened. I would go each day to the factory and sew the required garments without being called on to visit Tielo's office. Each night, I would lie there waiting for the torchlight to shine in my face, only to have the hours pass by in uncomfortable silence. It was the not knowing that was the hardest. Tielo left me in this uncomfortable space, where I sat with my thoughts second by second as the days ticked by. Something horrible was coming for what I had done, but the uncertainty of when or what that punishment was to be was almost as torturous as the act itself.

On a quiet day with few broken needles and little oversight, Vogel summoned us at our usual time to form up before we headed out to the front yard for our march. As we walked out the door, I saw the pole that Alma had been hung on the day she failed to make her quota. It was back, but this time someone new hung on it—it appeared to be a man. As we started to pass by, the frightened face stared down at me, and I broke from the line without thought to run toward him.

"Lucas!" I screamed as my legs pushed me across the dirt. I had hardly made it a few feet when the butt of a rifle slammed into the side of my face, and the force knocked me to the floor.

All I could do was look up into his eyes as Tielo approached me and leaned down to whisper in my ear, the same way he had done when I sat in the dirt at school after he punched me for knocking over his lunch.

"I told you that I would not forget."

I was lifted off of the ground and dragged back to the formation by two Schutzstaffel.

"March these prisoners back to camp. They need their rest, as I'm increasing their daily quotas for tomorrow by ten," Tielo commanded. His words caused panicked looks among the women, but there was not much they could do besides heading off in the direction they were herded.

I unwillingly did the same, glancing back every few feet to get another look at Lucas.

When he was out of view, terror gripped me. I did not know what Tielo might do to him on my account. It seemed like whatever I did, Lucas always wound up as collateral damage. Poor payment for his devotion to me.

I picked at the food we were given that night, sitting on the bed with great sadness. The others had noticed that I was all alone, and for the first time in my life in such a situation, men did not poke at me and call me names, rather they nodded in my direction as a show of recognition for my pain. Many of these strangers made gestures to comfort me, and some bravely approached to offer words of encouragement in Lucas's absence.

Even Vladimir walked over, putting his large hand on my shoulder and squeezing. "He will be back," he grunted, even though I was fairly certain none of them believed this to be true.

Still, in what was one of the darkest moments, when I felt the most helpless, it struck me that maybe I was never quite as alone as I had thought. Perhaps simply existing and showing my own humanity was enough for people finally and against all odds to see me and appreciate that while I might be different, I was still a person of worth.

I lay in the bed with these thoughts for several hours before the door to the bunkhouse opened and a trembling Lucas was shoved into the room. I helped pull him up onto our bed and rubbed his back as he sobbed into the night air.

"It's alright now, Lucas," I hummed, attempting to soothe his spirit. "You are alive, and that is all that matters."

"I don't know what I did. They came to the Plantage and took me without telling me why, and I was so frightened," Lucas replied through his tears.

"Shhh," I quieted him. "You don't have to talk about it, just rest."

And with that, he drifted off to sleep.

I lay there and looked toward the darkened ceiling, thankful that Lucas had been returned to me but worried that Tielo could strike at him again

THE NEXT MORNING, we had hardly been at our machines for more than twenty minutes when there was a commotion at the entryway to the factory. A sharply dressed Sturmtruppen arrived and demanded to speak with whomever was in charge. Vogel swooped in dutifully, her birdlike eyes peering from side to side in the direction of the soldier. It was not often the Nazi war machine sent representatives to the camps, and Vogel made sure to welcome this man as if he were *der Führer* himself.

The two of them whispered briefly before Vogel summoned one of the factory guards, commanding him to go bring Officer Tiegel.

Seconds later, the guard returned with Tielo, and the two saluted each other with fervor.

"These notes are from General Folger himself," the Sturmtruppen announced as he handed Tielo two pieces of paper.

At that, they saluted each other again, and the soldier departed

Tielo took a moment to open the larger of the two notes. As his eyes scanned its contents, Vogel practically broke her neck leaning closer and closer, trying to catch a glimpse of the words.

Tielo swiftly folded the sheet and acknowledged Vogel's curiosity by asking her to walk the factory floor with him while they spoke of the note's meaning.

As they neared my machine, I could hear the conversation. "With the United States entered into the war, they are conscripting new soldiers from households across the Fatherland."

Vogel's neck lifted in excitement, as her role in the continued war effort seemed clear. "And so the *Wehrmacht* army will be needing uniforms!" She declared with great pride.

"Yes, new recruits must have proper uniforms in order to properly represent the Reich, and our factory has been chosen to make them."

Tielo handed Vogel the larger sheet of paper he had read a few moments ago. "In fact, we have been given the very special honor of being chosen to produce the officer uniforms rather than just continuing to make this dour clothing for the camp prisoners."

Vogel straightened her back as she received the note from Tielo's hands, but neither seemed to notice that as the note was passed between the two of them, the second, and smaller, note that Tielo had been given by the soldier had fallen to the floor near my feet.

I stared at the note, then looked up and found Matya looking directly at me, for she had seen the paper fall as well.

There was no time to think. Matya suddenly began to fake a coughing fit, drawing the attention of Tielo and Vogel. I seized the moment and placed my foot on top of the fallen note, dragging it closer.

I had heard of networks within the camp who worked to give and get information to the outside world. Those who grew herbs at the Plantage passed notes back and forth between customers at the shop. Our seamstresses found ways to leave information behind on the streets of Dachau as we marched through each morning and evening. Inventory that was moved into the camp came with messages taped inside barrels, and messages went out between barbed wire and the fruits of slave labor. These bits and pieces were seized upon by an unseen resistance that managed to hide beneath the surface in all parts of the camp and country. Whatever was within this slip of paper, I would make sure it made its way to whomever could make use of this information. Playing a part, any part, however small, suddenly filled me with immense excitement, and my hands shook with nervous energy throughout the long minutes that Tielo and Vogel remained nearby and the note sat unsearched for and under my shoe.

"I can assure you, Officer Tiegel, that our factory will meet any task that General Folger demands. Our recruits will be well dressed thanks to our efforts," she trumpeted, as the two of them finally disappeared down the long row of workers and into the back of the factory, out of sight.

As soon as they were gone, I pretended to drop a spool of thread. I bent down and tucked the small note into my clog and under my foot. There it would rest until I had an opportunity to pull it out and read whatever message General Folger had intended for Tielo's eyes only.

I passed the morning in nervous anticipation. When lunchtime arrived, Matya looked around the yard cautiously before leaning over to me to whisper. She let me know that whatever I did, I was not to read the note here in the factory, but to wait instead until I was back in the camp. She felt that if I was caught opening the paper here, the consequences could be far worse, while the chances of someone seeing me unfold and read the paper lessened the farther I was away from the factory.

When Edna heard about what had happened, she informed me of a connection she had to a woman named Selma. Selma was known to always be up on the latest gossip from the outside world because she shared a bunk with Irena, whose sister, Eve, had been taken by one of the Nazi officers to live as his sexual mistress at a young age. Edna regaled us with tales of how everyone hated Eve, even Irena, because she was regarded as a traitor, but that Irena only played at her hatred for her sister. She understood that Eve was only trying to survive at any cost and that by sleeping with the officer each night, she was able to pick up information. Eve also had liberties that exposed her to servants who lived outside the camp, and these servants were able to bring messages of importance from the outside world via Eve's friendships with these household workers. So, while Eve was hated by many, few knew the role she played in sacrificing her own body to not only make sure hers was safe, but to become a key linchpin in the entire Dachau underground operation.

"This is why the girls are not killed off as frequently as the boys," Edna said, answering my lingering question. "Their bodies are of high value to the guards."

Fascinated with this information, I wondered if perhaps I might myself be undervaluing the forced sexual relationship I had with my own officer, unknown to anyone.

There was little time to think further on this, as Vogel ordered us back to work. The rest of the afternoon was spent with trucks of new fabric arriving, followed by the whirring of the cutting machines and the distribution of this new material to each of our stations. We were slated to begin changing over to army uniforms in the morning, and Vogel announced loudly that our overall quota each day would rise.

I made it back to the bunk before most of the other men that night. Thinking to seize the opportunity, I rushed toward the bed, pulled the note out from my foot, and hopped up, planning to unfold the paper and at last read its message. However, just as I was about to do so, all of the men began to return, so I rolled over and stuffed the note down into a rough hole that was torn into the side of the mattress Lucas and I shared. My plan was to take it out later that night when everyone, including Lucas, was fast asleep.

Yet the men had barely filed inside when a lower-ranked guard entered the dormitory and informed me that Officer Tielo had sent him to retrieve me. All eyes fell on me with suspicion, as this was not the first time now that this Schutzstaffel officer had called for me. Even Lucas, who had barely been inside a moment, looked at me with wary curiosity as I was marched out of the building.

My heart pounded as we got closer to the officer's building. I felt certain the only reason Tielo would call for me while it was still light was because he knew about the note. Who had told him? I went through a list in my mind of which women aside from Matya might have seen the note drop and seen me retrieve it. Edna and Alma knew, but none of this trio could possibly have been the one to turn me in. I'd thought I was sly in my covering and retrieval of the note, but clearly I had been careless. This would only serve as another excuse for Tielo to inflict his punishments on either me or, heaven forbid, Lucas again.

The guard dropped me inside of the building, and I made my way alone along the corridor to Tielo's room. The door was ever so slightly ajar, so when I knocked on it, it opened up to reveal Tielo sitting on the bed, reading through some papers.

"Go ahead and undress," he said plainly, his eyes remaining locked on the document in his hands.

I closed the door and walked across the room to where a single chair sat against the wall. A square mirror hung over the chair, and as I approached, my reflection caused me to stop and stare. I had not seen myself since we left Schöneberg what seemed like years ago. I almost saw a stranger. Gone were the days of dolls, and in their stead there were sunken eyes, patchy blond hair that was slowly growing back, and dry, cracked lips.

"You are still the prettiest boy on the block—the prison camp block, that is." Tielo chuckled as he came up behind me and lifted my arms above me and then pulled my shirt up over my head.

I had not seen him get up from the bed, so engrossed I had been in my own image. He then bent down to yank my pants to my ankles while I remained staring into the eyes of this ghost of die blaue blume.

My gaze was only broken when Tielo pulled me away by my thin arms toward his bed.

There was no mention of the note that evening, and I lay there while he used my body, vacant-eyed and unable to get the face of that poor thing I had just seen out of my mind.

How I missed my powders and creams, and the soft feel of satin and fur on my skin. What I would have given for another chance to flower and bloom. I felt a pain in my stomach at the thought that I had been stripped of who I was in a way no one here at Dachau could ever understand. They not only dehumanized me like the others, but I was completely deidentified, forced to live each day knowing that an intricately important and equal part of me that threaded through the core and essence of who I was had already been gassed and incinerated. The person left behind who stared back at me from Tielo's mirror minutes before was only half of who they truly had been, half of who I truly was, and I hated this place for doing it to me.

Tielo got up off of me, and I lay there as evening turned to night. Eventually, convinced it was the appropriate time for me to return, he pushed me out of the bed with his foot and ordered me to get dressed and leave.

I ARRIVED BACK AT the bunkhouse lost in a mixture of seething hatred and mournful sorrow. It was dark as I entered the building, and I tiptoed across the floor and pulled myself up into the bed.

A few minutes later, Lucas, whose back had been to me and who I presumed was by now fast asleep, whispered to me, "Why does that officer keep taking you at night?"

I was not yet prepared to answer, so I said, "I'm tired, Lucas. I need to get some sleep before it's time to go to the factory in the morning. They are increasing our quota as we switch from prisoner to army uniforms."

This did not quiet his lingering concern, and he rolled over to face me. "I saw the way he whispered to you when they had me hanging from that pole at the uniform factory."

There was silence.

"Why would they hang me at the uniform factory, Josef? And why would that officer appear to have so much interest in you?" he pressed.

"You are being silly," I groaned, exasperated from his line of questioning.

"Am I?"

At last, I snapped. "This is a concentration camp, not a pickup bar in Weimar!"

As I attempted to roll over and away from him, Lucas reached out and grabbed me by the shoulder. "Exactly. Which is why I'm so surprised that you are letting him spend so much time with you—unless you enjoy it!"

Lucas glared at me in the darkness, and I could just make out the fury in the whites of his eyes as he hissed, "Our lives are in the balance here. We never know if we are going to live from day to day, and here you are strutting your *fotze* ass off in front of all things an officer, just so you can get some Nazi *schwanz!*"

Without thinking, I reached out and slapped Lucas loudly across the face.

"This fotze ass is what is keeping your own ass from going back to Labor—or worse!"

The echo of the strike and my barked words caused some of the men to stir in their own beds. Not wanting to risk waking any of them up to witness this argument, I slipped out of the bed and stormed out through the bunkhouse door.

Dawn was already breaking over the horizon as Lucas came out to find me sitting on the cold ground, my eyes cast downward into the dirt just outside of our building.

He approached me and kneeled too, placing one of his hands on my knees.

"I had no idea," he said, full of remorse at his earlier chastisement.

"How could you?" My voice was soft. I looked up at Lucas and let everything that I had bottled inside of me these past weeks go freely. "The officer said if I did not do what he told me to, you would be killed. You will be killed. So I continue to do as he commands." I began to cry. "That's why he had you hanging outside of the factory. It was for my eyes, a message to me to prove his point. He wants to show his control over me, his lack of mercy, just like he did to me that day in Treptow when they held me down and he . . ." My words trailed off.

"In Treptow?" Lucas asked. The implications of what I said began to register on his face as he stood up incensed. It was a flash of the old Lucas, the one who would stand up to God if it meant saving me. "Wait. Are you telling me the officer here is the one who raped you back in Berlin before you came to live with Anke and me?"

His eyes bulged, and he looked as if he would explode.

"My God!" he shouted out. "And you have been giving yourself away so that I no longer had to work in Labor, but in the Plantage instead?"

Compassion began to replace his anger as his face twisted, and Lucas fell at my feet in tears to beg for my forgiveness.

"I told you that one day I would repay you for your kindness," I sobbed, laying my head on Lucas's back while he bent his face toward his feet and shook with each cry. "I meant it, Lucas. I will protect you the way you have protected me when I have been my most vulnerable."

We sat in silence until Lucas lifted his head up. Then we dried our tears and wiped our noses on each other's sleeves and laughed at our familiarity, where snot and love were one and the same.

"It's cold," I said at last. "Let's go back inside—I think we have at least thirty minutes to close our eyes before the Kapo comes, and I really need some rest as our quota now is quite large."

Lucas helped me to my feet, and we leaned on each other as we moved across the floor and lay down to embrace our short but emotion-cleansing sleep.

▼

THAT MORNING, IT FELT like there had been barely any time to rest in the bed before I was marched back to the factory for yet another day. As soon as I entered the building, Vogel nodded toward the steps that led up to the hallway with Tielo's office.

Her eyebrows rose over her hawkish eyes in suspicion, as by now she'd begun to wonder why this officer kept calling me to his office. It was close to the same look that the others passed my way, including Matya, Alma, and Enda, who all stared as I walked off in solitude toward those damned stairs.

We had only been separated for a few hours, yet Tielo was already calling me to him. "That *arschloch*," I said aloud, as I walked down the hallway in this never-ending nightmare.

When I opened his office door, Tielo was sitting at his desk, a cigarette in hand, his feet up on the desk in a position that was meant to imply his cool ease with his dominant role. It was all *brot und rosen* for the Nazi guards, but there was neither bread nor roses for us prisoners, only slop and shit.

"Have a seat, Josef," he instructed me, and he flicked his neck toward the thin metal chair with the bright orange cushion that sat in front of his desk.

As I sat, I automatically began to undress. I'd unfastened the first two buttons on my shirt before Tielo put his hand up in the air.

"Oh no," he interrupted, "No need for that." He swung his legs down off of the desk and sat up straight. "I do not want a release from you this morning," he said dryly as he leaned over and stubbed his cigarette out in an ashtray. Then he let out a final cloud of smoke into the air, watching it creep forward before it broke and fell all over me.

"I only want to inform you of a few changes that will be taking place so that you are well prepared."

Confusion spread across my face.

"First, I have made arrangements for you to spend some time with another officer, a friend of mine. Only one day next week to begin with."

"Another officer?" I asked, my baffled voice rising.

He ignored me for a few minutes and instead took that quiet time to take a glass and a small bottle of whisky out of his bottom drawer. When he had poured some into the glass, he took a sip. "Yes. He's a close confidant of mine. I shared with him the wonderful benefits time with you can bring, and he has an interest in seeing for himself if you can provide the same relief to him that you seem to give to me."

Tielo sat back and swirled the whiskey in his glass as he searched my face for the reaction he was hoping to obtain. I was so stunned I could not answer at all, just sit there in silence.

"Is this going to be a problem?" he asked playfully before lifting the glass and pouring the remaining contents down his throat.

There was no response that I could offer that would change the outcome or release me from his decision, so I dropped my head to my neck in humiliation and simply shook my head.

"Good!" Tielo erupted as he poured another drink into his glass and toasted me. "Oh, and now about your friend," he continued.

My head shot back up. "Lucas?" I asked with great alarm.

Tielo downed yet another drink and smiled. "If the officer, my friend, finds you satisfactory, then I plan to loan you to him on a more regular basis. But what of my needs while you are away?" His eyes narrowed. He was enjoying this, my squirming with nowhere to run and no one to save me from him.

Tielo stood up. "Well, that is where this Lucas of yours comes in." He walked around the desk so he could get closer and look down at me while I remained seated. "You see, I have decided that I will go over to the Plantage and have your little blond lover transferred to our factory here, beginning tomorrow."

I felt smaller and more insignificant than I ever had in his presence. At last, I could take it no more, so I flung myself to the floor at Tielo's feet and begged. "You can't, Tielo. Please don't!"

He pushed his boot out closer to my face and smiled as my breath fogged up the black leather. He stood there, waiting for me to continue the show that he had indeed anticipated.

"I'm begging you," I cried. "You promised me you would send Lucas to the gardens, if I only did whatever you told me to do, and I have! I've done everything. I'll do whatever else it takes. I'll go with your friend, I'll go with ten friends, just please don't do this to poor Lucas."

My words caused Tielo to laugh uncontrollably, and he flicked my prostrate body away with his foot.

"You are just as pathetic now as you were in Treptow." At that, his face became clouded over with spite and anger. "You are lucky I have kept you alive at all during this time. I didn't even do as much for your stepbrother, and he was my childhood companion," Tielo barked at me as I sat on the floor, gutted. "I saved you for me. I did not give a shit about you then, and I certainly do not give one now."

He began to pace the floor. "It's like this, Josefina. Your friend will join us here shortly, and he will be expected to do for me just as you do. That is all there is to it."

I had no time to respond, because there was a knock at the door.

"Only, I can't know for certain if your lover will measure up to you until I sample the goods," he stated as he walked toward the door.

He stopped as he got closer and turned back to me. "Oh, but know this— If your friend does not, shall we say, perform, I will kill him instantly."

He turned the knob on the door, and in walked Lucas.

I sat on the floor, stunned, as Tielo had just said that Lucas would not be leaving the Plantage to join the uniform factory until tomorrow.

"Come in, Lucas."

"Josef?" Lucas asked, seeing me on the ground.

Helplessly I watched as Tielo guided Lucas by his shoulder farther into the office. He yanked the chair he had been sitting on earlier out from behind the desk and dragged it onto the floor, close to where I sat.

"Have a seat on this chair here, Josef—I want you to watch every second of this," he ordered me, a look of twisted satisfaction spreading across his face.

"Please, Tielo," I begged again.

"What is happening here?" Lucas interrupted with great agitation. "Why are you on the floor, and is this that fucker Tielo from Treptow?"

Tielo wasted no time. In a flash, he grabbed Lucas around the neck and kicked his legs out from under him so that he now squatted on the floor, Tielo's hands closing around his throat.

"No!" I cried out, lunging across the tile toward Lucas.

"Make another move and I will squeeze whatever breath is left in him," Tielo growled, and I inched away, praying he would loosen his grip if I backed off. "Now get up off the floor and sit on that chair like I told you to before!"

I moved with trepidation, not wanting to antagonize Tielo into killing Lucas on the spot.

Once I was seated, Tielo released Lucas's neck. Lucas gasped for air and held his own hands up to rub the pain away from where Tielo had gripped him so tightly. The fearful look that he gave me and my impotence to stop what happened next seared themselves into my memory, as Tielo dropped his pants and stepped in front of Lucas.

Tears streamed down my face. I tried to close my eyes so that I would not have to witness the act, but Tielo commanded me to open them, lest he shoot us both in our heads after his release was complete.

When it was over, Lucas stood up and left, headed back to the Plantage for the remainder of the day. I sat on the floor for a few moments longer before I too was ordered to depart and return to my work.

I went back to the factory floor, where I worked as hard as I possibly could to make up for all of the time in Tielo's office. If I did not meet the quota, Vogel was bound to single me out, regardless of where I had been, or maybe especially because I was with the officer for a good portion of the morning.

In the yard later on, the women all swarmed me.

"What is really going on?" Matya pushed.

"If I explained it to you, either you would never believe it, or maybe you would hate me and call me a traitor like Irena's sister, Eve," I responded weakly, but this ragtag group had against all odds become my friends, and they swore that no matter what I told them, it could not be half as bad as the stories they had already heard and the acts of desperation people they knew had already participated in.

Reluctantly, I told them everything, starting with Treptow. I took them through my story with Lucas and my time in Schöneberg, and they listened without saying a word. I told them of the Rote Schwein, die blaue blume, and the raid. At last I shared my surprise at finding Marteen and then seeing Tielo Tiegel face-to-face after all of those years. Their eyes narrowed, and they leaned in with great intensity as I described what Tielo had done to me, how Lucas was the one who hung from the pole, and what Tielo was now forcing upon us both.

Alma gave me a sad smile and squeezed my leg to comfort me. Edna shook her head and asked aloud, "How can this world be so cruel?" Mayta stood up and looked toward the factory windows with a clenched fist and in a guttural Yiddish cursed Tielo, Vogel, and all of the Nazis across Deutschland with every colorful term known to any Eastern-European Jew.

For the rest of the afternoon they cast sad glances in my direction, followed by smiles and nods all meant to reassure me that no matter what Tielo did to me, I mattered to them and would never be forgotten.

Little by little, I inched closer to my quota, and occasionally, when no one was looking particularly closely in my direction, an extra pair of army uniform pants made their way into my pile. At the end of the day, I had the number I needed.

▼

LUCAS WAS SITTING ON the bed, staring into space with vacant eyes, when I came back in the evening.

"He has been like that for twenty minutes," Rabbi Horowitz informed me with a shrug.

"Maybe some sleep will help—not that it works for me," Vladimir added before walking away.

I strode over to the bed and said, "Hallo" as my hand touched Lucas's arm. He flinched, then turned his head to look into my eyes. When he realized it was me, he used his hand to remove my own from his arm.

Without a word, he rolled his body up into the bed and flipped over, giving me his back.

I climbed into the bed alongside him, but Lucas wiggled farther away so that we were not touching.

We sat there as the other men made their way to their own beds and the lights across the camp began to go out. I could feel Lucas as he shook next to me. I lay there and agonized over what I could say to make it better, but I realized there was nothing, so I remained silent.

Suddenly, something tugged at me, and I leaned over and eased my hand along the side of the mattress until my fingers at last found the same rough hole where I had stuffed the note only a few nights before.

In the dim light, I unfolded the small slip of paper that General Folger had sent over for his officer's eyes. I thought about its contents for a minute, then began to use my fingers to count the days of the week to myself.

At last, my path lay clear before me, so I jolted up in bed and smiled broadly at Lucas, poking him in the back.

"Lucas," I whispered with great urgency.

"Just leave me alone, Josef," he mumbled.

I could not accept the idea of us not discussing this tonight while time allowed, so I started to shake him with my hands.

"This is important. Turn around, please," I insisted. Lucas did as I asked, and as he did, I could see the salty tracks of his silent tears.

"Something terrible is going to happen tomorrow, Lucas, and I need for you to be prepared," I said.

"Could it be any more terrible than what has happened today? I'm tired. Let's go to sleep and discuss it in the morning."

He started to roll back over, but I would not allow him. "It can be worse, and it will be worse—that is why we need to talk about it while we can."

"I do not see how it could get any worse."

I sat up straighter. "You have a right to be upset, Lucas. I said I would protect you, and it seems as if I have failed. But I need you to promise me, right here and right now, that no matter what happens tomorrow, you will survive."

Lucas rolled his eyes. "You're talking crazy now."

He attempted once more to roll over, but I grabbed his shoulders with both hands and shook him violently.

"Promise me!" I demanded repeatedly, until at last Lucas relented and agreed.

"Alright, Josef, alright! Just let me rest. I am going through enough already, but whatever it is you say is going to happen tomorrow, I promise you here and now that I will live!"

Satisfied with his response, I lay back and allowed Lucas to roll over and fall asleep. I, on the other hand, used the night hours to think through my plan over and over again, each detail parsed out until I found that the morning had arrived and my chance at revenge was at last upon me.

AT THE BREAKFAST GROUNDS, I waved goodbye to Lucas as he walked off with the group headed toward the Plantage. Although Tielo had informed us that he would send over the paperwork today to have Lucas transferred, my mind was on Lucas's kind face. I thought back on his enduring generosity as he turned a corner and was no longer in my line of sight.

I reminded myself repeatedly of what I was to accomplish today and how I was to do it, and I spent the entire walk over to the factory hardening my resolve to see things through no matter the outcome.

As we entered the factory floor and headed toward our machines, Matya said, "You have the look of a warrior today. Is something about to happen?"

"I am finally going to make *der saftsack* prick pay."

Then I threaded my machine up and slammed my foot onto the petal. It roared to life, and I stitched with a fury as the minutes passed slowly by.

Vogel walked behind me while doing her rounds and nodded at my productivity so far, as my pile was stacked high and it was still only a few hours into the day.

At last, when the sun seemed to be nearing its height, I stopped sewing and reached down into my pants. Out I pulled the little note, which was now crumpled, and I unfurled it to inspect it closely one last time.

"Meet in your office for a factory inspection Thursday at noon- General Folger," was all it read.

"What time do you think it is," I asked Matya.

She looked up into the large dusty windows above the factory floor. "I'd say it's around eleven right now. Why?"

"Now that I ask, I realize it's been so long since I have even noticed the sky or the sun."

Matya shrugged at my strange answer, then went back to stitching on her own machine.

I crumpled up the note and tossed it into my mouth, where I began to chew it until every trace of it was swallowed. Once this was accomplished, I put the pair of trousers I had been working on down onto the pile and walked off from my machine, across the factory floor.

The seamstresses craned their necks to see what I was doing. Why would I walk away from my work without being instructed to do so. At the same time, they remained on the lookout for any sign of Vogel's swooping in to snatch me by the neck.

As I passed Alma, she turned around to look at me and exchanged her first full smile in the weeks since her punishment. It empowered me to keep moving forward until at last I found myself near the stairs that ran up to get to Tielo's office.

Both of Vogels' guards stood there, blocking my path.

"Where the fuck do you think you're going?" one of the Schutzstaffel asked me, as he started to remove his pistol from his belt.

"The officer has asked to see me," I answered calmly, though this was a lie.

"Let him through," the other guard chimed in. "You know the officer calls on this one quite a bit."

This satisfied the first guard, who placed his gun firmly back into his holster and stepped aside to allow me safe passage.

I walked down the hallway with great purpose until I stood just outside of Tielo's door. I closed my eyes for just a moment to steel myself. Then I took a deep breath, placed my hand on the doorknob and opened it, stepping in uninvited.

Tielo sat at his desk, reading some papers and clutching yet another glass of whiskey. He looked up at my appearance with great surprise.

"What are you doing in here?" he demanded to know.

I did not answer his question.

"I did not call for you today."

I shut the door behind me and imagined myself in a Helmut Käutner film, like the one Lucas and I had seen together a few years back in Berlin. Part doll, part movie actress, I stepped forward and purred, "Please forgive me, Tielo."

Tielo threw his papers down, then stood up. He tossed the drink back into his mouth and then came around the desk, approaching me with a look of alarm on his face.

"I insist on knowing what this is all about? Why are you here, Josef?"

Good. I wanted him to get all riled up and sloppy.

"It's only that over these past few weeks or months that I have been here with you, I didn't realize how much I have enjoyed our time together, Tielo."

My words caused confusion, and Tielo stopped his approach, but I took this as my own invitation to move closer. "I have finally seen that even after all these years we were apart, you were correct. When we were junge jugen, I really did lust after you just like you said back in school."

A small smile began to spread across Tielo's overly confident face. "And you are choosing to tell me this now . . . why?" he asked with a smirk.

I slid closer to him. "Ever since you told me yesterday that I would have to share you with Lucas, I have been filled with jealousy inside."

With a final step, I was right up on him, and I reached down and grabbed his swollen shaft through his trousers.

"I can't get the picture out of my head of you with him," I whispered, "you touching him . . . the way you let him pleasure you the way only I have been allowed to."

Tielo pushed me off of his body and declared, "This is not a marriage, Josefina," but I pressed myself again toward him, mustering up every bit of imagined passion that I could bring to bear.

"No!" I declared, "I cannot bear to share you," and I flung my body onto his and began to kiss him wildly.

Tielo hesitated at first, but then his tongue wrapped around mine and we threw ourselves onto the hard, tiled floor with abandon. We tore the clothes off each other, and I climbed on top of my captor and pretended to moan in delight while I positioned his arm to steal a glance at the watch on his wrist.

It read 11:59, so I threw my head back as if I had waited all of my life for this moment and yelled out, "Yes, like that, Tielo—yes!" Then I panted my final words to the man who had worked so hard to control my life, to ruin it even, with great and breathy delight. "I. Want. You. To. Never. Forget. This. Moment."

As the last word left my lips, the door to the office flew open.

"Right on time as scheduled, I am here for the inspection, Officer Tieg—" General Folger, a gray-haired, vicious-looking man in his late fifties, cut himself off abruptly as he looked down onto the floor to find his officer completely naked with his limbs entwined around a male prisoner.

"What is this?" the general yelled out with disgust, flanked by a group of soldiers.

Terror landed on Tielo's face for the first time, and I smiled at him while I soaked it all in. He had the same look that had been forced upon my own face at his hands on more than one occasion, and it was a pure delight to share this experience in return here and now, and at my doing.

In a dash, Tielo threw me off of his body and stood up. He saluted the General with both his hand and his erect penis. Not even "Kitty" could have had better comedic timing at Helmut Käutner's "World Conference" than I had managed to bring to bear on my own with this little scene fit for the big screen.

"General Folger," Tielo stammered. "What are you doing here?" Tielo reached to the ground for any piece of clothing he could to hold up over his exposed parts.

"I sent a private note to you days ago that said that I would be here for an inspection on Thursday at noon, but it appears you have had other things on your mind than the needs of das Vaterland," he growled.

The general turned to the Sturmtruppen who flanked him and thundered, "Army generals do not often come to camp factories. You would have thought they would have rolled out a parade for me, but instead I am greeted by an act of homosexuality!"

"Oh no, General," Tielo chimed in. "I am not a homosexual." His eyes scanned the room for something, anything to explain away this situation. When they fell onto his empty whisky glass, he rushed forward and grabbed it with one of his hands, holding it out toward General Folger.

"You see? He must have put something in my whiskey!" He tried to insist through his panic-shaken words. "Had you arrived but a moment later, this homosexual would probably have killed me, sir." He pointed to me, one last dash of hope on his face.

General Folger stood there and absorbed Tielo's words, looking back and forth between our naked bodies.

Then he yelled, "Grab him!" and his soldiers started to rush toward me while the general fumed, "I will have the dogs tear this shit-licking pig from limb to limb in front of the entire camp!"

Relief spread across Tielo's face. My plan, though well thought out, had failed. I had not anticipated all of Tielo's potential excuses, and he found the one that would bitterly seal my fate.

As the soldiers were just about to seize me, Vogel came into the room and addressed General Folger.

"Oh no, General, sir." She saluted. "I would not believe this officer at all, sir."

"I don't understand."

"You see, Officer Tielgel has this particular prisoner make visits alone to his office quite frequently, and with no explanation. And only yesterday, I learned that this prisoner has also been visiting the officer in his private quarters during the night hours. Now we at last all know the true purpose of all of these many visits," she concluded, puffing her chest up in enormous pride at presenting her damning case to the general.

"Do you mean to tell me then that this officer is in fact engaged in a homosexual relationship right here in the camp? Throwing this depravity and deviance around right into the faces of our good men and women who furiously work to obey der Führer?

Vogel nodded with delight at her skills, which surely made her something of a German Hercule Poirot to this powerful leader of great battalions.

It was enough to convince her superior, who ordered the Sturmtruppen to release me.

"Take the officer to the correction facility instead," he pronounced as he pointed to Tielo, whose chance to escape this situation of my making had now passed. "Have this creature that we once falsely believed to be an officer stripped of his badges, and prepare him at once for execution."

The soldiers grabbed Tielo by both arms.

"As for this one," General Folger said as he looked over in my direction, "leave him locked here in this room until the preparations for the officer are complete. I want to make an example of both of them, soldier and prisoner alike."

He turned on his heels and marched off, followed by Tielo, who remained in a state of undress as he was led out of the office.

Vogel was the last to leave, and as the door shut behind her, I could hear keys jangling, the lock activated.

I was secured in the room, but I was indeed alone, and Tielo was on his way to hell.

I sat down at the chair behind his desk where I poured myself some of the whiskey into the glass he had drank from only moments before. Then I sat back and smiled.

IN THE HOURS I spent waiting, I thought back on my journey. There had been many turns along the way, but I was satisfied that in the end I had taken control of my own destiny. Using the time I had, I started to rummage through Tielo's drawers, and when I found a rectangular mirror alongside a pocket comb he must have used to freshen himself up daily, an idea came to my mind.

I propped the mirror up against the empty glass and admired myself more closely than I had in Tielo's bedroom. To the right of the mirror sat Tielo's ashtray, so I reached out and pulled the dish closer to me. In my reflection, I noticed that in the corner of the room sat a small wood stove that he must have used to warm the space during the coldest winter months. I got up from the desk, opened its iron door, and dug around inside until at last my fingers pinched up a small piece of charred wood. I took this promptly back to the desk, where I sat and let out a gleeful laugh.

I dabbed my finger into the dust left behind from the cigarette ashes in the tray and rubbed the black-gray dust onto my eyelids one at a time. Then I held up the piece of charred wood and began to line each of my eyes, both on top of and under the lash line, until I saw the first glimmers of die blaue blume. I hadn't seen her in ages, so we gave each other a knowing wink.

When I was through lining my eyes, I used the last of the charcoal to darken my brows ever so gently, just enough to give some drama without overtaking the eyes themselves.

I studied myself as I lifted the mirror up off the desk so that I could move it around to get a better view from different angles. Something still wasn't right, but I could not think what was missing.

I heard rumblings outside of the window. General Folger's next move was approaching.

At last, I heard an old leathery voice that growled in my head, and I began to rummage through the rest of the desk drawers with frantic desperation. When I could not find what I was looking for, I looked down at the comb that had been in the draw next to the mirror and picked it up.

I ran my fingers along the spine and made two of my fingers into a vise that twisted until one of the thin teeth broke free. I then lifted this tiny piece of bakelite plastic that would be an adequate substitution for the sewing needle I had hoped to find. Quickly, I used it to prick my fingertip, and then I pushed on my pinky until drops of blood dripped down my hand and formed a small puddle on the desk.

"*Relax, my darling. It is only rouge.*" I could hear Sally's voice echo through time while I rubbed the blood from my finger up and down over my cheek bones.

"*Das rouge is power,*" she had said, and when I finished applying the deep-red fluid, I understood what she meant, for the face that looked back at me could stare down the fearsome Norse dragon, *Fafnir*, with its authority.

On a small bureau along the wall was a thin blanket used more as a tablecloth than anything, but I tore a small piece off and wrapped it around my head like a scarf. With the remaining piece, I fastened it around my body just as the keys to Tielo's office began to jingle one more.

"First you cower, then you flower, until at last you claim your power," I said as the door opened and Vogel and her guards approached.

Though she was visibly disgusted by my appearance, I saw a subtle admiration behind her vulture eyes.

Down the hall and stairway they led me, then through the empty factory floor. While it was not late enough for the group to have been sent back to the camp for the night, it appeared that they had been dismissed early, as no one aside from Vogel and her two guards remained.

The three led me to an empty vehicle, and I climbed inside. One guard drove, while Vogel and the other sat on either side of me, positioned so as to stop me in case I had any plans to flee.

Several minutes later, we pulled in front of the camp and I walked out under the metal sign one more time. *Work did set me free*, I thought to myself.

As we entered, we did not go in the usual direction toward the men's camp. Instead, I was escorted in between the administration buildings where I had first been checked into the camp upon our arrival from the transport train.

How much has changed, since I first faced the officer and his aide sitting at the table, as they decided each prisoner's fate.

When we pushed past these buildings, I looked out toward something of a field where a set of tall wooden gallows stood atop some scaffolding and stairs.

To my right ran a line of barbed wire and electrical fencing. It seemed to almost stretch on for eternity. All along the side of these fences stood hundreds, if not thousands, of prisoners, both male and female. They were a sea of gaunt images that one could almost mistake for a mirage, and not a sound could be heard from the camp aside from the whistle of a light eastern wind.

When at last they saw me, gasps rang out, breaking through the breeze, as the jaws of both the camp guards and prisoners alike dropped toward their navels. Some looked on with obvious disgust, while others wore looks of pride at my demonstration of defiance in spite of what was to come.

These people were but inches from me. The pathway to the gallows ran on a thin dirt trail directly past their haunted faces.

Vogel and her guards had handed me off to a set of Sturmtruppen, as the visiting soldiers outranked the guards and were following the orders of their leader, General Folger.

After only a few steps, I saw a smiling Alma, who stood alongside a quietly crying Edna. On Alma's other side, Matya nodded at me, her jaw set strong as if to let me know that I was a real gever with beytsim, and her confidence gave me courage.

The soldiers' pace pushed me forward briskly, and I began to pass by the men of my bunkhouse. I recognized Vladimir and Rabbi Horowitz in the mass of people, pressing themselves closer to the wire. It almost looked as if a tear had escaped the corner of Vladimir's eye.

Suddenly, out of the crowd of faces, Lucas burst through. He screamed my name over and over again. As he pushed past the others, he threw his arms out between the barbed wire so that he was only inches away.

"Why?" he cried, his fingers extended toward me as if he could scoop me up through the fencing and protect me from my fate. For a moment, as he reached out between those strands of twisted steel, our hands touched. It was long enough for me to deftly press something deep into his palms before I was forced to move forward. I left him sobbing in my wake. Turning back for a glance, I saw the rabbi comforting Lucas in the same way Lucas had done for him when Adam was taken from this world.

The trail ended, and we now turned from the crowd, walking to the top of a grassy knoll in the center of the field. We stopped at the foot of the gallows' stairs. I looked up to see General Folger and a mass of Sturmtruppen and Schutzstaffel of different positions and ranks standing atop the platform. It was clear that the general had not lied when he said earlier that he wanted to make a statement to all of the Dachau camp today. The position of the scaffolds on the hill were as Golgotha, and all around were only the heavens and the staring faces of both Romans and Judeans alike, who would all be made to bear witness to this crucifixion.

They turned me around to face back toward the crowd. There I waited as another lonely figure came into view. Step by step, Tielo Tiegel followed the same path I had just taken, prodded along by four Sturmtruppen. Tielo received only a singular look from the crowd, and it was of disdain. There was nothing for soldiers, guards, or prisoners to admire or pity about him and so their sneer was universal.

As he moved closer, I began to sing to myself, softly at first.

Love may come.
Love may go.
New love is like the falling snow.

Pushed off of the trail as well, Tielo began to make his way across the grass toward the steps. As he did so, my singing became louder and more joyous.

One minute it's there
and then it melts and goes.

At last I was face-to-face with Tielo. We stood at the bottom of those steps and looked deeply into each other's eyes.

But the memories fill your heart and it overflows.

I sang to him sweetly, and he looked back at me in horror and defeat.

Love may come.
Love may go.

I winked at him as my words faded into the wind.

General Folger stood up straight and addressed the crowd from atop the platform. A single microphone had been positioned on a stand. He tapped it with his finger and blew into it for feedback to indicate that it was active and that his voice would be carried through the speakers positioned all across the grounds of the entire camp.

Satisfied with the crackling feedback, he began to rant and rave in a furious voice. "Active homosexuality will not be tolerated at the Dachau work camp! Any deviance that takes away from the purpose of this camp, which is labor, will be punished harshly."

His message was meant to strike to the bone of all of his listeners because of what he wanted to prove here today—that it did not matter who committed the infraction. For prisoner and guard alike, the consequences would be fast, and they would be furious.

When he finished his thunderous speech, Tielo and I were led up the stairs to the center of the platform.

They placed nooses made of coarse rope around each of our necks.

I looked out into the crowd for Lucas. I found him just as he opened his palms and held up the upside-down pink triangle that I had torn off of my uniform earlier and had given to him when our hands briefly touched.

As he looked up at me, we smiled at each other across the field, its distance both short and long. Lucas and I would forever be bound. We were friends, we were lovers, we were family. We were triangles of color in a world of gray.

While today marked my death, Lucas would now be free from Tielo's threatened terror. He would not be subject to the repeated violations that I had been forced to endure. Lucas would not suffer the emotional deterioration that comes from having to surrender just a tiny bit more of one's soul than anyone else was asked to do at this death camp. Most importantly, at least for me, was the fact that Tielo had never had the opportunity to put in for the transfer of Lucas from the Plantage to the uniform factory. He would remain with his honeybees and herbs.

I gazed into the eyes of my lover, and I knew that I had at last kept my promise to keep him safe, in return for the favor he had once extended to me.

Live, I mouthed to Lucas, imploring him with that one word to defy the Nazis and somehow come out on the other side of their evil reign.

Out of the corner of my eye, I could see the general raise his hand in the air. I felt the floor fall out from beneath me, and the thick rope cinched tightly around my neck as urine released from my bladder.

My body shook with great force until it stopped.

Epilogue

The sun shone down bright and hot on my head as I snipped a piece of Genovese basil from the herb garden of the Plantage. I pulled a tiny speck off the edge of a leaf and popped the greenery into my mouth, letting the sweet and peppery taste melt onto my tongue.

It had been a long time since the scaffold, but how long I could not tell you. The seconds ran into minutes that ran into hours that ran into days, weeks, months, maybe even years. I had lost track of the exact date, but all at once it happened.

As I kneeled down in the dirt, a single gunshot rang out, followed quickly by the rapid tap-tapping of another, then another.

One of the garden's Schutzstaffel dashed by as he repeatedly yelled, "Lauf! Lauf!" to the other guards, and they obeyed. Each of them ran off from their stations toward one of the gates in the wooden fence that surrounded the Plantage.

A loud noise, like bone being crushed by a hammer, as a large green tank burst through the fence, running over one of the fleeing guards. Another fell on his face as a bullet tore through the back of his neck.

I stood up, bewildered by what I was seeing, and as I looked around the herb garden, other prisoners like myself started to wander toward me, all with the same look of confusion and disbelief.

There was a spinning sound, and then the top of the tank flew open. A man dressed in army green popped his head out of the hatch before he stood up tall on top of the armored vehicle. I could just make out the patch on his breast, with stars on a field of blue surrounded by stripes of red and white.

"You are free!" he announced in a language and an accent I had only heard before in the movie theater.

The man descended back into his tank, and it drove off through the other side of the wooden fence and onward to the camp.

Unsure of what to do next, I walked hesitantly toward the hole the tank had created when it burst through the Plantage's walls. Among the shattered shards of fencing, I heard a faint cry.

"Help me, please."

I leaned down and pulled planks and beams off of one of the older prisoners, one who also worked each day at the gardens. His thin, callused hand reached out, so I grasped it and hoisted him from the rubble.

"Thank you for helping an old stranger," he said weakly.

"There are no more strangers here," I replied, taking my first step over the threshold of my confinement and out into the world as a free human being once again.

Outside of the perimeter stood a row of houses, and I wandered toward them without thought. On my way, I stepped over the bodies of more than one Schutzstaffel, their faces frozen in death with the same looks of terror they'd replaced our own smiles with.

Reaching the door of one of the houses, I opened it and stepped inside a well-appointed parlor. There was no one there, so I just stood wide-eyed at the luxury. This had existed just beyond the barbwire fence that held us at bay like wild animals. Here someone had lived in silk-lined curtains and jeweled timepieces while thousands of us ate mush and washed in shit-filled latrines.

At the end of the room sat an object of exquisite beauty, a sight I had almost forgotten ever existed. Unable to help myself, I rushed to it and let my hands run over the fine wood of its lid as if I were caressing the back of my departed love.

Then I sat at the bench and pulled out from within my trousers the only thing I had left of him, a patch of pink fabric fashioned into a triangular shape. I held it up to my lips and kissed it as if my lips were gently touching his own, then I placed the pink triangle patch on top of the stand where the sheets would have sat.

My fingers fell onto the piano, and I played for him by memory, looking toward the heavens, knowing that he was watching from above and could see me.

"Thank you, Josef," I said through tears.

I allowed my hands to caress and stroke the keys as if they were touching Josef's body one last time. At his memory, my pulse increased and air filled my lungs. The music became as weather, its melody the wind that carried the clouds it had gathered up for a storm. Then the notes crescendoed and swelled in beautiful rapture before they burst like rain onto a sun-deprived plain and faded with a gentle, misty diminuendo.

"Farewell, my love," I whispered, and at last it was sunny once more.

▼

In addition to the millions of people killed by the Nazis for their religion, ethnicity, and political beliefs, untold thousands of homosexuals and transgender people were brutally treated and many were killed during this reign of terror.

www.ingramcontent.com/pod-product-compliance
Lightning Source LLC
Chambersburg PA
CBHW050401030726
47503CB00006B/1969